# Where are you, Anne Bonny?

Daniel Lance Wright

ISBN: 978-1-62420-100-4

**Credits**

Cover Artist: Designs by Ms G
Editor: Christine Young

Printed in the United States of America

# Chapter One

"Had you fought like a man you'd not be set to die like a dog on the gallows," Anne Bonny whispered. The convicted lady pirate couldn't bring herself to lift her eyes to connect with Jack Rackham's through the black iron bars. She feared giving in to romantic leanings. Eventually she did, pulling her gaze from the rough cobble stones of this St. Jago de la Vega, Jamaica prison floor and glanced beyond the vertical bars of the cell. Jack's silence attracted her attention faster than a scream would have.

As her eyes connected, "Stand straight, man! Don't be cowering. Ya hear me Jack? Replace that jelly in your back with a stiff spine."

Anne attempted advancing on the cell door to get into Jack's face with her warning but was yanked to a standstill by the leather bindings at her back.

The hulking guard holding her burst into bellowing laughter, releasing a spray of spittle into the side of her face. "The talk I've heard was not a'tall exaggerated. My God! You *are* an evil woman. This is the thanks you give Calico Jack? He's about to have his neck snapped by the hangman's noose, and he had the decency to offer the magistrate his life in exchange for yours. Now, he begs for your presence as his final request. How cruel can you be?" He slammed Anne's head into the bars, her face forced between them.

"Please, don't hurt her," Jack said. "She meant me no disrespect."

Unable to resist, hands bound, she could only stand, awkwardly leaning into the bars, face distorted.

Jack kissed her forehead then her lips. "I'm sorry, Anne."

"Me too, Jack."

"Nay to that; it's my fault... all my fault we're in this mess."

"Aye. That be true enough. Still, I don't wish to see you dead." Smashed against the bars, she strained to look back at the smelly sweating source of her discomfort, wanting to spit in his face.

The guard shook her hard. "Calico Jack must be daft or the devil guides your tongue," he said, still laughing. "You talk to him as if he's a bastard street urchin."

Finally, she was allowed to push away from the bars and stand straight. "He knows the mistake he made now that he's sobered and thought on it." She raised her shoulder and pressed it against her cheek wiping away the guard's disgusting salivary spray.

Angry lips relaxed. "Now, if you'd remove these leather restraints, I'd enjoy showing you how a woman can pleasure a strong man as yourself. My loins tingle each time I get the full look at you." *Come a bit closer so I might clamp my teeth onto that ghastly lip and rip it from your face.* She stepped closer but still at arm's length and relaxed her jaw, tongue dancing over parted lips. She looked longingly into his eyes.

Becoming mesmerized, he pushed his face toward hers then lucidity snapped into those dulled eyes. "I think I'd have a better chance of enjoyment...and of survival, stepping into a cage with an unrestrained she-devil." Holding her arms above the elbows, he spun her around shoving her toward the jailhouse door.

For an instant she came face to face with her captor smelling the stench of his foul mouth. Twisting her face into a queasy grimace, she kept her head turned away. But, even the rancid smell of all his recent meals couldn't erase the other disgusting aroma—unwashed human flesh within the confines of a crude tropical prison. The oily odors triggered a reflex to pull only enough air to stay conscious.

Time was of the essence. *Much needs to be said in the here and now but precious little time for it.* Forced away from her lover's cell, she craned her neck for a last look. "Now's your chance for redemption, Calico Jack Rackham."

The guard shoved harder, forcing her out of the cell house. She twisted her head side to side to keep him in sight a few seconds longer. "You may have failed at the manly thing to end up here but at least you can die like a man, without a whimper."Ya hear me, Jack? Without a whimper!"

The guard softened in a show of uncharacteristic concern. "By all that's holy, wench, give the man peace. He's about to be blue as the sea, dangling by his neck."

As unfathomable to the guard as Anne Bonny's rant seemed, she was sure Calico Jack understood; it was a backhanded show of respect for a life well lived by her measure, although angered over an act of drunken cowardice. Had it been otherwise, they'd yet be plundering shipping lanes in the West Indies. Remorse drove his spirit and shoulders into a slump.

Forced from the small freestanding structure into steamy Jamaican sunshine, she felt as though the foul smelling interior of the crudely constructed log structure excreted her with no more respect than bilious spew.

Struggling against bonds and captor, she strained for another look at Jack. Intuitively she knew it'd be her last. She glimpsed his sadness, an expression forevermore locked in her memory. Calico Jack disappeared behind the closing door.

While jerked about unceremoniously, another man equally repugnant came to complete the bookend set. Both pushed and pulled her between them making a boyish game of it until she stumbled and fell. The newcomer had been in the tropical heat too long. Curly black hair and beard glistened. Sweat streaked his deeply lined and tanned forehead. He straddled her then leaned over dripping perspiration on her face. Quivering from unsatisfied anger, she blew dust from her lips. "You stinkin' vomit-slick. If you yank me around one more time, I'll make a special trip back from hell to shove a rapier through your throat just to watch it come out the other side."

Bursting into boisterous laughter, they shoved one another disbelieving this woman's audacity in the face of hopelessness. The small one poked the larger one on the chest. "Ya be hearin' that, mate, we'd better be watchin' our backs."

"And our throats," the other said. He held his neck and made a gagging noise.

The larger man reached around the more jovial of the two and snapped her to her feet by the bindings. She grimaced from wrenched shoulders.

Gaze darting about the compound, she looked for escape clues, a way out. The area was strewn with small log structures apparently designed to keep dangerous prisoners isolated. Calico Jack Rackham must have been considered one. These smaller buildings faced the center of the complex where the main block of jail cells was housed.

Grinding teeth with pent up rage, Anne was forced along until they came to the central stone structure. One of the guards opened the door and shoved her, tripping down a narrow darkened corridor. Her eyes adjusted to the dimly lighted passageway. The massive stones mortared into the walls seemed to reach for her. The stockier of the two guards shoved Anne against the cool stone wall opposite her cell. A protruding stone hammered her ribs and forced air from her lungs in a violent rush.

Groaning over the weight of the door, the bigger guard clutched the handle with big square hands. He leaned away using his full girth to pull it open. The substantial hand-hewn hardwood door squealed on equally massive hand-wrought black iron hinges.

Anne resisted but was helpless against harsh treatment as she was slung inside, hands still bound at her back. Off balance, she tumbled to the rough cobblestone floor at the feet of her friend and partner in piracy, Mary Read.

The door closed and the heavy locking bar slammed across the outside of it into its sturdy cradle.

She gnashed teeth. "As the saints are my witness I'll make those two pay for their discourteous treatment of a lady." She spoke to the closed door. "I wager they'll soon regret underestimatin' me."

"Maybe. But your thoughts should be on greater problems than mindless dolts making merry with your misery," Mary said.

Anne noticed Mary perspired more than tropical heat should justify. "Love, I see gray in your face behind the grime. You sweat as a horse ridden hard yet lay perfectly still. Are you ill?"

Lying on her side, she nodded. "I'm hoping it's a natural thing, being with child and all." Mary pulled the sodden shirt away from her body to fan her burning skin. She pushed up onto an elbow then around to sit, groaning under her own weight. "My discomfort should pass. Don't concern yourself with me. Put your mind to finding a way out. As time slips away it will become clear that I am indeed pregnant as we wisely pleaded 'our bellies' to the magistrate. But, Love, the same passage of time will reveal you are not. They dare not hang me by law until the baby is born. I'll be fine for now. Your fate will be sealed quickly once the truth is learned. Those wretches might even remove your arms and legs before they kill you for deceiving them so."

Anne couldn't debate the wisdom. She nodded and scooted on her backside to Mary to have her restraints untied. She'd have her moment with those two guards, consequences be damned, even if freedom had to wait.

She leaped to her feet and spun to face Mary, yanking the loosened straps from her bruised and bloodied wrists. "I'll not even entertain the thought of leaving you behind if that's the point you're makin'."

"I knew that would be your mind. Understand, in my condition I'd make a cumbersome burden binding you to speeds unsuitable for escape. You need freedom to move quickly without a sick pregnant woman trudging behind." She mopped fevered sweat from her face with a loose sleeve.

Anne sighed. "All right. If that is to be the case, when I escape… and I shall, I'll return for you before the baby is born. I'll take you out of here so we might raise that child together far away from those who wish us harm…the French township of New Orleans, perhaps."

Mary closed her eyes. "Perhaps, but even if circumstances prevent it, do not fret. We've shared several lifetimes of pleasure and adventure in our brief time upon this earth. My life has been full. I wouldn't consider it a premature death even if I survive this fever to be hanged."

"You speak like a person knowing that life is draining away." She moved in close, probing Mary's eyes then stroked her cheeks with palms of both hands. Anne held her face steady to look for any possible lie.

Mary laid her hands atop Anne's. "You and I are women...intuitive beings. As such, I have a small voice telling me to prepare."

"What sort of gibberish is that?"

"I pray the voice is a product of this stinkin' Jamaican heat. But on the chance it's not, I urge you to find a way out and don't look back... don't come back either."

"That's crazy... just bloody crazy! You've stood under a full moon once too many times."

Mary blinked lazily as a weak smile came up. "Aye. That's certainly true enough."

After a moment, the burst of frustration evened out. She gently pushed Mary to lie down.

As Mary's head touched the straw pillow, "Both our chances are better if you leave without me. You must go alone this very night if you can. It's nigh thirteen miles south to the port of Kingston. Time will turn from friend to enemy by morning as the coming night yields to the light of day tomorrow. Don't give the bastards a chance to notice you're not with child."

Anne readied the debate but stopped short. "Even in sickness you think clearly."

Walking to a large stone mortared into impenetrable walls, she fingered a joint where imposing stones met. She allowed cunning free rein, thinking over variables that might end in freedom. Thoughts put movement to her feet. She glided laterally along the wall to the small heavily barred window and saw a small yard area void of grass by constant treading of feet. Gaze drifting to a nearby hut, she wondered what it housed. But it was the hut's lengthening shadow that held her interest, signaling the coming night promising deliverance of an ally, darkness. She hoped it would become as dark as the black heart of her jailer.

Anne whirled around. "You're right. We are women and better than all the men on this bloody God-forsaken island. We may have been swarmed aboard the Providence by Governor Lawes' men and brought in chains to St. Jago de la Vega, but overpowered in a surprise attack and being outsmarted are entirely different. There's no reason you and I cannot outthink even manipulate two guards who can't put together a single intelligent thought 'twixt them. By all that's holy, we can do this," she said pounding a fist into an open palm.

"Now that's the Anne Bonny I know and love." Mary forced a smile and snuggled her head into the lump of straw beneath her head. She was fast succumbing to dehydration, writhing about seeking elusive comfort.

The sight squeezed Anne's heart. She swallowed a sentimental lump. *Crying like a love struck child can help neither of us.* She ground fresh resolve between her teeth.

Shadows lengthened and melded with fading light. The landscape beyond the window changed. Coming darkness robbed color and a blue moon repainted the night. Anne waited and watched. The night stubbornly held heat and now breathed it into her face through the small barred window. Activity around the compound ceased. Movement and sound subsided. This Jamaican prison went silent.

"It's time," Anne said.

Setting the plan into motion, she removed all clothing and helped Mary do the same. Strategically, she positioned Mary on the grass-filled mattress, fully exposed to the small observation opening in the cell door. She knelt beside her friend so that her nude body happened to be equally bared to prying eyes. Adding legitimacy to nakedness, Anne dipped a wadded shirt into the oak bucket of drinking water and bathed Mary with it, mopping the length of her body in slow seductive strokes while caressing with the other hand. "Ya know, Love, I would've offered this even if it weren't part of the plan. Your skin's afire," she whispered.

"Though dulled by fever, your hand on my bared belly and legs is a welcome tingle." She touched her lips with two fingers and transferred the kiss to Anne's.

The sound of wooden heels came clacking down the corridor. The brief erotic spell crumbled. It wasn't necessary Anne add seductiveness to the stroking of Mary's body, only that she continue. It was believable because it was real.

Echoes of footfalls suddenly stopped. Anne needn't look to know eyes were on them. Shortly, an unintelligible but gruff whispering male voice signaled the approach of another set of boot heels.

Anne casually looked to the door. She saw two pie-eyed and likely salivating male faces crowd the small opening by the dim light of a candle one held. The brilliance of the moon streaming through the small window at the rear of the cell placed a silvery spotlight on their nakedness, illuminating them well enough to spark lust. The bait was cast. From the outset the plan showed promise.

Two low voices bantered beyond the door, bringing to mind fish circling impaled minnows.

Anne leaned toward Mary and kissed her stomach below her navel. Mary squirmed slightly and moaned for show.

Mumbling voices went silent.

The heavy wooden locking bar on the door shattered the quiet as it was lifted from its cradle.

The hook was set.

Squeaking hinges announced intention. The door eased open.

Anne looked up at the approaching men. "I apologize if I've disturbed you. I fear my friend has become aroused by the soothing caress of this wet cloth." She looked away from them and dipped it in the bucket then drizzled water over Mary's breasts. "Just because we are the captured and you the captors does not mean we cannot work together to satisfy basic human desire. We can all benefit. Don't you think?" In a measured way her eyes moved from

Mary's body to them. "If we are to hang anyway, what's the harm? Why would we not jump at the chance to feel closeness of men at least once more before we die?" She pulled her raised knees wide apart allowing full view playing the part in gesture and tone.

Judging by slackened jaws and saucer-size eyes, the acting job was suddenly superfluous. There rehearsed invitation plainly fell on deaf ears as the smaller of the two moved with lustful abandon. He ripped clothing from his hairy sweat-glistened body. His attention was fully on Mary. He straddled her.

Anne rose to face the other. "Now, how is it that I might satisfy *your* need?"

In the single second it took for his eyes to lock onto her breasts, Anne assessed the position of the rapier at his right hip and the shorter cutlass on the other. With the tips of her fingers she pulled his face up to meet hers. She parted her lips to accept his. *I'll be kissing you when it snows in hell!*

In a flash she reached across to his side and drew the short cutlass. With a catlike whip, she drew the razor-sharp blade backhanded across his belly, slicing open his midsection through the shirt.

Mouth agape, he stumbled backward into the wall then looked to the gush of blood and his exposed intestines. He whimpered and held protruding entrails in both hands. His was the face of a dying man, knowing the mistake he'd made and now too late to do anything about it.

Not waiting for death to come in its own time, Anne had a mission to complete with this one. Her mind reeled to every disgusting thing he'd done to her, throwing her around, spitting in her face—making a game of her feelings. She lunged for his rapier pulling it from his waist scabbard.

He only had time to moan pathetically.

Anne snapped the point to his throat, thrusting it entirely through his neck with both hands until visible on the other side.

"Oh my," she cooed. "That did feel good… just as I thought it would." She jerked his face near hers with the hilt of the rapier. She gave the man the kiss he so wanted. "Was it good for you, too?"

As the light of life flickered, his knees buckled. He went down crumpling into a quivering heap.

Now aware, the other guard withdrew and attempted a move to get on his feet but Mary reached down and latched on to his testicles and squeezed with all her might. He roared like a hungry bear. It gave Anne a valuable extra second.

The noise he made was all he had time for.

Anne whirled about, yanking his head away from Mary's face by the hair and slit his throat. She held fast to his hair until the threat passed.

The gurgle of foamy blood splattered into Mary's face.

Anne pulled him away and shoved him over onto the floor.

He pathetically tried to stop the bloody geyser with both hands. Desperate moves quickly reduced to full body twitching.

"His blood smells so much better than his breath, but I still don't care to taste it," Mary said, spitting and wiping her tongue on a forearm then lips with the back of her hand.

Showing no concern for lives ended, Anne took clothing she felt more appropriate for a getaway—boots, belt, scabbard, even pants, being cleaner than her own. While rushing to dress, Anne faced Mary. "When this deed is discovered in the light of day, tell them that you had nothing to do with any of this. It was all my idea. Do you understand?" Anne spoke fast, chopping phrases. "Tell them I did this over protest. You fought me to stop it. Say not a single word in my defense, sweet Mary." She buckled the leather sash of the cutlass scabbard across her chest. "I'll be back for you. I swear."

Bolting for the still open door, Anne abruptly stopped.

The probable truth stopped her faster than a closed door could have. Urgency vanished. She walked back to Mary. Wiping blood spatters from her naked friend's mouth; Anne Bonny looked into Mary's sunken tear-filled eyes and kissed her—the soft caress of a lover.

~ * ~

Legs aching from the fast nightlong march, Anne sat in the black shadows of streaming moonlight gasping for breath. She gazed at three vessels gently rising and falling in gentle swells in the island harbor. Legs dangling just above the water, she sat inconspicuously on the prickly rough-hewn planks of a dock among crates and barrels ready for loading. Valuable time spent recouping strength. She also needed time to shore up weaknesses in a new plan.

As precious moments of darkness passed and commitment to the task ahead firmed, she determined the best choice had to be stowing away on the vessel she recognized as a trading sloop. Experience told her that at first light it would sail for the mainland to the north, hopefully the American colonies. Having ransacked many such vessels, she knew it was likely unguarded.

Now fully committed, she rose and walked lightly along the dock back to the shore then made her way to a long protruding pile of stones in the water which served as a wave-break near the dock. She slinked along the massive boulders of the jetty parallel to the dock located on the opposite side of the narrow bay. She split her time watching her step and studying the sloop as it smoothly undulated, the anchor rope softly slapping against the hull. When she came to the end of the jetty, she listened for voices but heard nothing.

Easing into the water, the ripples disturbed the reflected moonlight on its surface sending them radiating in the direction of the ship as if pointing the way. With no splash or noise, Anne alternated between a dog paddle and breaststroke. She cut through the calm water.

The hundred-yard swim ended at the anchor rope. She shinnied up it to deck level then stopped to listen. Now she heard voices—a quiet conversation somewhere down the way near the stern. Hugging the rail she slipped over it onto the deck. Water pooled beneath her. She rested and listened.

Sitting long enough for breathing to even out, she crawled along the deck against the rail. Like a stalking cat stopping frequently to listen, she stayed below the plane to prevent casting a moon shadow.

Finally, she reached relative seclusion, a cranny between crates. The voices became distinct. Although whispered, she understood. One extolled the captain's quick work in port so they might be underway by dawn; the other reminisced of a woman left behind in Norfolk and would be happy to see her again.

She sat back on her haunches. *Norfolk, Virginia? Excellent!*

One said, "I feel better knowing Doctor Radcliffe's aboard. If we can have nothing but blue skies and fair winds, we'll know for sure God watches over us on the voyage home."

Sitting bolt upright at the mention of his name, she fell into a quandary. She thought Michael Radcliffe had abandoned her when she was captured and incarcerated. Or did he? *What business would Michael have aboard a trading sloop so far from the colonies?*

She'd heard no news of his whereabouts while in that Jamaican jail. Her mission to find a comfortable place to stowaway had suddenly modified to include finding Radcliffe's quarters. The sound of snoring indicated men asleep at various places on deck—many men. She mentally marked positions to avoid disturbing them.

Voices of the two still awake continued but began moving away and eventually went silent behind a closing door. She breathed relief, feeling more at ease. She tiptoed to the front of the ship where the Captain's quarters and cramped cabins were located. She stepped down into a short narrow passageway. It was more like a deep indentation in a wall. She turned sideways and stopped, standing before a door to her left, another was at her back and a third at the end of the passageway, all within arm's reach of where she stood in near total darkness.

Hearing voices beyond the end door, she figured that was the two men she heard. From the other two doors, she heard nothing. A faint light glowed from beneath the door she faced.

She pulled the cutlass resting against her hip from its scabbard and pushed the door until it opened a crack. Peeking inside, she saw Michael sitting at a tiny table with a single candle illuminating a journal. He concentrated on the entry he made. A scratch of quill on parchment was the only sound.

One giant step was all it took to end up behind him. She placed a hand over his mouth and the blade to his throat. "Why did you desert me," she hissed. "Of course I must add that's what men are driven by their jewels to do... have their way and move on."

Recognizing the voice, Michael relaxed behind her hand yet remained stiffly upright unable to move with the blade against his neck. "I did not desert you," he whispered hoarsely. "I went about the business of helping you."

"Explain yourself."

Drawing air carefully, "Late yesterday I completed negotiations and brokered a deal with Governor Lawes to have you released. His only condition was you leave the West Indies never to return upon penalty of the hangman's noose. You need to know your father had a hand in this."

One side of her lip curled into a sardonic grin. "Ah, the upstanding William Cormac of Charleston and, according to some, my father." Tipping her head low to rest her chin on his shoulder, she nuzzled her nose into his cheek. "What do you reckon he calls me these days; lesbian, traitor, or maybe just harlot? Surely, he doesn't refer to me as dear daughter. What say you to this?"

"Regardless of your feelings, he knows you are his only blood." He pulled his eyes as far sideways as possible. "Anne, I am no threat to you. Would you kindly remove that damn blade from my throat?"

She dropped the cutlass to her side. With a frustrated snort, "Could it be true I would have legitimately gone free this very day? Is this what you tell me?"

"Yes... within hours."

"Why would you do this for me?"

He eyed her from head to foot. Her red hair dripped seawater and matted to her head while wet clothing clung to her shapely body. "I've learned to look past the person you are and have given considerable thought to the person you could be. You're barely past your teens and many years of good life remain. But you seem bent on persisting in ways that keep you in life-threatening danger. Why do you do this to yourself?"

She smiled. "Why, Michael Radcliffe, is this your backhanded way of saying you care for me?" She quickly added, "You know better than most I despise owing for kindnesses. Each time I attempt to repay a debt of gratitude, it gets me into trouble and usually gets them killed."

"How's your friend Mark?"

"Mark?"

"Mary Read. You don't need to hide your affection for the woman, not around me. I've known for some time that Mark is her male alias."

"So you know my secret." She slipped the cutlass back in the scabbard belted to her side.

"It's not a well-kept one. But it doesn't bother me."

"Then I must beg your forgiveness for believing you to be like other men… having your way and running I mean." She drummed the handle of the scabbard with fingertips and raised a wary eyebrow. "I suppose I should thank you for not making an issue of it."

She turned and stepped away. "It seems I have complicated things with my actions this night."

"It would seem so."

She spun back and crossed her arms in a defiant pose. "Then I shall do what I do best, dress as a man and work as a man. I'll sign on to the crew of this vessel and work my passage to Norfolk."

Nagging images of Mary had dogged her through the night, but now new thoughts replaced those concerns. The ever-changing plan now centered on leaving the tropical heat of Jamaica to make a new life in the colonies and never look back. She had no desire to ever see that prison at St. Jago again. "You might be right, Michael. It may be time I find a new means of support and redefine how I think about adventure." She stepped toward the door adding, "If that's possible."

Slipping out, she allowed darkness to again spread its comforting cloak.

# Chapter Two

Hair and clothes clinging from the swim to shore, Anne kept an eye on the sloop still anchored in the bay as she waited in a short line of men. Dawn broke over Kingston before she dried. The quartermaster processed new crewmembers beginning at first light for the return trip to the colonies. A breeze penetrated the thin material of the damp linen shirt and up the legs of baggy pants bunched at her waist. She shivered and her stomach growled, having had no food since early yesterday. And that was mush she found a maggot in and refused to eat more than a couple of bites. Fatigue and lack of nourishment worked against her.

The slow moving line of men each made their mark on parchment swearing loyalty to the sloop and its command. Her gaze at the ship shifted farther out to the swells beyond the protected water of the bay. *Ah, the open sea. I feared my days on a ship were forever behind me.* Excitement to again slice through swells built. Desire sparked vivid imaginings; salt laden wind tickling her face, seeking out adventure, and freedom to demand the horizon give up her secrets.

The first rays of the rising sun warmed and lent a sense of well-being. She turned her face into its comfort. It soothed a gaunt malnourished frame, although each puff of morning breeze still brought gooseflesh.

Long shadows pointed inland; symbolism that chilled for a different reason. It told a story—one urging her to stay. Fidgeting, she wondered why—why such a strange notion? Was it for the sake of Mary Read or Calico Jack Rackham perhaps?

She slammed the door on sentimentality tugging at her. Getting away from Jamaica was a strict matter of life or death. Jamaica was hell. She'd not be trapped in it. She shook off contradiction—the first step in forgetting a former life.

The occasional drip of seawater from her fingertips should have been a source of curiosity if anyone cared to notice. No one did. *T'is a small blessin' for sure. I don't need pryin' questions about that or why my clothes are much too large for a 21-year old wisp, as myself.*

Earlier, emerging from the bay, escaping notice came strikingly easy. All eyes had been fixed on the quartermaster's table. Every man thought only of himself. Bumped and shoved about, Anne was dwarfed by the crush of masculinity vying for attention. Everyone on the dock jockeyed for the better place to be noticed by the man in charge.

She took no chance and bundled tresses tightly beneath a scarf given her by Michael. Remaining anonymous was not assured. If someone noticed her as a woman, the plan would crumble. She fretted, fearing the rising sun might reveal too much of her gender. The wet shirt clung hugging her breasts when against her chest. She pulled the garment taught away from her upper body. The flimsy material and the water-cooled breeze blowing through it were like a window on hardened nipples.

The quartermaster took names, directing those ahead of her to the top of the gangplank. There a sailor stood beyond the gangway giving further instructions.

A noisy clop, clop of heals upon the wooden dock approached from the rear, the added weight bouncing the planking in cadence. She didn't look. She didn't care.

A gruff male voice behind her yammered on and on about weather, the people of Jamaica, the integrity of the ship, and a myriad of subjects—none flattering. She cast a quick angry glance in hopes of quieting him, but no good.

The quartermaster accepted another just ahead of her. That one made a mark on the parchment list then shouldered a tattered duffel bag and marched up the gangplank. After a man whispered into the ear of the quartermaster hidden by a cupped hand, the man in charge stopped taking names and rose. He allowed the parchment to snap back into its roll. "Captain Peckary has sent word. We need no more."

Taken aback, Anne blurted, "But you must take me on. It's vital to your captain and crew that you do. You're incomplete without my services."

Folding his arms across his chest, a wrinkle of curiosity drew down. The quartermaster smiled. He eyed her from head to toe then back up.

From behind, the annoying oaf said, "What good could a small fancy man possibly be to a ship's crew?"

Ignoring the irritating hulk she nevertheless addressed his question, but directed the answer to the quartermaster stepping close, nearly toe-to-toe. "I can insure the safety of Captain Peckary against rogues, scalawags, and all comers who might wish him harm. That's the good I can do, sir."

The man posing the question planted a huge square palm in the middle of her back and shoved her stumbling into the quartermaster as he let out a spit-filled bellowing laugh.

The quartermaster shoved her back. "Sir, watch yourself." He straightened his tunic, realigning the gold buttons.

Feeling the buffoon, her face flushed crimson. Whirling about with no hint of hesitation, she drew her rapier.

In a blinding move, she hooked its tip in the hand guard of the rapier at the oaf's side and flipped it into the water before he could begin to prevent it. He hadn't moved at all and his weapon was already sinking to the bottom of the bay.

Bystanders whispered and laughed. A buzz of questions went up by those who'd missed it.

He roared, pumping the air with both fists. "I'll not have a smooth-skinned fancy man make a mockery of me!" From its sheath on the other hip he pulled a cutlass. With no finesse he swung the blade in a wide arc aiming at Anne's face.

She jumped back but saw no need to raise her weapon defensively.

He stumbled from momentum of his own flailing arm.

Keeping eyes locked on the hulk, she smiled and bowed with a measured head bob.

Men encircled them, preparing to enjoy a bit of early morning entertainment but the circle didn't have a chance to close.

Her adversary took a second, equally clumsy swing aiming for her neck.

In an amazing display of accuracy she positioned the point of her rapier so that his own inertial force drove the point entirely through his wrist.

His hand sprung open.

The weapon flew over the heads of ducking onlookers. He howled.

The cutlass clanked across the wooden dock.

Everyone fell silent—no jostling, no laughter. The only sound was the quack of a duck hundreds of yards up the shore. Then a din of hoots, hollers, and applause erupted. Even the men lining the rail on deck applauded.

Jerking the point from his flesh with a wet sucking sound, Anne flashed a grin at her aggressor, eliciting yet another roar from pain now steeped in humiliation.

Clearly wanting no more, he stumbled away holding the injured wrist close to his side. "I'll see you again someday," he muttered. "As God is my witness, there'll come a day of reckoning. I swear it."

"I need see nothing else," said the quartermaster. "Quite an impressive display, I must say." He looked to the captain up on deck.

The Captain nodded.

The quartermaster turned back to Anne. "I believe you to be a man of your word. Furthermore, I believe we now have just cause for one more in our crew. See to it that no harm comes to Captain Peckary from pirates, privateers, or hostile crew. Your position has been won by this show, but a single falter will end it. Is that clear?"

Anne courteously dipped her chin. "'Tis clear as this magnificent morning air, sir." She looked past him and up. The uniformed captain leaned against the ship's rail. He seemed to be a distinguished man, overweight and short. He stood next to Michael Radcliffe who also leaned on widespread hands against the rail looking down at her.

She touched her forehead in a show of respect for the captain.

He smiled approval then said something to Michael who nodded a response. Peckary walked away.

Michael, alone at the rail, clasped hands to his back, stood straight, and smiled. There seemed to be more in his expression than simple approval.

She lingered, admiring the handsome young doctor.

He lightly pinched the brim of his tall felt hat between thumb and forefinger in a small show of admiration and then followed the captain away.

Sailing out of Kingston harbor into open water of the Caribbean, the trading sloop set a course for the Windward Passage at the eastern end of Cuba. Winds were fair, just as that nameless, faceless sailor overheard the night before had hoped. The promise of a good voyage seemed assured. The course set was due north and would likely stay that way to Norfolk.

Anne Bonny assumed the name Andrew to complement the male disguise. Starting anew now seemed within reach.

"Andrew, your task will be simple in detail but may well turn difficult should my life be threatened," the captain told her, nose turned slightly upward. Standing at the bow he stared into the vast expanse of the Caribbean Sea standing.

Noticing how the bow keel neatly split the water, Anne took his warning in stride, "Aye, Captain. You need worry only about efficiency of the crew not your safety."

"These are dangerous times in which we live," he babbled. "All manner of scoundrels prowl these waters, looking for anything of value. No human life is dear to them. Do you understand my meaning?"

"Aye." It amused her that a short time ago the words applied to her. She knew well his meaning.

The days belonged to Peckary, the nights to Michael. Stealing away from her tiny sleeping space in the open up on deck, Anne slipped away in the dead of night down to Michael's closet-size cabin to share his bunk. She stayed until dawn—a pattern quickly set—a pleasant diversion the first uneventful week under sail. But on this morning that changed.

"Ship! Vessel off the starboard bow!" came the shout from up on deck.

Anne abruptly awakened in Michael's arms, realizing she'd overstayed. Jumping to her feet from the bunk built for one, she frantically covered her womanhood but she needed more time—time she didn't have. She abandoned the ritual of binding her breasts with a strip of cloth in favor of getting her shirt on fast.

"The craft is hoisting the skull and crossed sabers," shouted the same voice. "Prepare for battle!"

Running from Michael's cabin still tying her hair into a scarf, Anne leaped up the one step onto the main deck. She spotted Peckary looking around, his face fraught with pathetic cowardly fear. "Where the bloody hell is Andrew?" he demanded of the men scurrying about on deck.

"Here, Captain. I am here."

"Come be at my side, Andrew. Now!"

Joining the captain at the rail she watched the approaching vessel as Peckary queried, "Our cargo is of no great value, just a few barrels of spice and dried fruit. Why would our ship be made a target?" Fear squeezed beads of sweat from his furrowed brow, trickling down his temples to ample jowls.

"I cannot say, Captain, unless we have been mistaken for another."

"I'll not put this ship or crew in jeopardy over a few barrels of dried fruit and precious few canisters of spice." He turned to his first mate. "Run up a white flag. There is no need to risk cannon fire."

Anne looked upon the approaching ship confused, believing she knew every pirate ship in these waters yet did not recognize this one. It was a topmast schooner new to these waters. *If it's booty they seek, anger at leaving empty-handed might drive them to kill us anyway.* She looked at the captain. He'd made an asinine decision by her reckoning. The crew of a ship under the skull and crossed sabers would not reason. Their own sordid desires born of soulless hearts would be all that mattered.

"Keep your weapons in their sheaths and scabbards," the captain yelled to the crew. "Make no threatening moves. If we allow them to search, they'll realize their mistake and leave."

The aggressor vessel turned broadside, gunwale flaps open and canon rolled out to the ready position. The ocean current and rolling swells pushed the larger ship into the smaller sloop within easy boarding distance. Men spilled onto the already crowded deck of Peckary's sloop, faces of the marauders concealed behind scarves and rags.

The captain opened his arms wide, almost as if he welcomed them aboard. "Look about and take what you will. There's nothing of value and certainly nothing worthy of the effort it would take to remove it."

"Value to one may be worthless to another," said the one in the lead.

The voice rang familiar.

Walking toward her and the captain with weapons in each of his two big hands, he said, "I know what I'm after and, yes, you do have it aboard."

Glancing to the stairwell, Anne noticed Michael had come up on deck.

A hostile appearing move by the masked invader seemed aimed at the captain.

She drew her rapier.

"No, Andrew!" Peckary shouted but too late.

All hands on deck filled with every manner of weaponry—knives, cutlasses, sabers, swords, pikes and clubs.

Anne engaged the leader as the captain dropped into the background. The crew had no choice but swarm the invading force and attempt to repel the unwelcome guests.

Confusion heightened. She lost sight of Peckary.

Parrying with this large masked invader demanded full attention. She backed into the wall of the quarterdeck again glimpsing Michael. He hunkered beside a crate without a weapon.

She tossed a cutlass in his direction. It bounced across the deck. She shouted, "I pray you'll not cower like Calico Jack! Defend yourself!"

He crawled on hands and knees and snatched up the weapon then leaped to his feet and took on the nearest man. Though skill lacking, his courage was not, swinging wildly disallowing a counterattack.

Anne put herself at a disadvantage without the cutlass. She thrust and swung the rapier.

The much larger man parried with the occasional slash from the long knife in his other hand trying to connect with her body. Although she was quicker, his power and additional weapon began showing advantage. She stumbled backward.

The big man swung with mechanical efficiency. The cutlass finally connected with the blade of her rapier just beyond her hand. It flew free, clanking on the deck.

It was clear he'd not be leaving before separating her head from her body.

She growled in pain as she fell into the sharp corner of the crate Michael had been hiding behind. Breathless, she rolled to her back.

Blinded by the sun, she threw her head to the side and noticed Michael losing ground to the man he fought. He fended off cutting blows but he'd soon be against the rail with nowhere to go.

She attempted to scoot on her back but rough splinters of the deck planks penetrated her skin and held fast.

The big man straddled her. "I know who you are, Anne Bonny. Governor Lawes will pay well for your return, dead or alive. I choose dead. I'll pickle your sorry carcass in a barrel of brine until I collect." He raised his rapier for a killing thrust.

"If you already know I'm a woman then you should recognize these," she said, ripping her shirt open, exposing her breasts.

Delaying the killing thrust for a fractional second proved too long.

Anne sent a foot sailing into his crotch.

He froze, breathless.

She saw the puncture wound on his wrist, realizing whom she fought. He careened to the side holding his jewels.

She rolled the few feet across the deck to her rapier and with blurring speed threw it as a spear from the flat of her back.

The point found its mark, dangling from between his ribs over his heart.

He gasped then fell dead.

Panting, "That certainly proved a deadly fascination." Suddenly realizing the chance she'd taken, she looked about to see if anyone had noticed the stunt that saved her life. Every man had his own confrontation to deal with—no one seemed to notice. Taking only time enough to tie her shirt, she leaped up to join the battle.

Somewhere from within the crush of male bodies, a voice shouted, "He's been killed. Let's get out of here."

The clink and clank of metal upon metal ceased.

Men separated like a receding tide. The invading force leaped, some swung on loose ropes, back to their own ship.

Looking about, Anne saw Michael breathing hard and blood spattered, otherwise unharmed.

Upon inspection, the battle had been fierce even if brief. Mortally wounded men writhed in pools of blood moaning for aid—help that would prove futile even if it were available. She ran up to the quarterdeck. Peckary cowered behind a barrel. "Are you well, Captain?"

"I am, thanks to you Andrew. I'm grateful you acted over my protest. I think that scalawag planned on skewering me."

Using the point of the rapier like a cane, she dropped onto one knee and steadied with it. "I believe I know why they attacked, sir."

"What might that be?" From his hiding place he chose not to move just yet, surveying the ship for lingering hostiles. Finally, he emerged from behind the salted pork barrel.

"If you check the identity of that man lying over there, you'll see it is the same one I angered at the dock in Kingston. I believe he sought revenge."

"Humph, a terrible lot of trouble for a little revenge."

"That is my thought as well." She acted mystified by the attack then rose and slid the rapier back into its scabbard. Turning away, a half-smile curled her lip, cozy in the thought it had been credibly explained.

Looking down at the big man lying dead with a spreading area of red on his chest, she realized how easily it could have ended with her in chains and transported back to St. Jago and the gallows. The air suddenly smelled sweeter.

# Chapter Three

Standing at the bow of the trading sloop, Anne looked to the horizon and what she sought finally came into view, Norfolk. It could have been the chilled north wind of this early March day that the sloop tacked in to, but Anne chose to believe it was the sight of the colonies that took her breath—a vision until this moment she thought she'd never see again. While sweltering in that Jamaica prison with the cloud of the hangman's noose hovering, it seemed unlikely this opportunity would ever come again, but there it lay growing on the horizon.

Mary and Jack crossed her mind, grating away some of the joy. Calico Jack was probably already dead and Mary Read might not live long enough to see her baby or the noose.

The crew had not prepared adequately—woefully unprepared for cold blustery winds after spending time in the tropics. Men huddled in every available space to block the chilled wind. The sloop continued tight, riding high in the water, slicing the rolling Atlantic swells. Occasional spray misted over the bow. It felt warmer than ambient air.

Clearly feeling safer now, possibly lackadaisical, Captain Peckary waved her away as she approached to stand at his side. "I don't believe it's necessary you remain so close, Andrew. You've fully earned your passage and I'm grateful. But the sight of Norfolk calms my spirit."

Anne tipped her head courteously and went on. She spent more time with Michael. Peckary, of late, made it easy. Quiet talks with her lover appeared as nothing more than friendly banter between men. She approached Michael standing alone at the bow rail. "Care for company, Doctor Radcliffe?" she asked in a bold voice for anyone to hear.

Looking at her, then beyond for prying eyes, "If that's what you wish... Andrew." He smiled.

They watched the coastline grow large. Her grip on the rail tightened. Excitement increased. The pull of the city's charm swelled within her. Desire to return to a calmer polished life appealed to her, far from filth and grime of living with the dregs of humanity. At this moment, she wanted to leave all that behind, thankful to be alive.

Such refinement was not unknown, but once upon a time it suffocated her and drove her into a pirate's life. Circumstances of her early teens compelled her to run from that life of privilege. Now, watching Norfolk swell over the bow, she felt drawn to it. She'd gone full circle in her short life.

"The future, Michael, what does it hold for us?"

"Whatever we choose." His eyes connected with hers. "We deserve it and can damn well demand it."

They discussed plans and possibilities. Enamored by such talk, Anne was drawn to abandon the ruse she guarded. She wanted to speak as a woman, to show her feminine side. She had to be Andrew a short while longer. Amorous leanings must be controlled in favor of stealth, speaking in hushed tones, facing away from the crew. Discovery meant death. The charade had to be maintained to the end of the voyage. Even then anonymity had to remain supreme or plans could be dashed. She was a wanted woman—a criminal on the run. To forget that would be a self-imposed death sentence.

The crew scurried about. Captain Peckary barked orders to furl mainsheets for a controlled entrance into quieter protected waters of the bay.

"Do you think your father would like to see you home in Charleston?" Michael whispered sideways as he gazed across the choppy ocean waves that slapped the hull with hypnotic regularity.

"Possibly, but there is a bigger question ya should be askin'; do *I* want to be there with *him*?"

"Do you?"

Although inviting the question, she wasn't prepared to answer it. But opinions of her father, William Cormac, had softened since she'd last seen him in Charleston; now remembering good times, the rift between them not so important anymore.

She fingered the hardwood of the ship's rail, smoothed slick from many months of clutching hands. Pondering her father, now that she approached her twenty-first year, desire to bear children and start a family seemed reason enough to look upon him in a renewed way and leave differences in the past. *Am I softening?* The pain her father caused couldn't be forgotten but hopefully set aside.

Still, she had to get past his heartless act of throwing her out of his house over her marriage to James Bonny. It motivated her to do things she'd come to regret—retaliatory actions resulting in charges brought in Charleston for attempted parricide, arson, and conspiracy against the king's authority. *With a bounty on my head in Jamaica and Charleston, it would be wise to keep my identity known to no one beyond my circle.*

Looking to Michael, she chose words carefully and spoke slowly. "Even if I should believe my father and I could reconcile, freedom and possibly my life will always be in jeopardy around Charleston. Aside from that, placing trust in a man who once turned his back on me is not an easy thing to do."

It occurred to her people she would have readily trusted with her future remained in Jamaica and were most likely dead by now—Calico Jack by the gallows and Mary by fever. In sidelong glances, she wondered about Michael's loyalty. With some urgency, "Are you willing to stay with me? Can you see the years ahead with us together, an inseparable couple? Can I trust you to defend me in word and deed? Have you considered consequences of fathering our children? Does it…"

"Stop the questions. Have I not proven myself? Do you believe it trivial that I sailed from Norfolk to Kingston to bargain for your release?" He smiled yet still unable to look her in the eye for secrecy's sake.

She glanced and saw truth in that smile but wanted to hear it.

He snaked his hand down the rail to cover hers.

Snatching her hand from beneath his, "Now is not the time to risk everything on questionable loyalties. Are you willing to give me a solemn vow and give it at this very moment?"

"Hold this in your memory forever..." Michael fixed a gaze at the rising landscape ahead. "...You came into my life and walked away with my heart. You have it locked away and hold the key. This act of romantic thievery may have been many months back; still, I am without control of my heart. If your desire to be with me is a mere tenth of my wish to stay with you, or even a fraction of *that* miniscule number then eternity may not be long enough."

Anne continued gazing straight ahead. "You do realize, don't you, even without the blessin' of a church I consider those words a vow of marriage?"

"Then together let's consider my solemn vow to be just that."

"I fancy a kiss," she whispered, "Just to seal the deal mind you."

"What might Captain Peckary say if he saw me kissing 'Andrew', his courageous protector?" Not waiting for a reply to the jest, he placed a finger to his lips and transferred the kiss to hers. Both continued looking into the icy wind at the growing port of Norfolk. Michael drew a deep breath and released it in a prolonged sigh. "I fear that will have to do... for now."

~ * ~

The pristine metropolitan atmosphere of Norfolk stood in sharp contrast to seedy tropical pirate lairs, neat rows of storefronts, and colorful clapboard houses with manicured yards and white picket fences lined proud and straight. Although accustomed to rundown, unkempt and rotting structures of the Caribbean where tropical climes transformed new to old in months, she wondered how she could've ever viewed that as normal.

Gawking at the stylish garments of passersby on Norfolk streets, it occurred to her how novel it appeared having come up from a part of the world where style of dress was strictly utilitarian. Raised into wealth, Anne well remembered such things but it now seemed dreamlike that she'd ever been part of it. Before circumstances changed, it hadn't occurred to her the opportunity to return to such a life would ever come again. But now it was all around her.

Men in tall beaver felt hats with frilly ruffled shirts beneath spotless and wrinkle free coats in bright colors; women in full dresses, some twirling parasols and giggling at every utterance of men at their sides. Unlike the first time in this world of status and money, it no longer seemed repugnant. She wondered why it ever did. On the contrary, it beckoned.

Having less reason to fear recognition in Norfolk, Anne allowed Michael to dress her in the finest clothes. Dolled up, she made a fetching sight.

Weeks passed. It was a time of good food, wine, and perusing the finest shops in Norfolk. She discovered the lifestyle had to be relearned, although familiar from younger days living with her father. Life among the wealthy was an art. Never the one to shy from challenges, she studied mannerisms and worked at presenting the perfect presence. Before long she spoke the language of the privileged, talking of things with feigned interest as any good socialite should. Becoming comfortable blending into elite circles of Norfolk, reorientation would soon be complete. She relaxed, prepared to enjoy life at the opposite extreme.

Stopping before a huge ornate mirror framed in gilded swirls around fleur de leis located inside the foyer of the Regal Hotel, she examined her reflection. Ringlets of coiffed hair spilled from beneath a dainty hat that matched a burgundy velvet gown.

Michael handed his tall hat to the attendant.

He paused and took in the reflection with her. "Heavenly... absolutely heavenly," he said.

"Is this how you envisioned us, Michael?"

"Better." He was clearly enamored with the presence they made together. He kissed her cheek and took her hand. They walked arm-in-arm into the ballroom which served as the main dining room. The Regal Hotel housed the most excellent restaurant in Norfolk where local residents of means congregated.

The meal matched ambience. Afterwards, they shared quiet conversation unaware a man sitting at the table behind Michael overheard them discuss locating a permanent residence.

"Sir?"

Michael seemed annoyed by the interruption and did not respond.

"Sir," the man repeated. "If I can have a moment, I might be of help with your quandary over a permanent residence."

Michael finally turned and with a quizzical flip, "Is that so?" He cocked his eyebrows high, waiting for the stranger's version of wisdom. "By all means, please share your knowledge."

After an introduction, the stranger befriended Michael. As the conversation progressed, Anne watched Michael become interested. She remained wary, not as quick to accept a stranger's word. She quietly questioned motive. *The hearts of men like him are not that big. He's up to something.* Nevertheless, she didn't interrupt, playing the role of quintessential highbrow lady allowing her male escort to handle the conversation.

Regardless what she thought about the stranger, Michael became enthralled with the story the man rattled on about. This seeming gentleman described lands and adventure for the taking out west in wilderness territories held by the French near a wide river called the Mississippi. Anne smiled at his condescending explanation of location. She knew well where the Mississippi River was, having sailed past its mouth on many occasions in the Gulf of Mexico.

"Every week new groups of pioneers assemble and head west to create fortunes, traveling together for safety," he told Michael. "But be forewarned, opportunities are not without end."

As the man excused himself to find new ears to bend, Michael looked to Anne, "What do you think? Does our future and fortune lie somewhere beyond the colonies to the west? Is it possible we can leave this lifestyle behind?" He gestured to the lavishness of the Regal and to the manner of dress that surrounded them.

"You're asking me? Are you daft?" She laughed aloud, drawing attention from patrons. She noticed their stares and placed a handkerchief to her mouth and hacked in a subdued lady-like way as if merely clearing her throat. She then leaned across the table and whispered, "Is there an adventuresome streak buried within you, Michael? How absolutely novel that would be." She allowed the question to hang, musing with a smile and wrinkle of curiosity. "I may have underestimated you. I thought you were happy amongst this finery. Norfolk offers a genteel way of life, much more to your likin' I thought."

"It is to my liking. Still, it's only one way." The tone of his whisper became serious. "Do you not find yourself looking over your shoulder wondering if, or when, you'll be found out?"

Holding cut crystal stemware to the light, she swirled wine in the glass and watched the sparkle go crimson, "You are perceptive, Doctor Radcliffe. I'll grant you that." She took a sip then set it on the table, following it down with her eyes, thinking. "Have I made it that obvious?" She glanced side to side. "Indeed, I'm painfully aware. How could I not be?" Her voice was soft and even. She leaned across the table, whispering lighter yet. "Wanted by the law, as I am, I become suspicious of looks that linger or attention that cannot be explained..." She tipped her glass toward the stranger. "...Such as your new friend over there offering up tales of wealth out west beyond the colonies." She sipped.

The man now demonstratively engaged another couple.

"Then I'm compelled to say that finding our own piece of heaven far from prying eyes is worthy of consideration."

"Piece of heaven, you say?" The words held a comforting ring. Feeling a glow from the wine, a sense of femininity she feared lost long ago emerged.

Anne reveled in tenderness Michael so willingly offered. "I need consider nothing. If the father of our future children wishes to head west, I shall be at his side." She tossed the last swallow of wine to the back of her throat in a single gulp—most unladylike. She smiled because she didn't care if people saw or what they thought. That rosy glow escalated toward full-blown inebriation.

"It's time to call it an evening." He offered his glass in the manner of a toast and took the final swallow. "It would seem we have a plan."

~ * ~

Anne stood aside and watched Michael in two days time, convert possessions into gold, retaining some things and purchasing necessary provisions. Even then, it required ten packhorses. Their total worth rested upon the backs of animals. It seemed Spartan by standards she had so quickly become accustomed to. The lean muscles of the horses flexed mightily under the weight—all roped together single file in a pack train.

Just as the stranger at the hotel had said, a large number of people and horses eager to move out assembled on the outskirts of Norfolk. Anne wondered how many had been seduced by that stranger and still thought him dubious. That didn't matter anymore. She figured it was just one more example of a lifelong distrust of men.

Taking a position within the line, she and Michael waited for word to leave. As they did, day one turned into day two. In that time the number of people more than doubled.

Looking across a sea of expectant pioneers from the lower branch of a tree, "There must be three hundred or more people here," she called down to him as he stood by the horses keeping them soothed. "My heavenly word, the number of horses must tally to the thousands."

The call finally came back from the head of the line to move out. The trek west began. Animals hundreds of yards ahead began to move. As she dangled her feet from the branch of that tree, she noticed a few oxcarts and flimsy carriages. *Fools!* She shook her head at the stupidity. *They'll be useless before Norfolk sinks from sight.* She leaped from the tree to join Michael.

The length of pack animals and wagons moved slowly. The hardiest of the travelers in the snaking line walked alongside animals and wagons. Few seemed willing to leave possessions behind. Anne figured some pack animals would be dead of exhaustion soon if their loads weren't lightened.

Walking slow but steady, Anne noticed near the overloaded oxcart ahead of them a young Indian girl, apparently a servant. She neither talked nor smiled. Head down most of the time, Anne never caught her making eye contact with anyone. It was as if she counted steps—every day, all day long. It reminded her of those days confined at St. Jago. She counted days, hours, even minutes, but hers was of confinement not working as slave labor. *Then again, what's the difference?*

After three days observing the young Indian girl, Anne caved to curiosity. Quickening her step to catch up, she was now bent on striking up conversation, bored with the monotonous pace. "Hey you," she called out. "My name is Anne. And you?"

No answer came.

Undeterred, Anne broke into a jog to close the gap. "Don't be shy, girl. What's your name?"

The girl snapped a glance over her shoulder but quickly dropped her head to watch the ground beneath her feet. "I am Little Feather," she said, response subdued. After a few seconds she glanced again, this time making brief eye contact.

Anne slowed to a fast walk and wondered about the girl's situation. She was very young and seemed overly skittish, maybe afraid of displaying behavior that might be construed as disrespectful. Her appearance was so young Anne wondered if she had reached her teen years.

Curiosity took another leap. She accelerated her pace catching up to the girl and walked alongside. On closer inspection, the girl may have been in her teens, but barely.

Anne examined her profile. "How did you come to be in the employ of those people?" She nodded in the direction of the man and woman tending the oxen of their two-wheeled cart. Anne paid them little mind but noticed when the man snapped the flank of an oxen with the flimsy end of a cane rod to keep it moving.

"I am Iroquois. The Flatheads stole me away, holding me prisoner for two winters. Once I reached a profitable age they traded me to these white people in exchange for weapons. The Flatheads are the enemy of the Iroquois." The girl glanced repeatedly at her masters. "The Flatheads have aligned with the English. My people, the Iroquois, have found no cause for an alliance. The Iroquois resist. My tribe sees whites as greedy, wanting to control and dominate everything."

"Then I was right. You are a slave."

A shout came from the man walking ahead of them, "Girl, you'd better stop falling behind and get back up here now or feel that leather strop across your back again."

"Again?" Anne became instantly angry. "What in blazes did he mean by 'again'?"

"I'm sorry. I must go," the girl blurted. She ran ahead to resume her position nearer the oxcart.

Anne didn't drop back. She followed and thought about such a delicate young girl beaten by that ass of a man.

She became angrier and took off running until she came upon him.

She grabbed his shoulder and spun him around, "Your name, sir, what is it?"

"John Tilford. But what business is that of yours?"

"Because, Mister John Tilford, if you *ever* touch that girl with anything other than a warm blanket on a cold night, I shall treat you so harshly that you'll beg me for the comforting sting of that leather strop on your own back. Do you understand my meaning?"

At first, the unwelcome advance incensed him. His face began to harden.

But his anger couldn't match Anne's. Her lip twitched. Dancing eyes flashed fire.

Indignation turned to hesitant fear. He backed away. "What is this girl to you?"

"She's a human being you bloody twit! And she damn well should be treated as one, not an errant pet, beast of burden, or a draught animal like those oxen you keep popping with that cane." She stared a few seconds longer then turned to leave but couldn't let it go.

She whirled back around, poking him in the chest with the rigid point of a finger. "As you treat her, you shall also be treated. Remember that, you fool."

The man said nothing, dumbfounded by the forwardness of this lady hellion dressed in man's clothing. Anne wore black britches to just above her ankles and matching boots that came up to meet the hem. Above that she had on a white linen shirt that fit loose and billowed with the slightest breeze.

She went back to their lead packhorse. Michael walked beside it. "Do you think it wise to be drawing unwarranted attention like that?"

"Oh, it's warranted all right." She fumed, unwilling to forgive or even let anger go. After a moment she settled. "Who are the Flatheads anyway? What manner of people are they?"

It's a tribe of Indians that calls themselves Iswa. The English know them as Catawba. They're ruthless and savage but usually just toward enemy tribes. There's a loose trading alliance between them and the colonists."

Looking ahead at the young Indian girl going about her chores, "Their alliance be damned," she muttered. "The Catawba are now enemies of mine."

The days became an endless creak and rattle of carts, punctuated by occasional whip cracks over oxen becoming lean from sunup to sundown exertion, only allowed to graze overnight. A packhorse whinnied a protest. The scenery changed grudgingly, fooling the eye on occasion, appearing to repeat. Children played, adding an enjoyable sound to the mechanical grind of wheels and the bawl of an ox. Natural obstacles such as creeks, hills, or dense foliage slowed progress, sometimes taking entire days to find ways around, over, or through. Wheeled vehicles systematically failed. Axles didn't last long in rugged terrain. Forward advance never slowed nor sped, failed carts left abandoned on the trail. The number of wagons diminished. Draught oxen became food.

Now two weeks out of Norfolk, Michael busied with horses while Anne grew content enjoying the company of Little Feather. By most accounts they'd only traveled about a hundred miles. Walking together, she learned much from the youngster about medicinal qualities of various plants and others used as food—things she would have never learned aboard ship. Anne noticed a twinkle in the young girl's eye. She saw desire for independence.

This day was coming to an end. The sun sank below the horizon. Light of day dimmed. Exhausted travelers stopped at the first relatively flat clear spot and made camp to prepare the evening meal. As if darkness created it, the glow of campfires popped to life along the entire length of the assembled would-be settlers.

Playing the role of dutiful wife, Anne prepared food and handled other daily chores.

A disturbance from the other side of the Tilford oxcart caught her ear.

"You'll do as I say and you'll do it now!" A slap of leather on bare skin she plainly heard following the demand.

Knowing full well the situation, she sprang to her feet and sprinted toward the sound. She heard an anguished wail then nothing.

Rounding the front of the wagon, the sight was like someone had taken a slow match and touched the powder of her anger. Little Feather sat on the ground cowering, digging heels into the dusty earth, scooting backward on her buttocks to relative safety beneath the cart behind the wheel. She refused to cry out.

John Tilford moved threateningly over her, holding the strop high overhead. Ready to swing again, he appeared most angry that she refused to cry out.

Without feeling a need to further assess or even slow down, Anne ran at Tilford. Teeth clenched and a growl building in her throat, she leaped high into the air, feet first.

She planted both heels in his back transferring momentum to his body knocking the wind from him.

He slammed the ground rolling in a cloud of dust.

The leather strop flew from his hand.

Before Tilford regained wind, Anne snatched up the leather strop and straddled his pudgy body.

She swung wildly, landing blow after blow indiscriminately with loud pops of the leather.

"Stop! No more!" He shouted, anguished.

Although his pain evident, her lack of concern for his well-being was equally obvious. She continued whipping the man even after blood streaked the white of his shirt.

Mrs. Tilford sobbed, begging her to stop, tugging at Anne's shirt and shoulders.

Anne thought only of revenge for Tilford's treatment of Little Feather.

It took the tug of the young Indian girl at her shirttail to stop the savage attack. Anne glanced and saw Little Feather had crawled to her. "Please Anne, no more."

Michael appeared out of the dark stepping into the fire's orange glow. He'd finished bedding the horses. "What's happening here? What's the ruckus?"

"Who is this woman? She dresses as a man, possesses the strength of a man, and fights with the savagery of a beast. Is she Satan cloaked in feminine skin?" Tilford wailed, writhing on the ground.

Fiery contempt spilled from Anne, rabid slobber strung from between clenched teeth as she huffed. Her nostrils flared ready to go at him again. She threatened with a false start, wanting to beat the bastard more. Pulsing knuckles worked on the strop, not satisfied to call it even just yet.

Michael raced to her side. He attempted soothing her.

Anne would not be so easily returned to calm. But finally, she threw the strop onto Tilford's bloodied torso and grabbed Little Feather's hand, leading her away, "Never again must you suffer the sting of that strop or even the unwanted touch of a man… any man! 'Tis a solemn promise I'm makin' to ya, girl and as God and all the saints are witness, I'll be makin' sure of it!" Intense anger always deepened her Irish brogue. Mussed and curly red hair matched her face beneath the grime.

Searching from horse to horse, Anne found the one she sought. She rummaged beneath a canvas until she uncovered the stash of blades rolled in the dry, protective shroud of multi-layered oilcloth. The collection included three cutlasses, a rapier, and an assortment of six shorter knives. Bundled with them were two flintlock pistols, loaded and kept dry, ready to fire.

She chose two of the cutlasses. Little Feather's training began in the glow of the campfire.

Days passed. Anne identified three types of eyes that watched the training night after night; curious eyes of disinterested people in search of entertainment, admiring eyes like Michael's, and of course those who watched warily like the Tilfords.

Although she'd given far too much of her identity away, each time she looked into Little Feather's eyes, conviction deepened that she did the right thing. She relished growing boldness in the pretty young Iroquois and watched the youngster with burgeoning affection.

Anne came to realize fluttery feelings for the girl must be tucked away and not revealed. To Anne, love was love. Gender made no difference.

# Chapter Four

The long pack train turned southward through rugged and sometimes impenetrable terrain. More time was spent searching for passages west than actually traveling that direction. A dense stand of oak and hackberry trees and boulder-strewn outcropping on the flats near the base of the mountains had some people, including Anne, grumbling about traveling in circles. Weary pioneers had to stop yet again for a path to be cleared. Looking back to where they'd come from, it was easy to see the road forged.

While they lay idle, waiting for the latest impediment to be removed, the powers that be thought it wise to discuss the situation. They realized how important ongoing agreement and contentment was. Meetings to air grievances were a regular event. No decision was forced upon any man; all action taken was by consensus, but among men only.

Anne's resentment grew. Her opinions were taken lightly then summarily dismissed only to be addressed later by a man and acted on. Although never a direct snub, attitudes and actions implied she should remain quiet and stay with the women. It frayed a rather fine thread of self-control. Pretending to be the submissive wife became laborious.

"Sir?" Anne blurted over the rumble of many conversations.

Ignored, she raised her hand and waved. "Sir, if I could address the gathering, it might prove helpful to our cause."

The leader orchestrating the meeting offered Anne a tired look. "Yes, Missus Radcliffe, what is it?"

"We start each mornin' makin' great progress, but it grinds to a crawl late in the afternoon *every day*. Would it not keep a perk in our step if we stopped mid-morning and mid-afternoon to rest instead of pushing on to exhaustion each day?" She looked around at all the bearded men. No one commented.

"Not prudent," the leader finally said. "We must squeeze the good out of each day or a six-month trip will turn into ten months." Having dismissed the concern even before he'd finished talking, he was already scanning faces looking for questions then added, "Is there anything else?"

Already on her feet, she spun to walk away. "Fools... all you fat-bottomed, hairy-faced old men are idiots," she muttered as she marched away then came the worst insult of all. One of them asked, while still within earshot, "I wonder if resting a couple of times a day might not increase our pace enough to make up for time spent at rest?"

There was no joy in hearing her idea develop legs. She'd had all the talking down to she could tolerate. Kicking arrogant asses now seemed more like a plan than a fantasy. She had to get away from the gathering before she followed through.

A short time later with more of the trail made passable, the caravan resumed snaking through treacherous landscape.

Anne's tolerance of the entire ordeal thinned. How long would it be before she exploded and attacked someone again, she wondered. Escape from those tendencies came by way of daydreams—imagining salty breezes in her face and a ship under her command slicing through ocean swells with a cutlass on one hip and a rapier on the other. This image calmed her—a special lure not easily set aside, nor did she want to forget it. Someday she'd be back to it. This unpleasant journey made that goal top of mind.

Carefully picking a way southward, the leaders searched for a passage through the formidable line of peaks that abruptly rose just west of the flats they traveled. Delays and numerous detours pushed back arrival by weeks. The guides seemed lost. But she'd heard a consensus murmured that it might take extra months to make it to the Mississippi River. As yet, no way through the mountains had been sighted.

On a sunny morning that began the third week of a time-wasting southward trek, a fetching sight interrupted Anne's nautical imaginings. She walked close behind Little Feather. Her gaze upon the form of the young Indian girl became intense. She admired the girl's proud straight posture. She enjoyed watching the newly acquired cutlass in its scabbard, dangling from a leather strap slapping her back with each step. Anne breathed desire for the girl—a small fire dutifully doused. She sighed wistfully over the unrealistic yearning. It was far out of step with fulfilling her maternal instinct with Michael.

Anne took pride in Little Feather's new take-charge attitude. The girl was no longer Tilford's slave but a paid employee. It was a move clearly aimed at keeping Anne away from them, nothing at all to do with fairness.

The girl had now tasted freedom. She split her buckskin skirt and re-stitched it as pants, emulating her new friend, adding painted markings signifying Iroquois warrior status. Little Feather grew bold; even to the point of debating old man Tilford over how to accomplish demanded tasks. Otherwise, the Indian girl never complained.

*Little Feather keeps a wary eye on old John Tilford. The man cannot hide anger over his impotence in the matter.* Whenever Tilford spoke to Little Feather, he glanced around first to establish Anne's whereabouts. She noticed and enjoyed it.

The pack train stopped. Word filtered back that a narrow passage had been found by advance scouts less than a half-day's travel ahead, wide enough for people and horses but not surviving oxcarts.

News of a way through the mountains brought cheers down the line. If true, they could turn west and cross the mountains as they expected to do three weeks ago.

Carts were stripped and loaded on the backs of draught oxen. The crude vehicles were abandoned. Bovines would later be slaughtered for food if necessary. If not, the oxen and milk cows would begin herds. The pack train grew lighter. Little of the original cargo was left, shed along the way.

After a brief stop for the noon meal, they trudged onward. Anne saw people and animals far ahead turn into a narrow canyon between two peaks. Word came that the line meandered for about two miles.

When she and Michael had their turn to enter it, the so-called canyon was little more than a broad washout that took eons to cut rising precipitously on both sides. The promise was that it opened into a fertile meadow less than five miles ahead, the planned campsite for the night. They were told to expect easy passage for many miles once they cleared this canyon.

Heat and dust turned oppressive within the narrow channel. Anne cast cautious eyes to boulders above them on the steep slope to their left. Some were ominously perched, appearing poised to tumble. *By all that's holy, I pray those stones stay right where they be.*

But she suddenly saw those rocks from a different perspective—good places to hide. Centuries of erosion suddenly became the lesser concern. Instinct slapped her hard and drove gooseflesh from the neck down. Intuition brought back that fateful day aboard the Providence when the ship was boarded by soldiers under orders from Jamaican governor Lawes. This gender-specific sensitivity would not relinquish its flutter.

Other than the squawk of straining leather straps, the click of hooves upon rock, and the occasional bawling protest by a whipped ox, no other sounds were made. It seemed everyone had reservations about this canyon.

A gnat buzzed by Anne's ear and that caused her to notice sounds of nature had been quieted—but by what?

The distant screech of an eagle added its voice.

"Michael, come forward and walk where I can see you." As she spoke, her eyes scanned the slopes. "I don't like this place."

Unconcerned, he complied, moving forward to take up a visible position on the opposite side of the lead packhorse.

She glanced to Little Feather. The young girl's gait had changed. *Can she sense it, too?* She jogged to catch up. "Is there a change in the air or does my mind play tricks?"

"Something is not right." Little Feather's eyes swept the boulders above them. "An Iroquois elder once told me that ill will and deadly intent will thicken air before a presence can be seen or touched. I sense that heaviness now."

"Draw your cutlass, girl. Hold it close to your side. I fear your training will soon be tested."

Anne trotted back to a specific packhorse and retrieved blades from the rolled oilcloth. She walked alongside the animal. Its load swayed to unevenness in the trail. Dust puffed from beneath its hooves and boiled lazily up to join the brown haze hovering above them. Once she secured the rapier in its scabbard to her side, she slung the cutlass in its leather sheath over her shoulder, letting it hang at her back by a leather strap. She removed the two pistols. She trotted ahead and caught up to Michael. She held out the pistols to him. "Take them." She then pulled a shorter knife from her belt, "And this, too. Something is not right about this place."

Smiling, Michael threw his arm over her shoulder. "It would seem the walls of this canyon are closing in on your mind."

Miffed by the response, "Michael Radcliffe, I've not survived harrowing times by going unprepared and ignoring my gut! Take the bloody pistols!" She shook them at him. "This is no time to be cracking wise."

He took them from her and shoved them both into his belt. He slipped the knife inside his shirt. "I suppose caution is good." Still, he showed no concern, turning attention to the lead packhorse and clucking his tongue at the animal to maintain an even pace.

A towering thunderstorm cloud appeared over the peaks ahead. The shadow of it marched across them. "The darkenin' sky portends more than rain," she muttered. Choking heat and dust rose in ever-thickening brown clouds from hundreds of horses.

Feelings of imminent danger persisted. She wouldn't be comfortable until this narrow canyon opened into that broad meadow. Adding to apprehension was the agonizingly slow rate of travel. Desire to bolt and run remained strong, but if she did, where to? Her muscles twitched and flexed at every sharp sound like a racehorse at the starting line.

Within the half-hour, wind from the thunderstorm channeled through the canyon, kicking up blinding dust. Downdrafts signaled the approaching storm. Horses whinnied protests at the abrupt change in the air. It carried coolness, blown through a rain shield several miles ahead. Thunder became audible. The sky darkened further and cloud-to-cloud lightning sent out webs of electrical discharges.

Upon whistling wind, a shrill sound came to her—a human cry followed by frenzied voices.

Among the confusing buzz one word came to Anne clearly: "Attack!"

Leaping onto a nearby boulder she strained to stand tall. She saw human forms spilling from the mountainside to the frightened people and horses below.

She needn't strain for long as figures appeared in a wave on the slopes above the entire length of the caravan.

She noticed the misshapen heads of the attackers, all with a painted black circle around one eye and a white circle around the other with the bottom portion of the face painted solid black. "What manner of demon is this?"

"Iswa!" Little Feather yelled. "Iswa, the enemy!"

Disbelieving what he saw, Michael stared into the swarming horde. "This cannot be. The Catawba are friends of the colonists."

"Stop doubting the obvious and arm yourself, man. The time has come to fight or die!"

Pulling the two pistols from his belt, he leveled one, aimed at the nearest screeching attacker, and fired.

The warrior spun away.

Another sliding down the steep slope from behind a boulder above him jumped in right behind the fallen man.

Michael shot him with the other pistol.

The swarming warriors left no time to reload. He tossed the firearms to the ground and withdrew the eight-inch knife.

A third appeared from behind another nearby boulder. The screaming, crazed warrior squared off to Michael wielding a stone axe in one hand and a club in the other.

Michael had no choice but to engage him. He swung the knife fiercely.

Three others descended upon him.

A wild melee of swinging knives, clubs, and tomahawks ensued. Quickly overcome, Michael went down in a spray of blood.

"Michael!" Anne yelled, as she slashed the throat of an attacker.

Running to his aid, she speared the nearest screaming savage with her rapier.

She glanced in response to a war cry behind her and with a backhand slash of the cutlass, felled another.

A passing glance at the gruesome remains of the man she called husband was all that was necessary. The battle had become for her life only.

Little Feather ran in her direction.

She noticed beyond the Indian girl the Tilfords had already been disabled. They lay twisted and unmoving. "Come here! Quickly, girl! Stay at my back. It's our only chance."

Lightning flashed, accompanied by crackles and booms, now almost constant as a curtain of rain approached.

Fiercely fighting back to back, the two prevented surprises on the other and gradually made their way to a crevice barely wider than shoulder width in the canyon wall.

A particularly deafening crash of thunder split the air as the sky darkened to a dusk-like dimness. Wind stirred dust, blinding their attackers.

Anne shoved the girl into the natural fissure. "Get behind me and stay there!"

The tiny space blocked wind and dust. It provided advantage by allowing only one attacker at a time. Anne viciously disposed of each that attempted to engage her, slashing with the cutlass in her left hand and lunging with the rapier in her right.

Bodies piled. Rain fell in torrents.

The scene appeared biblical. But Anne did not wield the jawbone of an ass and these hideous attackers weren't Philistines but heathens all the same.

An indomitable will to survive pumped adrenaline through her body into her weapons. Defeat never crossed her mind. She fought from behind the pile of bodies that lay at her feet.

From one of the felled warriors, a club came whizzing up and struck her across the shin. She heard a snap. A searing pain bolted through her leg below the knee. Tremendous agony brought tears but did not slow her blades.

She hopped laterally to support herself against the rock wall maintaining presence of mind though blinding pain made her head spin.

She lost balance. As she went down, she thrust the rapier one last time into the eye of the next attacker who climbed over the top of human flesh she had lain to waste.

Anne glanced and saw Little Feather reach over her. The girl swung her cutlass at the blinded Indian, slicing him open. Eviscerated entrails spilled from his belly. He fell on top of Anne. She couldn't move.

Struggling to free herself, she heard a banshee-like screech.

A club whizzed toward her head.

Little Feather screamed.

Anne saw a flash then pain streaked from her head to her neck.

Oddly, her thought was not about pain but how wonderful cool rain felt in her face. Still aware of the fight above her, she no longer could open her eyes or make any one of her three good appendages move. Suddenly she became consumed by bliss and passed caring. The din of battle and storm receded. Thoughts whirled away in a montage of images—then nothing.

# Chapter Five

People talked. Flies buzzed. Children laughed. Cool dampness swept across her face. Anne woke to strange smells and blurred vision—no sense of place or time. Detached from self, it was as if she inhabited someone else's body. She strained to open her eyes but the lids seemed weighted.

She finally got them open. Framework of a crudely constructed arched ceiling came into focus. Another swipe went across her brow. She now recognized it as a dampened buckskin patch. Her eyes flicked to its source, a young girl. Several seconds passed before recognizing her new Iroquois friend, Little Feather.

Vision sharpened. Memories flooded her awakening mind—Michael, the expectant settlers, and those satanic looking Indians. In a gravelly hiss, "Where are we? Why are we alive?" She coughed then dragged a dry tongue across the roof of her mouth. She fingered the fur-covered hide beneath her, peripherally trying to identify it.

"Your courage in battle earned you the right to live. It's their tribal law to reward courage in battle, even the enemy. But, that show of courage also marked you as valuable. They plan to barter you back to the whites." Her chin sank to her chest. "I will be sold back into slavery or traded to enemy tribes holding Iswa prisoners."

Anne attempted pushing up to sit. "I think I'd be safer staying with these heathens." She groaned and fell back. "Oh sweet lord, the pain…" Her voice trailed. Her hands were numb and dead. Tingling returned to them. She lifted her arms and worked the fingers. She then made a fist with blood-encrusted digits. The hands seemed to be in working order.

As she fingered the bloody lump on her forehead, she said in a raspy voice, "I can't allow that to happen, nor can I allow them to enslave you again. Both are out of the question." Rubbing stiffness from her shoulders, Anne rolled to her side to sit up. But the jarring movement sent a pounding throb through the lower half of the injured right leg. Grinding her teeth in misery, she saw a splint of two sturdy slabs of bark lashed to her leg.

"It is good you dwelt for a time with the spirits. The medicine man who realigned the bones in your leg dealt with you harshly. If you are to be a means of exchange, it is to their advantage the merchandise is in good order, meaning that you are able to walk."

As pain eased, Anne examined the swollen gash on her forehead with a feathery brush of fingertips. "This will heal into a lifelong reminder of that clubbing." Suddenly, she realized that she may not be alone in her pain. "What about you? Are you well?"

"Yes, but everyone else is dead. You and I were the last left alive. Once you fell the fighting stopped. The Iswa stopped attacking. I laid my cutlass down and attended to your needs." She lowered her eyes. "I—I thought you were dead."

Anne noticed the look and stared at Little Feather a long second then changed the subject. "How long have we been here?"

"The sun has set once and now has risen once."

"Then it is little wonder even the unbroken bones complain." She completed the painful quest to sit upright and examined surroundings. The roughly octagonal building was constructed of sturdy logs, covered over with bark and reeds. "Can you understand the language?" She continued looking about.

"I was forced to live with the Iswa many weeks before they sold me to the Tilfords. I learned it. Yes, I understand them well."

"Why did they attack us?"

"Frustration over the tribe's dwindling numbers. This is only part of the greater tribe. This group broke away, refusing to accept the colonists' opinion that Iswa were lesser humans. They want nothing to do with whites or even members of their own people who do. They settled here believing themselves free of white settlers. That's why they attacked. They were quick to anger when whites were discovered moving through territory they claimed as their own." Little Feather smiled slightly. "It's interesting they want to trade you back to the colonists. They may not like the whites but they like their weapons."

A sturdy tribesman stormed in and without overt animosity, grabbed Anne by her thick curly red hair as if she were chattel and dragged her screaming and cursing through the opening into the dusty central yard of the village.

Hurling obscenities, shrieking in pain, Anne rolled and twisted, shoving her writhing body along with her one good leg, attempting to lessen pressure on her scalp. Weakened as she was, her defense was poor.

Little Feather rattled off something in their language. Whatever it was she said did no good. To this Catawba warrior, it was just a chore that needed taken care of.

Another tribesman grabbed the young girl by the arm and yanked her. She stumbled onto her belly then rolled over onto her back. She was dragged squirming on her butt into the yard after Anne. Their treatment, it was quite clear, was as livestock, property, nothing more.

Dropping Anne before a post buried deep in the ground, the warrior bound her hands to her back then strapped her to the post with several rounds of braided rawhide rope. Looking up through dust covered eyelashes, she huffed and snarled. "You've sealed your fate with that stunt!" She spit in his face.

Spittle dribbled down the Catawba warrior's cheek. He continued unperturbed, giving the straps a couple of hard tugs, checking his handiwork. He got up and walked away with no more emotion than if he had just tied off a sack of corn.

Enduring the same consequence, Little Feather was bound to a boulder some distance away.

"Why are they doing this?"

"They want us in full view so escape is less likely. Your tenacity in battle may have saved your life and mine too, but it also made them cautious. They are wary of your fearlessness and take no chance that your cunning may be equal."

Bright sunshine beat down as morning turned to afternoon. Anne weakened. Throbbing head and leg pounded with each beat of her heart. Heat took a toll as well. Pain and thirst became unbearable yet nothing she could do about either. The huts formed a rough circle around the post where she sat bound. It hurt and was humiliating but endure it was all she could do.

Continuously trodden ground had beaten away grass and weeds leaving a powdery dust over the entire common area of the village. People walking by kicked it up and any breeze carried it to Anne and Little Feather, settling on their clothes.

She watched a chattering gaggle of women butcher an ox taken from the wagon train. They hung strips of meat on three racks constructed from saplings, corners of the racks secured by rawhide strips. Insects swarmed them and the meat. Lying nearby was an infant with a small split log strapped to its forehead, presumably to permanently flatten it as the skull matured and hardened.

One of the women glanced often as she systematically cut meat into strips with a stone knife. She seemed particularly interested in Anne. Anne was weak and listless. She noticed but didn't care. Eventually, the woman approached with a gourd dipper and a clay pot of water. The woman smiled. That seemed odd. She held a full dipper to Anne's parched lips.

Anne sucked the precious fluid down.

The woman then stood, smiled again, and tossed the remaining water directly into Anne's face. Wanting desperately to slap the woman, Anne tugged at her restraints.

"It's not what you think," Little Feather blurted. "It was kindness, just a way to cool you." The young Indian girl accepted a drink, too then thanked her.

Anne's chapped lips were split, providing yet another source of discomfort. Subtle cool streamers of air mixed with sweltering heat before the general cooling of evening set in. Even an aching head, throbbing leg, and numbness of bound hands couldn't keep Anne awake. Aside from that splash of cool water in the face, this was the first comfort she felt. Her body went limp and her head wilted forward until her chin rested on her chest as she drifted into a light sleep.

A puff of warm air and that unmistakable feeling of closeness abruptly pulled her from slumber. Even before her eyes opened to the moonlit night, anger welled against the presence. The plan was set. She would bite the nose entirely off whomever this happened to be, simply for daring to come so close.

Sensing anger and startled by Anne's sudden jerk when she woke, a curious wolf jumped back then stood unmoving.

The skittish animal's legs twitched, ready to bolt.

But, oddly, it held its position. Sharp canine senses must have indicated absence of threat.

The beast eventually lost curiosity, backed away, turned, and casually walked to the drying racks where the fresh meat hung. While occasionally glancing back to Anne, it stood on hind legs and reached one of the longer strips of meat. After several failed attempts, it finally pulled the strip from its hold and gulped it down.

"I thank Providence I didn't get a mouthful of *that* snout," Anne mumbled. She then turned to see Little Feather fully awake. "That beast could have eaten my face entirely away. Had that meat not been hanging there, my face may have fared no better than ox meat."

Upon closer inspection, the brightness of the blue moon made it easy to see the animal was female with full mammary. Eating her fill, the she-wolf yanked a final strip of meat from overhead. She loped away, disappearing into the forest.

The breaking dawn brought a jumble of chattering voices when it was discovered the racks of meat had been robbed. Anne awoke to a Catawba brave crouching on the ground checking tracks beneath the rack where only a paltry amount of meat remained.

Angered, the brave sprang to his feet speaking abruptly to the woman who had been so kind to her the day before. The woman dropped to her knees and pleaded with outstretched arms.

He snatched a hefty stick from the ground and whipped the woman, becoming frenzied, slobber stringing in rivulets from his bouncing lower lip.

She cried in anguish yet he wouldn't stop.

He continued whipping even though she'd gone quiet and still. He had beaten her senseless.

Anne jerked and squirmed against her restraints. "You crazy lout! She had nothing to do with it!"

The warrior beat the woman until he tired of swinging the stick. After a final brutal swing, the brave threw the stick to the ground and looked to Anne— lunacy in his eyes, drool dripping from his chin. He ground the squaw's face in the dirt before storming away. He yelled orders in that guttural language to others. Men and women watched with bland expressions as if it were commonplace, an everyday occurrence.

*They act like animals.* "I have never before seen such cruelty," she told Little Feather.

"Preparing food is the job of the tribe's women. It does not matter how the meat came to be missing. It is the responsibility of the woman. According to custom, it is the fault of the woman that it's now lost. He gathers men together to hunt down the wolves and kill them. Instinct will bring them back again and again in search of an easy meal."

"Damn their laws and traditions! That maniac will someday know my wrath." Anne's faced reddened to match her curly hair.

The squaw lay semi-conscious until midday. Drying blood caked her mouth, nose, and one eye. Flies gathered and began the timeless process of looking for a place to lay eggs. She lay unconscious for hours. When she did regain consciousness, she lay unmoving for some time.

The brave who had beaten her returned with other hunters and dropped wolf carcasses on her then threw a clay pot of water on her and dropped a flint knife in front of her face. She groaned and pulled her body into a tight ball, covering her head. She feared another beating.

Anne could do nothing. The dazed woman was expected to skin the wolves. Her face had swollen into a grotesque caricature.

Darkness descended by the time she completed the task. She stumbled away injured and exhausted.

The only food given Anne or Little Feather all day happened to be a few spoonfuls of mush made from a variety of crushed seeds. Anne's stomach rumbled and growled in need of more nourishment to heal properly. Pangs of hunger stayed with her into the night. She couldn't sleep. Looking to the brilliance of the moon, she wondered when an opportunity to escape might occur. She was confident it eventually would, simply a matter of when.

She detected movement next to a hut across the yard. Fixing a gaze on the shadow, she waited to see if a trick had been played on her vision. Eventually, she saw the outline of a wolf emerge, hesitating and cautious, head hung low. It stopped frequently to sniff the air. Anne noticed low-slung teats. It was the same animal from the night before.

"Well, lass, I wager your pups are dead and the rest of your pack is over there with their skins stretched tight. You've now been set adrift as we have."

Looking to Anne with a curious head tilt, the wolf briefly paused when it heard the gurgling emptiness of Anne's stomach. It moved on to the framework that held taut wolf skins. Sniffing the remains of her family, the animal whimpered. The she-wolf dropped her head and walked in a tight circle, mourning.

"Make no sound, love, or you shall be found out and killed, too. I'd take no joy in seeing your skin hangin' beside those of your pack."

As if understanding the warning the animal made no more noise. It stopped and again looked at Anne. Its head tilted one way then the other, curious about Anne. Cautiously, it approached.

Anne pulled her good leg up and leaned her head against the post she was bound to. She became suspicious of the animal's intent. "Now what interest am I to you?"

The wolf slowly stretched its neck to put her nose near Anne's face and sniffed.

Anne stiffened. In a slow deliberate way, she turned her head to the side in case the next move was a sudden snap of sharp canine teeth on her face.

Apparently satisfied, the animal backed away and went to the drying racks. She circled one, looking for a way to retrieve meat that hung higher than before. The beast tried reaching morsels dangling above by standing outstretched on hind legs but no good. Clamping jaws onto one of the sapling angle braces at the bottom corner of the square frame, she tugged. Nothing moved.

The wolf backed away, circled then went at it again. This time she tugged repeatedly in rhythmic fashion. The rack swayed. The action wrenched the brace from its binding. The entire structure listed into a parallelogram. The meat was suddenly within easy reach. The wolf gulped down as much as she could hold.

The growl of Anne's empty stomach prompted the animal to pause and take a quizzical look. It pulled another strip of meat from its hold and approached.

Anne watched, nervous. *What motivates a wolf to approach with meat in its mouth? Am I to be desert?* She sat motionless. As the animal came close, Anne pulled her head as far back as she could. Again, she turned her face to the side. The animal placed the strip on her chest just below Anne's chin, licked her cheek then backed away. Anne drew a deep breath and exhaled. She looked down at the meat. "Have I become your surrogate pup? Is that it?"

Anne worked her head until she snagged the meat between her teeth. She chewed, moaning. Any other time raw meat would have disgusted her but now the taste was exquisite. The long strip gradually disappeared into her mouth as she chewed. Swallowing repeatedly to capture and retain the last smidgen of flavor, she licked her lips. "Sweet lord, if my body wasn't racked with pain that would have been orgasmic."

Her wandering eyes fell again on the wolf. "If you believe me to be your pup, then I shall call you Momma since maternal instinct drives you."

Anne hadn't considered consequences of the wolf's actions but Little Feather did. "The squaw will be killed if the meat is discovered missing again."

"Then I hope our new friend, Momma, does not hold against me what I'm about to do." As loud as she could, "Get away from here! Run! Don't come back or your hide will join that of your family!"

Momma scampered into the night.

The noise awakened the village. Rustling bodies and voices turned into a gathering in the central yard. Taking the lead was the woman beater. He examined the rack, teeth marks on the sapling brace, and tracks. He assessed the noise saved the remainder of the meat. He shouted orders to the squaw with the puffy bruised face. She pulled a knife and cut Anne's bindings to the post then offered Anne a warm smile, no translation necessary. In it, Anne saw that the squaw knew the shouting saved her life. She cut Little Feather loose as well.

The brave was not as gentle. He unceremoniously grabbed Anne by the pants belt and dragged her into a hut, retying her hands to her front. Another dragged Little Feather in to join her. The squaw put a bowl full of meat, berries, and seeds in front of them, bowing slightly, smiling again then leaving.

As the brave finished binding her, Anne looked into his eyes. Knowing he couldn't understand, she cooed, "Just because you're feelin' obligated, ya need to know it has nothin' to do with you or your stinkin' tribe. And do ya know what that means?" She smiled in a loving way. "It means I still plan on slittin' your bloody throat." She batted her eyelashes and held a dreamy look.

# Chapter Six

Imprisoned in the Catawba village everyday was like the day before and likely to be the same as the next. Anne's tolerance was about exhausted. One day ended another and began like a wheel—no beginning, no end. Staying alive occupied waking thoughts; that and living long enough to get revenge on Woman Beater.

*Boredom crushes the life from me. How many weeks has it been?* She attempted calculating passage of time starting from the day of the clubbing then dragged to the village of this splinter group of the Catawba tribe, but she couldn't.

Villagers grew comfortable with Anne and Little Feather's presence. Security, nevertheless, remained tight—the hut guarded day and night. Anne took little comfort in no longer being the village oddity. Bright red hair didn't amaze as it once did. Hardly anyone stopped to stare anymore.

This familiarity grated Anne to a raw edge because it meant she'd been imprisoned too long. Contempt for the captors increased with each new day denied freedom. Anne looked to every nuance as opportunity—each deviation in routine a chance for escape. But even the most promising she couldn't act on; she had no weapons and remained bound. In a constant state of bloody rawness, her wrists would be scarred for life. Aside from Little Feather, she trusted no one, and underestimating the Catawba would get her killed.

With Little Feather's assistance, Anne came to understand the language better. Even when she couldn't determine exact meaning, she understood enough to garner intent. Understanding was the first step in outwitting them.

"By the saints," Anne wailed with a grimace. "Don't you bloody people do anything in a gentle way?" The medicine man paid her no mind as he probed her leg determining if the tibia had knitted. With a decided lack of finesse, he poked, kneaded, and turned the leg one way then the other. "Be careful or you'll snap it again you heathen idiot!"

Understanding his muttering to mean *good enough*, he pulled a short flint knife and cut bindings that had secured the bark splint in place. Sudden increased blood flow down her leg stung then she felt warmth flowing through veins long starved.

Later, pain subsided as vessels dilated carrying the necessary volume of blood through them. Comfort increased; so did questions. Speaking to her leg, "Okay, my lovely, just what can you do for me today?" She gently moved the leg about and then bent the knee. Stabbing pain shot through it. "Oh, so that's how it is goin' ta be. Twice in this life I must teach you to walk."

The squaw entered, having become quite comfortable in Anne's presence. Charged with the care of the tribe's precious merchandise, she cut Anne's hands free and urged her to stand. Anne frowned up at her and shook her head. She had no intention of doing anything until the extended deep massage was complete, an ecstasy only imagined at the beginning of this day. She rubbed until the needles-and-pins tingle subsided.

The squaw knelt beside her and examined the bloody wrists. She unfolded a buckskin patch. In the center of it was a dollop of fat that had been mixed with something green, a forest herb perhaps. The Indian woman daubed it onto Anne's wrists. The woman's gentleness surprised her. "You have the touch of a loving mother." Anne nodded approvingly. "Thank you. It is the first kindness I've known in this wretched place." The squaw didn't understand the words but plainly did the tone. She smiled.

It seems they prepare you for a journey," Little Feather said.

"So it would seem." She gave her leg a final rub. "I've lain looking up at that ceiling for weeks. Now, I finally get a closer look… a simple pleasure for sure." Using the center support pole of the hut, she began the arduous task of pulling herself to her feet. After a time she became fully erect and attempted putting weight on the injured leg. To her great surprise no pain seemed associated with the application of body weight. But once she attempted a step, atrophied muscles twitched and failed. She collapsed, spiraling to the ground.

She believed the squaw to say, "Do it again." Then she poked hands into Anne's armpits and pulled her up.

Walking hands up the central post, she struggled to her feet then hopped around on her good leg to face the woman almost nose-to-nose. "What do they call you?" Anne asked, using the Catawba language best she could.

The woman did not pull away. Instead she seemed impressed with Anne's growing command of the language and rattled a response.

Anne frowned with a quick headshake then shrugged. She looked to Little Feather. "What does she tell me?"

"She says her name is Cantawekaedalanea. It translates to The Noise That Is Made When the Wind Disturbs the Trees."

"*Canta…Cantawee…Cantaway.* She laughed. "Surely she doesn't expect me to use that. Life's too short."

Looking to the squaw, Anne thought for a second then clumsily attempted to speak the language. She finally gave up. In English, "How about I call you Windsong? I once knew a galleon by that name. Ah, a finer ship I've never seen. Its name conjured beautiful thoughts."

Little Feather offered a quick translation.

"Wind…song," the squaw said, enunciating carefully. "Windsong," she repeated rapidly then offered a broad smile. She nodded approval. Windsong didn't dwell upon it, again urging Anne to walk.

The remainder of the day, Windsong and Little Feather walked Anne about in a circle within the confines of their prison, exercising the leg. It responded favorably. As the sun oozed below the horizon, the leg began to ache. Therapy ended. Windsong left, leaving Anne and Little Feather alone.

Aimlessly drawing circles in the dirt floor, "Are we about to begin a journey back to the colonies?"

"I've heard the Iswa chief speak of the wisdom of making a trade before news of the massacre makes it back to the colonists. They fear their bargaining position will drop to nothing should they be found out. They desire to trade us for weapons then return to fortify their village before that happens."

"Foolish savages. Should the colonists discover my identity they'd not only receive nothing, I'd likely be shot or hanged…them along with me. Excrement has more value than my hide."

Exhausted, she scooted on her butt against the wall of the hut. Her head fell back against the cedar sapling frame shingled over with birch bark on the outside. As fatigue set in, she gave her thoughts free rein wondering about the future. She longed for the sea but feared dying in these woods hundreds of miles from the nearest salt water. Getting back to a world she felt mastery over became the goal. *Whatever it takes, that's what I must do.*

Suddenly, she sensed something at her back and sat upright.

Looking through a tiny separation in the bark siding of the hut, she saw Momma the wolf.

"Well, my darling. It's nice to see you again."

The kind sound of her voice drew a whimper.

"Shh. Quiet now. You don't want these heathens knowin' you've returned."

Anne pulled strands of the loosest bark away until a tiny space widened enough to poke the very tip of a finger through. She rubbed Momma's snout. A warm tongue lapped at the appendage, wetting it. "We may not be in this place much longer. I think you sense that. Is that why you've returned?"

She rubbed the wolf's wet nose for a moment longer then dropped her head to see through the hole, looking directly into the eyes of a wild animal that showed signs of understanding. "So, sweet friend, how do you see my capture playing out?" Anne asked the wolf in such a way that Momma did a quick dance on her front paws.

Astonished, "You do understand, don't you?"

~ * ~

The leg strengthened. Tribal elders allowed Anne to move about the central yard under guard but with no assistance. Walking about happened to be a therapeutic indulgence that allowed her to think clearly—to plan without interruption—escape the goal. There could be no other consideration. It had gone from possibility to inevitability by her calculation.

Protesting exclusion, Little Feather wanted to join her friend in the yard for those walks. But the protest earned a hard backhand slap in the face by Woman Beater. The young girl was forced to remain in the hut.

On this day, Windsong joined Anne in the exercise ritual and walked with her. A warrior laden with spear, knives, and a tomahawk dangling at his side, followed closely, but Windsong had learned enough English to converse. It was rough but understandable. Anne saw it in Windsong's eyes; the squaw felt liberated, unfettered by the confines of her own language. She spoke freely without fear of reprimand, a seed Anne had every intention of nurturing. "Windsong, where are my cutlasses and rapier?"

Not understanding those words, she merely looked confused.

Anne made tiny slashing and lunging motions with her finger.

Recognition brightened the squaw's eyes. Holding a finger close to her front, she pointed to Woman Beater then to his hut.

"Aye, the reasons mount why I should put that man down," Anne muttered as she looked across the compound to where he stood talking with others.

Signs of preparation for an overland journey continued around the village. Women pounded dried beef, suet, and course raw sugar together to make pemmican, a highly concentrated food source rich in nutrients yet taking up little space. The men fashioned flint points for arrows and spearheads, lashing them to hardwood shafts children gathered from the woods.

Anne noticed English influence. A few of the men carried tomahawks and knives with black iron blades. Although much of the clothing was made from furs, skins, and leathers, a few of the men sported colorful cloth shirts or rags that had been fashioned into a type of headdress. It was likely things taken after the massacre.

The sun shone brightly but the late summer breeze bore an unmistakable feel that seasons were about to switch. Forests of green would soon be cloaked in autumn's colors. A month, maybe six weeks, and first snows of winter would hamper foot travel. Anne assumed the journey would allow the Catawba to complete business with colonists and make the trek back to the village before the bitterest cold set in.

"I want to teach you a new word, Windsong..." Anne told her, "...freedom."

"Free...dom?" Windsong formed the word carefully.

"That's right. Freedom. It means doing as you wish, going where you wish, and being master of your own life."

Windsong appeared not to trust her grasp of English well enough to capture the essence of what freedom was all about. "Freedom?" She placed a fingertip between Anne's breasts. "With freedom, who protects you?"

Anne smiled. She reached for Windsong's hand and placed it on the scar left by the clubbing on her forehead. "I have been beaten." Anne then transferred Windsong's fingertips to her own scars left by Woman Beater. "You have been beaten. What's the difference?" Anne suddenly dropped the smile, becoming intensely serious. "Believe me, my sweet, your chances of survival are better if you provide for yourself. This *protection* will get you killed. Can you understand that?"

Pursing her lips, Windsong stared for a long moment. She nodded faintly. Anne couldn't be sure how much the woman grasped.

Looking around at the group of huts encircling them then back at her guard with clear contempt, Anne summed up her daily lesson. "You're intelligent. You have heart. You deserve better. It's worth the risk I consider you my friend."

"Friend?"

"Yes, friend."

Windsong knew full well the meaning of this word and squeezed Anne's arm a little tighter as they continued the walk around the village common. Her eyes moistened.

# Chapter Seven

Woman Beater examined provisions and weapons of the assembled men, angrily scolding those unprepared. Women and children stood quiet and obedient near respective huts and waited. Wind swirled dust through the open central yard of the village. He stopped the tirade long enough to turn his nose into the wind like an animal catching scent of the coming change of seasons.

In words Anne recognized, he announced, "We go. Time grows short." The wind shifted and now came in from the north. Dust stopped swirling and now blew straight south—an almost magical punctuation to his order.

She hated the man but he was an interesting study. Woman Beater was dog-ugly. Yet she believed he saw himself worthy of deification. His dark, ruddy red face bore pits and scars. Add in that hideous flattened forehead and a gnarled nose broken numerous times and it was amazing he didn't frighten his toddler child. *I'd like to break his bloody nose again.*

His child had the flat forehead, too; all the males did. They proudly displayed the disgusting head slope from above the eyebrows to the hairline pressed into their skulls as infants. *Hideous is normal to those poor children. My actions will be dictatin' whom I'm to be and how I'm to live; not mashin' me damned head flat.*

One of the braves tied their hands then bound them together at the wrists with a long single rope, the end of which was tied to the tail of an ox. As the ox went, so they went. Teeth clenched, jaw muscles working, "I promise you, our days as chattel grow short." Unalterably, she stood directly behind the massive bovine's anal aperture and hoped for tight bowels waiting to begin the forced march east.

Windsong ran from her hut and in an unusual display of disobedience and pleaded with Woman Beater. Anne understood none of what she begged for.

"Windsong pleads to go along as protector of the merchandise...us. I think it might be her way of escaping."

At first shocked, Woman Beater recoiled in surprise but then lived up to the title Anne bestowed upon him. He slapped her then with balled fist knocked her to the ground ordering her back to the ranks of the women and children.

Anne took out after him but only a single step later she hit the end of the rope. "You ugly, arrogant ass!" she yelled.

The startled ox yanked her off her feet. Then the animal's tail stiffened and from beneath it oozed feces. She suddenly realized it was only the precursor to a full load. She rolled left just before grassy green excrement splattered on the ground next to her.

Veins bulged on the sides of her head as her face went deep crimson. She exploded, "Your time on the face of this earth is predestined and I, sir, am...your...destiny!" She followed with a shrill scream flushing a nearby flock of egrets.

"Anne, look," Little Feather said.

Windsong lay holding her swelling cheek, but she bore an oddly pleasant look. Then pride swelled in Anne as Windsong said, "Freedom." The quiet strength of this Catawba beauty quelled Anne's fiery temper and filled her with hope.

One of the braves slapped the ox on the back, jerking Anne then Little Feather forward. They watched Windsong as long as she remained in sight. "If I have to tiptoe through hell, I'll know you again, friend," Anne mumbled as Windsong disappeared behind them.

~ * ~

The first few days out proved uneventful but exhausting. Walking without free use of hands was a constant struggle for balance. Anne and her Iroquois protégé engaged in long conversations of wishes and dreams; things that took their minds to other places and times for brief periods of relief from the grueling trek.

On the third day at dusk they stopped to make camp. The long rawhide rope was removed from the ox's tail and used to bind the two to a tree. Hands were left free enough to eat as cakes of pemmican were dropped into their laps. They devoured a portion, setting aside the rest for later.

Anne yawned. "I'll be your pillow if you'll be mine."

The young Indian laid her head on Anne's shoulder, snuggling down and sighing.

Anne pressed her cheek gently into the top of the girl's head.

As Anne drifted into a light sleep, Little Feather whispered, "It doesn't matter that we are bound to a tree, I feel safe in your presence."

The day ended. The moon rose. Anne was seduced into slumber by the flattering words of an Indian maiden.

Some time later, Anne was startled awake. She opened her eyes in response to an unknown stimulus. She cautiously moved only her eyes and looked to her right but kept her head still. When she looked to her left, there stood Momma. She relaxed. "Well, good evening, my darling." Using only fingertips, she reached inside her shirt and removed a chunk of pemmican and offered it to the she-wolf. The canine stretched its snout and sniffed. "Go ahead. Take it. It's only fair. You certainly nourished me once upon a time."

Momma lightly gave the chunk a stroke with her tongue then snatched it from Anne's fingertips and mauled it between her teeth and gulped it down.

"She sees you as an ally," Little Feather said, now fully awake but still resting upon Anne's shoulder.

"And I see Momma's presence as a sign."

"Of what?"

"An omen that—"

Momma suddenly bolted and ran into the forest.

"By the saints, what got into her?" Straining to see through tree-filtered moonlight she saw nothing but suspected that one of the Catawba men might be approaching.

"Look over there," Little Feather said barely above a sigh.

Straining to see into the shadows, she concentrated on a space between trees where the moon illuminated a patch. She finally saw movement low to the ground. It was indeed a human form, crawling.

"It might be a warrior from a rival tribe," Little Feather said, fidgeting, tugging at the knotted rope on her wrists.

"Easy lass," Anne whispered. "There's nothin' to be gained by fear."

Anne looked to where the Catawba men were bedded. She saw no movement.

The form quietly darted from one tree to the next, pausing briefly giving time to assure secrecy. Anne tried picking out detail. But even a brilliant moon couldn't erase black shadows where the intruder chose to stand. The only discernible feature was that the person did not have a flattened forehead. *Not Catawba. But who might it be?*

Finally making it to the large tree next to the one they were tied to, the stranger stood motionless. Anne wanted to call out but curiosity must wait or risk waking her captors. She hadn't determined yet if that would be wise or not.

The person lowered to the ground and crawled behind the tree that held her and Little Feather. Twisting side to side, Anne tried to see behind them, uncertain if a tomahawk might split their skulls. But one word put them at ease. A blackened face appeared beside Anne and whispered, "Freedom."

Windsong sliced through the ropes and freed them. Without conversation, they followed her into the woods, marching north long enough for the moon to move from their left to their right. Along the way Anne noticed

Windsong had taken a chapter from Little Feather's book of how to dress for freedom. She'd split her buckskin skirt and stitched it back as leggings. Freedom demanded ease of movement and protection for lower extremities.

Anne felt personally responsible for these precious friends. She put herself in position of protector because she was the one that had convinced them they'd be better off on their own.

Climbing a short boulder-strewn rise, Windsong dropped off a steep embankment beside a tangle of vines. She pushed them aside and retrieved a bundle. She then tossed it up to Anne. Untying a leather strip, Anne unrolled the tanned cowhide. Revealed were food, knives, bows, arrows, and spears. But something else happened to be in the cache, Anne's beloved cutlasses and rapier.

Throwing arms around Windsong, she pulled her into an embrace. "I am no longer Irish. Little Feather is no longer Iroquois. And you, Windsong, are no longer Catawba. We are just free women, belonging to no one... clan, tribe, or cult. Do you understand? Free!"

The three marched north for a time then turned east, trekking in the direction of the Carolinas, roughly parallel to the route Catawba braves took. Anne thought on a plan. She was confident she now had the wherewithal to give it life. Adding to that boldness, she looked to the ridge above them. There, in a small clearing, a particularly strong moonbeam illuminated the fourth member of their party. Momma the she-wolf matched their pace.

Confident they'd be pursued, Anne refused to rest and did not allow dawdling. After captivity covering most of two seasons, determination to remain free had hardened to stone, and she was bent on putting safe distance between them and the warriors. They marched through the night and well into the next morning.

Head hanging heavy, Little Feather announced, "I have wrung the good from our brief slumber of last evening."

It was midmorning. Anne finally acquiesced to a break. "The moon will be almost as bright again tonight. We'll rest through the heat of day and be on the move late this afternoon through the night. Agreed?"

Little Feather and Windsong looked at one another and nodded.

"I pray the warriors did not discover our absence until after daylight."

Slipping into relative security of a space overhung by jutting rocks and camouflaged by a curtain of vines, the three shed weapons and provisions then dropped to the ground. Sleep came quickly.

Anne woke to a beetle crawling across her bare ankle then noticed the sun had shifted to the setting side of the sky. She heard the gurgle of water and rose to follow the sound, leaving her friends to sleep. Down the hill, through dense undergrowth appeared an inviting sight, a narrow creek of crystal clear fast flowing water.

Dropping to her knees at its edge, she drank of the chilled fluid savoring each swallow. She couldn't remember ever having drunk water sweeter, treating the experience with reverence. The thirst she quenched went beyond the physical. She quenched an exhausting desire for latitude, for indulgence, for privilege—for freedom. Renewed vigor coursed her body.

Walking on a short distance, she came to a boulder splitting the flow pooling calmer and deeper water behind it. Willpower to remain vigilant suddenly went elsewhere. She removed boots, pantaloons and blood stained linen shirt. Squatting naked on the bank, she washed away months of grime ground into each piece then she slipped into the water. Iciness gripped her, squeezing breath from her lungs pressing out a girlish giggle.

Momma appeared on the other side and drank her fill then sat on her haunches. The wolf seemed to enjoy watching. She even smiled, in a wolf sort of way, panting, tongue dancing in her open mouth.

"Isn't this wonderful, Momma? I never thought the simple pleasure of a bath could be so heavenly."

Anne whirled around in the water, luxuriating in the cool feel of it against her skin. Finally, she noticed Windsong and Little Feather watching. "There's no reason to deprive ourselves of this pleasure. Let's make use of this piece of paradise while we can."

The two hastily shucked buckskin breeches and tops, sliding into the chilled water. As the grime of the trail floated away, so did concern. They laughed and played like children. Worry over the passage of time melted away as they wallowed in a version of heaven on earth.

Momma napped, the animal occasionally raising her head in response to a giggle or a splash. But then, quite suddenly, she jumped to her feet and threw her nose into the air.

"Look, the wolf senses something," Windsong said.

The canine paced left then right then walked a tight circle before moving back into deep cover.

"We must heed the warning," Anne said. She climbed from the water meandering and picking her way through the brush back up the hill to where they shed clothing.

Little Feather and Windsong followed.

The sound of voices carried on the wind.

The sound of talk grew stronger then stopped. When it resumed it was subdued.

They had been discovered.

"Our weapons," Anne whispered, "We must get to our weapons."

The voices became a marker of the enemy's position.

They hurriedly dressed.

Methodically, the warriors moved in the general direction of the campsite.

"You two stay here," Anne ordered, "One person will make less noise and work faster."

Crawling so fast through the undergrowth she seemed to slither like a snake up the hill. She made it to the cowhide roll encasing weapons and food. Leaving the bundle rolled tight to avoid the clank of metal, she hurried back down the hill to where she'd left Little Feather and Windsong.

Belting the rapier around her wet, clinging shirt, she threw her fiery red and sodden hair aside then poked her head through the leather sash holding her cutlass scabbard, buckling it securely. She then shoved three short knives into her belt. Taking the leather strip that had bound the cowhide roll, Anne cut it into thirds and issued lengths to her friends. They uniformly tied strips around their heads to hold wet hair from eyes. Advantages would be few, outnumbered four to one.

Little Feather pulled her cutlass from the pile and strapped it on. Windsong filled her fists with arrows, a bow, a spear, and a flint knife.

"We are only three and cannot overtake sixteen in a face to face fight," Anne said, prefacing an idea. "Little Feather, climb that ridge. Windsong, go back down near the creek. When you hear me hoot then you hoot too, Windsong. Little Feather, you wait for a short time and then cry out as loud as you can. We must separate them. If timed well, maybe we can split them into manageable numbers."

Once the two were out of sight, Anne waited. Even though the voices were whispers, they grew sharp. Drawing her rapier and holding it in her right hand she withdrew the cutlass and held it backwards in her left hand, blade forward, her personal version of battle mode. Throwing her head back she let out a primal scream, hoping to raise hackles and freeze the Catawba in place.

Jumping into the adjacent clearing, she made ready for an assault as the entire party appeared over the rise. They yelled out their own battle cries. "Now, Windsong. Now, or I am dead," Anne growled through clenched teeth.

Running full bore at her, the sixteen Indians slowed when they saw only one. Then from the direction of the creek, Windsong yelled out a Catawba word that Anne did not recognize. A number of men responded and peeled off, running down the hill. But it was not enough.

Ten, maybe more, prepared to engage Anne when above her Little Feather let out a screech. Not a single one broke rank to respond to Little Feather's call. Obviously, the heathens remembered the battle in the mountain pass and saw Anne as the bigger threat.

"Bloody hell," was the only thing she had time to shout as the first armed brave arrived with stone ax raised. Speed and accuracy disposed of him quickly, lunging once with the rapier then back-slashing his throat with the cutlass.

Backing against a large tree, Anne attempted to battle in a way so that she need not worry about an undetected rear approach. She held one at bay to her right just beyond the tip of her slender rapier. At the same time, she slashed with the cutlass at another to her left, leaving her belly exposed.

A spear wielding man lunged at her screaming as if the battle might be over in a flash.

Anne had a different idea, slapping the approaching spear aside with a clang of her cutlass and continuing that motion taking the razor sharp blade slashing the belly of another attacker to her left.

That forced the now stumbling spear handler to impale himself on her rapier just as the brave to the right brought down a tomahawk landing on the shoulder of the spear handler. He collapsed against Anne giving her the necessary time to withdraw the rapier and jam its point through the neck of the one holding the tomahawk.

The battle was confusing and fast. Two more hands were needed. The two she had were not moving fast enough. She scarcely had time to react to each advance.

She couldn't find enough time to draw a full breath. Anne slung her head around, catching sight of Woman Beater.

He charged. He leaped. The self-avowed leader threw his full weight behind a war club, bent on pulverizing her skull.

Anne recognized the weapon as the same type that had broken her leg in that previous battle—maybe the same one. She felt the sting of a memory pain in her leg. *Oh, no. You shall not break another bone of mine, you Son of Satan.*

She bolted away from the tree to take the fight to him, as every injustice flashed in her mind—the broken leg, dragged by the hair and, the vilest of all, the senseless beating of Windsong. With a stroke that could never be duplicated in speed or accuracy, she severed the club wielding hand and both went flying out of harm's way. The move cost her the protection of the tree. It left her back dangerously exposed. She saw the shadow of a knife raised above her.

She heard a whistling thwack. Spinning around she found herself nose to nose and looking directly into the shocked, staring eyes of a brave. An arrow had penetrated his back and all the way through the left side of his chest—the stone arrowhead visible to Anne. He still held the knife high in a death-dealing pose.

Then he collapsed, no longer a threat, as Windsong yelled, "Freedom!"

From above, Little Feather dropped from a boulder to join the fray.

The triad stood back to back to back. They felled two more.

Only one remained. As his eyes darted about, his thought was clear upon his face; he realized he was the last one standing against three determined women. He scampered over the hill. A handless Woman Beater stumbled after him.

Breathing heavily and sweating profusely, the three did not move, uncertain if the battle had indeed ended. Wary eyes searched nearby trees and bushes for new faces to appear. None did.

"What do you think?" Anne huffed. "Will they be back?"

"I think we have lost our value to them," Little Feather said.

Windsong collapsed.

Tossing weapons aside, she and Little Feather dropped to the ground on each side of her. Anne noticed blood streaming from a hole in the buckskin that covered her belly. She raised the garment to reveal a deep gash, exposing the multi-colored veins of her intestines.

Putting her nose close, she sniffed. She raised her head allowing it to fall back on her shoulders, anguished.

"What is it you smell?" Little Feather asked.

"The acrid contents of her belly. She is poisoned. I can do nothing. Nothing!"

Through pain Windsong uttered the same Catawba word she'd screamed earlier that Anne could not translate. An unusual calm replaced the pained look on her face. She reached for the leather sash across Anne's chest and pulled her close. "You...Little Feather...me...we are free?"

"Yes...free." Anne's eyes filled with tears. She turned to Little Feather. "What is that word she uses?"

"It is the Iswa word for freedom. She wanted her attackers to know in their own language her intention."

When the day ended, so did Windsong.

## Chapter Eight

Dawn the next day, a sad task lay before Anne.

It began to rain. Large drops splattered the dry ground in a miserly pattern. It seemed even the rain sought to fall only on surfaces not infected by melancholy. Gloom left nothing untouched in this battle of the greater eternal war between forces of life and love and that of death and hate.

Steel-hard toughness bred into Anne could not stand against heart-rending dolor. She and Little Feather scattered wildflowers over the lifeless body of a liberator they barely had a chance to know. Windsong lay serenely prone inside the leather coffin—still a hint of smile upon her lips. As the light of life left her last night, freedom was hers and she knew it.

Succumbing to the weight of sorrow, kneeling alongside the corpse, Anne's head pressed into a grieving bow. Little Feather's head hung as low. They folded the cowhide that once held provisions over the lifeless Catawba woman who not only discovered freedom and what it meant but also gave them theirs. She disappeared beneath the leather fold in which they wrapped her.

Rain fell harder and became indistinguishable from streaming tears. Lightning flashed then thunder crackled and boomed.

Anne didn't flinch. She placed stone upon stone over the body, in this place that was now Windsong's grave. "Storm clouds and death follow me, Little Feather. You'd have a better life... nay, a better chance of just surviving if you stayed far away from me."

"Responsibility for life resides with the soul in which that light shines," Little Feather said. "You merely fanned a flame that already existed. You nurture the same flame in me. Your presence inspires me. It is not a curse." She looked to the leather roll holding Windsong and clenched her hands together over her heart. "It was her choice. It is my choice as well."

A mournful howl went up as the two looked to see Momma sitting on her haunches high on a ridge some distance away. The animal sensed loss and sounded those feelings.

"You see. Instinct tells even the she-wolf to keep a distance. She knows well the grim reaper follows me as do storm clouds that appear when a friend falls." Locked in grief, Anne refused to be swayed.

"Grieve the loss of a life but don't let it create blackness around you that blinds you to the truth." Little Feather placed a final stone upon the grave then rose. "Now, I'll tell you how Iroquois eyes see this..." She paused and stared at the oblong pile of stones. She spread her arms wide. "...Our friend did not die a broken woman or join the spirits sad and weakened. She joined them empowered as a free human being. Lift your head, Anne Bonny, and know that Windsong experiences the ultimate freedom." She faced Anne and gestured skyward. "Our friend has called upon the great spirits to send this rain. There is no sadness in rain. It signals rebirth. You are given the gift of a cleansing shower with water straight from heaven to wash the blood of your enemies away. Windsong has sent her blessings upon you just as she did with a gourd dipper of water into your parched face.

Anne's eyes followed Little Feather's attention to the sky. Rain streamed from her chin down her neck. She tried looking beyond the rain, above the clouds, all the way to glory. "Holy Father, I have no right to be askin' due to my lack of innocence and all, but please take Windsong into your lovin' arms. As for me... well, I understand it's too late and I cannot relive my pathetic life. But standin' before ya is a true heart, worthy of goodness."

The rain stopped. A ribbon of sunlight pierced the turbid cloud-filled sky, illuminating the clearing where they stood.

"Windsong tells you it's time to stop mourning and to continue our journey."

# Chapter Nine

Getting over the mountains to Charleston before snow clogged the passes seemed unlikely. Nevertheless, the pace remained casual as Anne and Little Feather enjoyed the freedom of not having to look over their shoulders. Without Catawba warriors on their trail and the colonists believing she was dead, Anne felt secure—the first time in a long while.

Little Feather became a veritable fountain of survival information. She taught Anne the art of snaring rabbits and to track peccary and dear plus other skills necessary when the pemmican supply ran out. The young Iroquois identified edible wild onions and lambs quarters greens in rain-filled meadows—even snacking on berries along the trail became commonplace. Also, the young girl pointed to a plethora of plant life suitable for treating and curing ailments.

"I may become heavy on my feet if this wild bounty continues," Anne said, pushing a tree limb aside, revealing a broad grassy clearing and a view of the mountains in the distance. She held the limb until Little Feather passed.

"The mountains will use up energy quickly." The rocky outcropping at the base of the mountains appeared reachable in another day's walk. "Food may become difficult to find in the high country. The days grow short and snow will always come first to the mountains. We are not prepared for weeks of searching for passages over them."

Reluctantly, Anne agreed to use a few of the precious warm days to stockpile food and fashion warm garments for the arduous journey into the high country. Traps and snares netted rabbits, possums, raccoons, and even one worthless porcupine. Little Feather discovered a shed set of deer antlers. She taught Anne how to rattle them until a would-be rival buck appeared to claim its territory but instead got an arrow. They got venison and a warm cape for the effort.

Meats were hung to dry, as were skins. Warm garments were fashioned from hides, including mittens, snug headgear, shoulder drapes, and fur covered leggings and boots.

On this late autumn morning, the two woke to a strong north wind whistling through the woods carrying a bone-biting chill. Northward flowing clouds thickened, obliterating the mountains in the dull gray cloak of a winter sky. Brilliantly colored seasonal foliage shook loose from trees and swirled to the ground in a noisy rustle. The season entered the throes of a timeless ritual of change.

A day passed then two. Only then did clouds move on allowing the sun a chance to squeeze random rays through to the ground. A plan-changing sight appeared before the final scudding clouds cleared away. Snow blanketed the mountain peaks all the way down the sides into those areas where passage were assumed.

Disheartened, Anne cursed the weather. If the mountains are clogged with snow then what? Was Charleston by springtime even possible now?

Little Feather had a pragmatic outlook—the circle of life, all things in their season, readily accepting that it'd be spring before they could begin such a formidable journey with hope of success even survival.

"This is a warning to complete preparations. We must winter here," the young girl said. "We may still have warm days ahead but snow here is only weeks, maybe days, behind the mountains."

Confiscated tomahawks and Anne's cutlasses had become construction tools. Sunup until sundown for three days, they cut saplings, lashed them with reeds, vines and stringy cedar bark between two massive oak trees creating the framework for a hut. Birch bark was then stripped and layered on it in such a way as to shed water while efficiently blocking wind.

Blustery north winds pushed wildlife to prepare as well. The animals of the forest remained on the move, eating, building a fat layer that would carry them through lean times of winter. That made it simpler to lay in a larger stock of meat, furs, and skins. Once the hut was complete, more time was given to gathering seeds, nuts, and berries. It became a daily ritual right up to the day that proved the investment in time had been wise.

The north wind no longer teased with gentle cool fingers. It stung exposed skin with frigid blasts. Dreary gray clouds hung low.

Huddled within the hut, Anne looked about at hide pouches lining the highest cross-members of the enclosure all loaded with dried meats, nuts, berries, and seeds. All the while a small aromatic fire at the center crackled lazily. "If you'd not been here, Little Feather, I would now be somewhere high in those mountains hungry and dyin' from this wretched cold. Without you, I would've done the foolish thing and gone on. I'd never have survived 'til spring."

A particularly hard gust popped the hide flap covering the entrance. Snowflakes forced their way in, revealing a familiar face standing beyond the portal. Momma poked her snout beyond the flap. Anne noticed. "Come in, my darling. Join us by the fire." The invitation was not accepted.

Throughout the day, the wolf reappeared at the opening frequently but only to sneak a peek then wander away. Momma became increasingly bold, coming farther inside with each appearance. Daylight dimmed and the wolf eventually became comfortable standing for extended periods at the opening. Wind increased. Snow blew at blizzard strength and that became the wolf's motivation. Although skittish, she finally came inside the hut and moved to the opposite side, turned once then laid, snout perched on her paw. She snorted in a satisfied way, stirring dust beneath her nose. Her reward for bravery was a hefty dried strip of rabbit Anne tossed within inches of her nose. The bonding of different species was complete. Momma saw Anne and Little Feather as her pack.

At first light the she-wolf left the hut, presumably to search for breakfast. Within the hour she returned with a partially eaten and bloody rabbit carcass, dropping it before them. "It appears the maternal instinct remains strong in Momma, feeling she must keep us nourished." Holding up the remains, she added, "So we shall save our preserved meat for another day. Now, we feast on fresh rabbit." She skinned and skewered the rabbit with a branch, supporting it over the small fire. Momma moved to her place inside the hut and napped.

After a short time, the wolf snapped her head up and sniffed the air, fixing a stare at the opening to the hut with those intense gray eyes. A guttural growl escaped from deep in her throat. In the blink of an eye, the wolf was up on all four paws. One side of her upper lip rose and twitched as if about to snarl.

"What is it, Momma?" Little Feather asked.

"The Catawba warriors may be back," Anne said. She pulled her cutlass from the scabbard dangling from the wall of the hut.

"I don't think so. We're of no value to them any longer. They view revenge as meaningless unless profitable. In this cold it'd be uncommon to consider."

With no warning, a hungry mountain lion charged through the flap but quickly recoiled hissing and snarling when it saw Momma.

The wolf snarled. Hair on her neck stiffened and stood out. Momma lunged at the big cat, responding with bared fangs and a warning growl of her own, drool dripping from her open mouth.

Momma made choppy but aggressive advances on the big cat, apparently trying to bluff it into backing away.

Muscles in Momma's haunches trembled, a clear warning for the feline to leave.

But the cat's focus was elsewhere as it tried to ignore the wolf. It moved on Anne threateningly.

Going on the offensive, the snarling slobbering wolf attacked, attempting to clench her jaws on the cat's throat.

The cat was too fast. It recoiled away from bared canine teeth, swiping with extended claws as long as Anne's little finger. The claws made solid contact gouging flesh from Momma's side.

Momma yelped and jumped back.

"The rabbit!" Little Feather yelled, "Throw the rabbit at it!"

Although injured, Momma attacked again but staggered as Anne threw the skewered partially cooked rabbit at the head of the mountain lion. She hoped to stab the sharpened skewer stick in the cat's eye but failed.

Anne came off her knees and sprang to her feet to bring her cutlass into the fight.

Little Feather grabbed the wrist of the blade wielding hand. "Leave it be. It just wants the rabbit."

Hissing a warning to the pair, the cat appeared to be coming at them but stopped at the steaming hunk of meat and snagged it with long yellowed teeth then withdrew from the hut. As it did, its eyes remained fixed on the women. Its snarl reduced to a throaty rumble as the animal trotted away with its prize. The smell of it roasting had tempted the big cat beyond its natural fear of humans.

Anne turned to Momma. She fell to her knees and crawled to her friend in a non-threatening manner keeping her body very low. "Easy, my darling. I just want to check your wound."

Momma pressed her back into the wall of the hut and whimpered.

Lying flat on the ground, Anne extended her arm its full length to touch the bleeding gash. "The claw has laid her open a length longer than my hand."

"I'll go down to the creek where the willows grow," Little Feather said. "I need the bark to help with her pain."

Anne didn't understand but realized Little Feather knew much more about the woods than she.

Little Feather wrapped in a long deer hide and covered her head with a crude bonnet of rabbit fur then cautiously left the hut. Anne stayed behind gently stroking Momma, gaining the canine's trust, yet careful not to make sudden moves that might cause the animal to bolt or, possibly attack.

As soon as the young Indian girl returned, she stripped the tender white pulp from the inside of the willow bark and ground it into dried venison using stone upon stone. Rolling the mixture into a gooey ball, she handed it to Anne. "Give it to Momma."

Anne laid it at Momma's mouth.

The wolf sniffed, licked it then sniffed again.

Anne backed away to lessen the animal's hesitance.

As she moved away, Momma watched. The wolf relaxed as Anne receded to the other side of the hut near the fire. The canine sniffed the meaty concoction laying on the ground once more then snapped it up between her teeth and gulped it down. She sniffed the ground and lapped up remaining morsels with the tip of her tongue.

"You'll feel better soon," Little Feather said then smiled. "And thank you for being our friend.

In the days following, Momma became a full partner. The wolf received an equal ration of meat allowing her ample time to heal.

Days ground by. Snow deepened.

Anne stuck her head beyond the hide flap that was the door to their hut and saw that piled snow left only a small crescent opening near the top of the entrance. *Heavenly saints, this strips the soul of vitality. 'Tis no better than that Jamaican jail cell just the opposite extreme.* It suddenly occurred to her that a few moments in steamy Jamaican heat seem quite inviting at the moment.

Storms swept in from the northwest like waves of the ocean. Ice and snow didn't have a chance to thaw between fresh blasts. It piled higher. Fresh meat became difficult to find. They hunted everyday to preserve stores.

The monotony of winter days knotted Anne's gut. She again dreamed of standing at the bow of a ship, velvety salt air filling her lungs. She woke, the image still fixed in her head. The joy of it vanished with the gray light of just another day buried in snow.

As the wind howled, Anne sat by the fire sharpening her cutlass with a stone. She scratched the letters A and B on the upper portion of the blade, gouging deeper and deeper so the initials might never wear away.

"What are those marks you carve into your long knife?" Little Feather asked.

"The first symbol of each of my names…A for Anne and B for Bonny." She pointed to each. "They're called initials."

"I have seen that before. The Tilfords used it." The girl understood the explanation if not those particular letters. "I wanted to ask them about it before I met you," she said then hung her head in shame, "But I feared the lash too much."

Anne nodded. No need to respond. The Tilfords would never be a threat again, massacred with the other pioneers in that mountain pass. "It is the written language of the white man. Many similar characters when linked together represent spoken words in my language."

"Can you teach me?"

"After all I have learned from you, how can I refuse?"

With renewed purpose, winter days became a shared learning experience as the mind-sharpening endeavor filled seemingly endless confinement waiting for spring.

# Chapter Ten

Finally, days lengthened. The sun warmed the earth as it filtered through on afternoon breezes. Snow cover responded; drifts shrank and receded in flatter areas—wet by day, crusty and slick by night.

Anne's mood improved. She spoke of a plan once they arrived in the Carolinas, Charleston in particular. The focus shifted from day-to-day tedium of survival to a way over the mountains.

She and Little Feather shared excitement of liberation from long cold nights. Goals now seemed reachable—objectives that went beyond that range of mountains. Life back upon open seas and breathing salty air was no longer idle wishing or nighttime dreams. It was a plan. If a tenth of the things she chatted up came to pass, it would still be a dream fulfilled.

Anne wandered through the awakening forest, enjoying the sun's warmth although breezes carried a residual chill. She noticed Little Feather examining something in her palm. "What're ya holdin'?"

"A sign of rebirth...of spring." Opening her hand, she revealed a delicate blue blossom and then held it out to Anne. The sun streamed through the canopy of the forest making the blue petals striking.

Smiling, Anne gingerly took the blossom from the girl's hand. Bold color lifted her spirit further. Now, only shreds of an icy layer remained in darkest shadows hiding from annihilation. *I can't remember a time that filled me with more joy than this small blue flower does at this moment.*

Not having a calendar, Anne believed she neared the first anniversary of her return to the colonies aboard Peckary's trading sloop. A scant few weeks later she left Norfolk with that fateful pack train of settlers heading west. The year had been fraught with dramatic and painful change—so much so it seemed impossible outside of a nightmare. *If I hadn't lived it, I wouldn't have believed it. How is it that I'm alive and so many others are not?*

The high adventure seemed to have encompassed more than a single cycle of seasons. Puzzled by it all, it worked on her in a way that seeded a mindset—a different way of looking at the world incubating in the womb of concepts. Although the ultimate optimist, Anne's confidence showed cracks.

The small flower slid from her palm to the ground. Her shoulders slumped. Sudden insecurity drove her to turn away from the young Iroquois girl.

"What drains your spirit?"

"I'll be fine, love."

Now that a cloud of negativity hovered, she mired in darkened thoughts. Sauntering away, she glanced back at Little Feather. *Will I be able to protect the love of my life? Or will trouble again find us?*

A sudden clear image struck her. One in which Little Feather was no longer in her life. She spun back and stared at the girl. Little Feather knelt and picked up the blue flower, sniffing it. Such a thought scared Anne.

Ruthless had never been a word Anne used to describe her actions. Instead, she viewed every action as a means to an end, refusing to allow anything to stand in her way. Until recently she possessed the uncanny knack for never looking back at the blood trail she left. Gazing at the young girl, it occurred to her it wasn't her own bloody history that dogged her but a clear vision of a bloody future. She resumed her stroll through the woods contemplating just that.

Maternal instinct coupled with a need for more and closer human contact gave her pause. She wondered if she had become a pariah that meant death to anyone daring to stand too close. In the isolation of the winter hut

Anne had come to realize her thinking and way of life needed to change. But that was like trying to step from one dinghy to another in a hurricane—possible but extremely dangerous and no guarantee of survival in either.

She plucked a blade of new grass and peeled strips from it as she leaned against an oak tree. Her mind locked on to the concept of becoming a lightning rod for death to friends and loved ones. *Those that have died before me, had they never known the name Anne Bonny, is it possible they'd still be alive?*

She shuddered and tossed the grass blade to the ground and attempted wiping away the frightening thought by cleansing open palms on her pantaloons. Mary Read, lover and friend—Calico Jack Rackham, lover—Michael Radcliffe, lover and planned father of her children and finally, Windsong, friend and liberator she scarcely knew.

She again looked to Little Feather. *Sweet Lord, girl, is your life at risk just by knowin' me?* She noticed Momma the she-wolf coming around a tree a few feet away. *And what about you, love? Has your life lost value by stayin' at my side?* She dwelled upon the worrisome belief that their collective futures were inexplicably in her hands.

"Lines of concern mark your face," Little Feather said. "That should be reserved for elders of a tribe."

"It's of no concern...really," Anne said, with a dismissive wrist flip. She walked the few feet to a small knoll and sat, drawing knees to her breasts encircling them with her arms. "I ponder the journey over the mountains, that's all." She propped her chin upon stacked fists. "The time has come for us to challenge them."

Anne forced her thoughts onto positive pursuits and sprang to her feet. "Let's get on with it, girl. We have a journey to prepare for."

Preparations were quickly taken care of. Provisions compactly stored in hide rolls, pouched for ease of transportation although strength to carry it all would be tested in steep terrain.

Momma took a position on the nearest high ground sometimes in view, sometimes not. Anne knew she'd drift in and out of their sight as a phantom always close but not too close watching over her adopted family. She took comfort in the wolf's presence even more so than having a lookout high atop the yardarm of a ship. The animal's senses were keen. Anne trusted the canine to provide warnings of impending danger offering time to react.

The early spring sun warmed her face. She looked at the mountain range ahead awed by it, admiring its beauty yet respecting it as a formidable obstacle. Marching ever forward over and around obstacles, she kept an appreciative eye on snow-capped peaks but paid particular attention to those lower areas between them as possible passages.

They came upon a reed-thin stream. It flowed swiftly and noisily from the direction of the mountains. "If we follow this stream, it will take us to a pass cut by water through the peaks," Little Feather said.

With each passing hour they walked, the stream size and noise increased as it rushed to lower ground.

"The melting snows feed the river," the girl explained, pointing to where the river overflowed its banks, swirling around brush and rocks—areas above the water line at other times of year.

"Look," Anne said, pointing up through the pines lining both sides of the roaring river. "It's a waterfall. The area should make a nice campsite."

Little Feather offered a quick nod, "Then that shall be our goal to finish this day and set up camp."

Arriving, Anne noticed the narrow horseshoe-shaped canyon had been cut by countless millennia of falling water from a great height. Sheer cliffs rose hundreds of feet, trapping mist that hung in the air between vertical stone walls. A permanent rainbow at its center fluttered and played upon the drifting spray. The water crashed into the pool from a distance of several hundred feet up. Shouting was necessary to be heard above its roar. But the continuous nature of it was more pleasant than annoying. Along the banks, grass textured as fine as moss collapsed under its own lush weight, creating a thick downy-soft mat. A few stately pines stood guard on the canyon floor on both sides of the agitated pool, but nearer the fall it was void of dense growth.

"Aye, sleep will come fast and easy this night." She pushed and fondled soft grass with her foot.

Little Feather surveyed the precipitous canyon walls cut into the mountainside. "The way to the top will take careful consideration or this mountain may be inclined to hurl us back down."

Anne's eyes followed Little Feather's up. "Your concern is well-founded." She slipped the layers of pouches and hide rolls off her shoulders. "For now we eat and rest to build our strength to even the odds." She dropped down to find food stored within one of the hide sacks.

The young girl mimicked her, throwing all she carried to the ground. "Look over there." She pointed to the pool's edge. Momma had appeared and lapped up cool water.

"That wolf mystifies me. How is it she can magically appear from thin air to be at our sides?" Anne chuckled then went about building a campsite.

The sun disappeared behind the high cliff. Light dimmed then faded. Softness of the grass beckoned. Fatigue pulled them down.

Anne woke to gentle nudging of a small hand. "Wake up Anne," came a breathy whisper, "Lay very still. Make no moves."

"What is it?" Anne asked in a rather sharp tone, irritated at having been pulled from such a wonderfully sound slumber.

"Shh."

Suddenly Anne heard a grunt, a sniff then a snort. The ground vibrated from heavy and very close footfalls. Moving only her eyes, she looked about. Lying on her side she saw no moon, darkness near absolute. Mist blurred the stars. "What is that sound?" she whispered.

"Bear," Little Feather said, breathing the words directly into Anne's ear. "Hungry... just out of hibernation... lie very still... human flesh may tempt it."

Anne heard the animal rooting within scant feet of where they lay. She believed she heard it mauling the hide roll holding their only food. Instinct, not wisdom, guided her. She flinched, wanting to protect their food source, arrogantly believing she could control the situation with a cutlass.

The sound now was no longer grunts and snorts but a growl.

"Anne, please..."

The warning fell on impulse-deafened ears. Anne sat bolt upright before she had a chance to understand the poor choice it was.

The ground thundered beneath them.

She strained to see into the darkness, as the growl grew into a roar loud enough to override the noisy waterfall.

Gaze darting, she looked frantically about then directly at the source of the sound.

Above her was the outline of a massive animal standing on its hind legs set against the barely visible mist-obscured stars.

Losing any reason to remain quiet, "By the saints, what monumental blunder have I made?"

"We are marked for a meal," Little Feather shouted. "Run!" The young girl sprang up and bolted before Anne could even roll to her feet.

Anne strained to see into the blackness.

By the sound and vibration of the ground next to her, she determined the behemoth had fallen back to all four paws upon the ground and gave chase.

Little Feather squealed in pain.

The bear roared.

"Little Feather, where are you? What's happening?" Anne shouted.

Then she heard a thump-whoosh, thump-whoosh in the grass. It was accompanied by a familiar snarl then recognized it as another animal running through the deep grass. "No, Momma, don't!"

Angry animal sounds suggested the wolf had engaged the bear. An animal kingdom version of all-hell had just broken loose very close to where Little Feather made her last sound.

A knot yanked tight in her gut not knowing if her young Indian friend was alive or dead. She heard nothing from her.

Sounds were confined to the ear-splitting roar of a bear and savage snarls of a wolf underscored by the constant waterfall.

Mere seconds had passed when a shrill canine yelp split the air followed by the dull thud of a body hitting the ground. Then, save for the waterfall, no sound at all.

Anne sat unmoving and speechless for tense seconds then, "Little Feather?"

"Over here. I dared not call out as long as the bear was so close. I have not been harmed but my ankle will stiffen and swell."

"Is it gone...the bear I mean?"

"I cannot say. I heard the sound of its heavy paws lessening in the distance." She moaned. "Maybe the lack of meat on our bones was not worth the fight."

Anne remained down and crawled to Little Feather. Sweeping arms found something else on the way, the sticky-wet fur of Momma. Groping hands examined the animal. The wetness had the metallic smell of blood. The animal's body was covered in it. Resting a hand on the rib cage, she felt Momma's breathing, shallow and labored. "Oh, my darling friend, what have you done?" It occurred to her that had she never moved, this incident might have been avoided. She cried out, "What in bloody hell *have I done?*"

Snuggling close, she placed her body next to Momma, spooning the injured wolf to keep her warm. Her mind raced, searching for ideas but other than keep her warm there was nothing she could do. Momma would have done the same for her.

Beyond reason the night became darker.

# Chapter Eleven

They climbed, one foot then the other, slowly. Anne looked down the ascending rock shelf from where they'd come from straining to keep Momma in sight through the boiling mist of the waterfall. The wolf still had not moved. Its condition had not changed. Hope was gone that the animal would ever be up again. Blood loss and damage was just too great from having been partially disemboweled.

Nevertheless, Anne kept looking down, hoping Momma would overcome the odds.

It took Little Feather's insistence that she leave the canine behind. Anne grudgingly acquiesced laying food near the wolf's snout. It was an irrational impulse to want to nurse the animal back to health. Momma was going to die.

*Goodbye, love. You'll live on in my sweetest dreams.*

The trail they ascended jutted from the sheer canyon wall and snaked upward, now becoming steeper. They took it slow remaining ever mindful the two-foot wide surface could be lethal with a single misstep. They crawled more than walked as the incline became more severe. Progress could be measured in inches up the treacherously narrow ledge.

Anne reached back and took Little Feather's hand helping her around a bush jutting from a crack in the cliff wall. The young girl's swollen ankle was weak and undependable.

Stopping to breathe for a moment, Anne mopped sweat from her eyes. She attempted an encouraging smile. "We'll be up on that plateau while the sun still hangs in the air."

Little Feather stopped crawling and leaned to her right looking down over the edge—straight down to the mist-obscured treetops in the canyon below. "We make good time."

Readjusting hide rolls and pouches, Anne urged Little Feather to stay close behind. She resumed climbing. After a time they came to an area almost flat allowing them to stand upright and walk a few feet.

Little Feather forgot to watch her footing and stepped on loosened rock chips.

She braced with the other foot but it was on that weakened ankle.

It wrenched sideways.

She slid backward, arms flailing.

Rocks and gravel spilled down the mountainside.

She teetered, listing toward the edge desperately seeking to regain balance.

Anne grabbed the hide roll strapped to the young girl's body and yanked her back against the sheer rock wall. "Damn you, girl!" Anne shouted in anger. "Watch your step! I'll not lose two friends in the same bloody day!"

The echoing rebuke hung in the air.

"Move around and climb ahead of me. I want to keep my eye on you."

As they climbed on, the roar of water crashing into the pool below faded. It left a quiet that rang in Anne's ears, broken only by the occasional caw of a crow, screech of an eagle, or merry chirp of barn swallows building mud nests in the crevices of the cliff wall. The final obstacle came into view, a waist-high boulder lodged in the rock shelf.

"Almost there. Just one more little problem and we'll soon be standin' on flat ground." She swept streaming sweat from her brow. "Once over it, nothin' else stands in our way." She pointed to an inviting level area above them covered in grass and trees—just up and over a small boulder and they'd emerge in a river valley between mountains. *Oh blessed sure footing, I ache for thee.* She grinned at the poetic longing for something as simple as flat ground.

As Little Feather tentatively searched with a sweeping hand, she apparently discovered a secure handhold and placed her stronger foot in the lead. Anne palmed the girl's buttocks shoving her to its top.

The stone crunched and seemed to shift slightly.

They froze.

The boulder moved again, this time noticeably.

"Jump!" Anne shouted.

Little Feather launched her body to a grassy patch and exposed tree roots above, just below where they needed to be. She latched onto the rough bark of one of the gnarled woody appendages and regained safe footing beyond the shifting stone.

That extra pressure sent the boulder sailing from its perch taking a chunk of the trail with it. Its absence left a five-foot gap in the rock shelf, Anne's only route to the top. The crashing boulder reverberated through the canyon when it landed. A throaty echo died reluctantly, as if to mock them.

All was quiet, ominously so. Even the small birds quieted. Looking to her right, the drop was a thousand feet or more. Anne peered over the edge directly ahead. The gap in the trail extended down some distance before closing off to a crack and nothing but a vertical rock wall to her left.

"Suddenly, my balance and ability to leap are the only talents that count. No men to defeat. No beasts to conquer. Just leap without falling. That's all it should take to win this day. Right?" She puckered then pushed out her lower lip. She nodded slowly. "Simple enough...don't you think?" She tried to remain light showing her humorous side but courage was fading.

"It's only a short distance. Why do you hesitate?"

"Aye, a wee distance." Her breathing became shallow and rapid. "But only a single chance to get it right, you see. I'll not be havin' a second swing with a cutlass at this enemy."

For the first time, Anne inadvertently showed Little Feather that even her courage had limitations—a glaring frailty now on display. She tore her eyes from the gap in the trail and glanced to see Little Feather smile.

"And just what might you be grinnin' at?"

"Run two steps then jump. It should be of no concern for a woman of your bravery."

"I think ya might be enjoyin' a good look at my misery." Anne sucked in a lung full of air along with some courage. "Okay...two steps then jump, huh?"

Anne tossed the provisions and weapons across then backed down the ledge two steps. She briskly rubbed warmth into her palms then touched her body with the sign of the cross. "I hope the saints are smilin' today."

Losing all pretense of a hardened woman, she suddenly transformed into a frightened little girl, squealing like a prepubescent lass.

She ran then jumped.

Little Feather caught a flailing hand and held it tight in one hand while clutching a tree root. They grunted. They twisted. They struggled. It paid off. She pulled Anne up onto the grassy surface. Together, they climbed the final few feet to rest on very solid, very flat ground covered in downy soft grass.

Rolling to hands and knees, Anne laughed. After time to recompose, she rose but still untrusting of the strength in fear-weakened legs. After a quick test on bent knees, she smiled and bounced upon her toes. "A flat surface feels strangely wonderful." The smile relaxed as she looked back to where they'd been. Beyond the mist of the canyon below, the area where they spent the winter was plainly visible. It seemed too close to have been a two-day walk from where they now stood.

Her gaze shifted to the boiling mist of the canyon. Anne thought about the wolf. She held Little Feather's hand. "Momma has earned a place in my thoughts and my heart for the rest of my life."

"Yes, mine as well."

Grudgingly, Anne turned her back on the past and faced the future. Ghosts and images from bygone days were becoming cumulative, layering in her head. She squeezed her eyes shut, sighed then opened them to the path ahead.

They stood in the lowest point between formidable peaks on the banks of a monstrous river that continued swelling with melting snow coming down in many small rivulets from higher up, all flowing into the channel spilling over the cliff's edge as the waterfall.

"We should have one maybe two days of easy walking."

"When survival is not the focus, the beauty and bounty of this place makes the heart soar," Little Feather said.

"I'll be grantin' ya that. But I'd be happier in the low country on the other side. Better yet, aboard a scudding galleon upon the high seas."

Dropping to her knees beside the raging river, Little Feather scooped water into her hand and drank. "No sweeter water is there in the entire world than that born in the mountains and cleansed upon the rocks."

As the young Indian maid espoused virtues of the mountains, Anne glimpsed movement among the pines. Not trusting her eyes, she watched for a while but saw nothing. She dismissed it. "Of course when death looms large from thirst, water from a muddy hole would be as sweet," Anne countered then remembered a clay pot full of water thrown into her face by Windsong once upon a time.

The young girl dried her hands on her buckskin breeches. "It's the simple things that offer the greatest joy."

Her memories and Little Feather's words couldn't be debated. Anne simply nodded.

A rustle in the brushy undergrowth behind her perked her ear.

Suspecting movement only seconds before, she was not inclined to deny her senses this time. She rushed to retrieve her cutlass from the hide roll but didn't make it.

A scream burst from the woods.

She spun around.

Woman Beater charged her, rambling loud and angrily in the Catawba language.

The weapons were out of reach.

She faced him unarmed.

Anne's forte was speed not strength. She sidestepped, forcing him to stumble. The healed-over stub where she'd severed his hand presented balance problems. The screeching warrior fell and rolled over the grass.

Not waiting to see what he'd do next, she dove for the hide roll, fumbling with its bindings but couldn't untie it fast enough.

The maniacal savage rolled her over and planted the points of his knees on her arms above the elbows, pinning her to the ground.

He rattled something.

She assumed it was cursing. With each word came a spray of saliva into her face. Although armed with a flint knife meant to be used on her, his ability to keep Anne pinned with a handless arm was clumsy.

The time it took to position the knife for a killing thrust offered a valuable second.

Little Feather dove and knock him off Anne.

Angered even more and now distracted by Little Feather, he leaped to his feet and charged the girl.

She ran, back-stepping toward the river, never taking her gaze from him. She attempted to emulate Anne and sidestepped the charge.

Her speed lacked Anne's snap and gave him time to throw out the good hand as he stumbled by. He pulled the young Iroquois girl in close and wrapped her up.

Together they went over the edge into the roiling water.

"Little Feather!" Anne yelled.

The young girl bobbed and rolled out of control in the rush of icy water. Anne ran flat-out to stay ahead of Little Feather as she was swept along, tossed about in the raging water.

Woman Beater had less control with only one hand. He tumbled to the center of the river where it flowed faster.

Little Feather managed to stay nearer the bank, although unable to find anything to cling to. She clawed at moss-slickened rocks and limbs.

Anne snatched up a long tree limb, scarcely breaking stride to do so. She sprinted with all speed to get ahead of the young girl. As lungs were about to explode she dove headlong to the water's edge. Lying flat, she extended the limb as far out as she could.

"Grab it, love! Grab hold!"

Little Feather got a hand on it.

The girl's weight and force of the water dragged Anne to the water's edge. She rolled onto her buttocks and dug wooden boot heals into anything that might provide a hold—rocks, roots, even the mud.

Little Feather whipped around and slammed into a large rock, expelling breath in a loud wheeze. But she hung on. The same boulder that took her wind provided a place to plant a foot against the current.

Tension eased on quivering arms strained to their limits. Anne gained advantage. She pulled hand over hand, inch by inch. She tugged until Little Feather came into less turbulent water next to the bank then pulled her onto dry ground.

Exhausted, they lay together watching Woman Beater thrash about. He bobbed and rolled then shot over the falls screaming.

"Where, in the name of all that's holy, did he come from?" Anne asked, still panting. "How did he make it to this high ground with only one hand?"

Chest heaving, gasping for breath, Little Feather wrung water from her hair. "I don't know. But he shouted that you were responsible for his being driven from the tribe. Missing a hand he was viewed as incomplete and of no use."

"I saw him as incomplete and a troublesome idiot when he had both hands," Anne said. "It's hard to believe he came all this way just to kill me."

"That proves you are no ordinary human." Bone-weary, Little Feather pulled herself to her feet. "I must change my opinion that Catawba warriors do not seek revenge. That's certainly what he sought."

## Chapter Twelve

Anne and her Iroquois protégé drew closer to Charleston. The lady pirate's focus narrowed as anticipation heightened. Her pace quickened. Girlish excitement fluttered her stomach. Arriving back among her people was now within reach.

But another yearning figured in to that excitement—the lure of the open sea. Every breeze, even clouds racing across the sky, kindled visions of standing at the bow of a ship under her command slicing high and tight while holding her face against a strong wind blowing through her curly red hair. She was becoming obsessed, speaking at length about it with Little Feather.

The girl hung on each story, mystified with the concept of spending months aboard a floating vessel, no land in sight, just water horizon to horizon. Readjusting the weighty stock of provisions strapped to her back, "We are from different worlds. Time has come that I know about yours. I want to hear your thoughts and dreams, all of them. You speak often of the big water and the strange places you've traveled to. Why is your spirit so drawn?"

Anne climbed over a massive rotting pine tree fallen across the path laced with thorny leg-grabbing vines. "For one thing, all obstacles I encounter on a ship are known to me before I confront them." She unwound vines from her legs and feet. "Out here, all enemies and obstacles leap from behind boulders and trees…each one new, different, and unpredictable." She stopped to survey the path ahead and looked up to the high canopy formed by towering pines.

"Aside from beasts of the forest, surely those you encounter must be as difficult to deal with as Iswa warriors."

"True. But there's one major difference; seafarin' men think only of selfish pleasures. A sailor's brain and his jewels tend to share thinkin' responsibilities." She laughed. Most times I can make the latter true and outwit them. Catawba men are practical, actin' accordin' to survival needs and harder to sway from their purpose. Sailors are easy for a woman to manipulate." She frowned. "Catawba savages see women as bloody livestock."

Little Feather kicked pebbles from her path. "Is it your plan to return to that life?"

"Aye. My stories betray intent. I've given it much thought. Unfortunately, opportunities are limited. I'll not be movin' about freely in Charleston lest I be arrested and hanged. I did not leave there some years back in good stead with the keepers of local law. I regret that now."

Three days of easy travel passed since the waterfall. The mighty river they followed dwindled as elevation increased. It shrank to little more than a spring dribbling from a crack in a cliff wall—the source. Drinking from its origin, they marveled for a time at its humble beginning.

The trail became more downhill than up. Anne glimpsed the low country on occasion through the pines as the path descended. Anticipation drove restless feet. She calculated another day to put the mountains behind them.

Anne drank in the tightening bond with Little Feather. It made the journey bearable. Closeness metamorphosed into behavior that would be viewed unacceptable by societal mores of the day.

Little Feather's hero worship made her accessible to Anne's tender advances. It also provided the young girl courage to be inquisitive. "Are there people in Charleston you count as friends?"

"I wish I had an answer for you. I don't but it's a risk I must take. I'm willin' to believe my father has forgiven me and may do favors on my behalf. I grow confident since Michael told me that he paid for my release from that stinkin' tropical prison in St. Jago." She glanced back. "It's a risk I'm willin' to take but it's a big one." She ducked under a limb.

Little Feather dipped to avoid the same branch. "It's not a risk you take alone."

Pondering the comment, "Then let's discover together if there's promise in a meeting with my father."

# Chapter Thirteen

Springtime in Charleston; it was a great day for a brisk walk to shake winter blahs.

"Mister Cormac?" a man said from some distance as he trotted up to stand face to face with William Cormac. "May I have a word with you, sir?" He took a swipe at a passing butterfly.

"It would seem you are bent on having that word," Cormac said, annoyed that his stroll had been interrupted.

The aggravation was as much for show to keep a beggar at a distance. Cormac knew him, a pitiful elderly man in tatters without home or family. He extended his walking cane to keep the old man at least that distance away to check the rancid odor carried upon the breeze. The sight and smell reminded him the old man lived on the streets and had no future. He softened his stance and expression, now inclined to show pity as he had sporadically done by giving the guy an occasional stipend for food. He reached into his vest pocket and fished around with his fingertip. Abruptly, "Is it a coin you wish?"

He planted the point of his gold-tipped cane on the walkway between his widespread legs leaning over it aggressively, not wishing to appear an easy mark. He tapped the cane upon the cobble sidewalk, indicating his desire for the old man to hurry and get to the point.

"Not without giving you something of value first. I wish to favor you with information for all your kindnesses, sir." He wrung his hands apologetically and hunkered low so he might look up humbly into Cormac's face.

Looking to the position of the morning sun, Cormac blurted, "Then get on with it, man. I have business soon and would like to finish my walk first." He feigned agitation by looking away to watch an aggressive blue jay scold a squirrel that happened to be too close to its nest in a huge oak tree.

"I overheard Francis Alexander speak angrily of you. It seems he learned of your visits of late to his wife at their plantation while he was away on business. If you weren't aware of this information, I felt it might be important that you know."

Suddenly, Cormac lost all expression of displeasure, replaced by disturbed interest. Flipping his cane into his armpit, he folded his arms. "Where is it that you heard this?"

"I slept under the stairs in an alley beside town hall. I was awakened by angry words through an open window above me this morning. It was Alexander beseeching a group of city fathers to deny you patronage of your law practice."

Expecting anger over bleak news, the old man backed away and meekly looked down to his shuffling feet. "Alexander is a powerful man in Charleston. I fear he may have support of influential folks in this matter."

Reaching again into his vest pocket, this time in earnest, Cormac retrieved a coin and flipped it to the old man. He hesitated momentarily then pulled another, pitching it to him as well. "Your words are troubling but welcomed. Thank you."

The old man bowed deeply, turned, and quickly walked away.

The warmth of this spring morning and the chirp of birds and chatter of squirrels lost its charm. His mood darkened and the stroll turned into drudgery placing one heavy foot in front of the other. He sulked. Lack of willpower had gotten him into trouble. He altered his course and walked toward his buggy.

Having lost his beloved mistress, Mary Brennan, who died at a young age, he found the attention of Katharine Alexander a bit too inviting. She was plain but quite charming. Lack of physical beauty didn't prevent indulgence in a forbidden affair. At the time he felt helpless against her beguiling ways. She wanted it and she started it but he went along with it. Even then he realized lust was an infectious disease that would eventually bring him down. Many times he tried to break it off with Missus Alexander. But having no other to turn to, she was convenient. It took weeks to finally deny her advances. Now, months later, it had come back on him just as he feared. Alexander had the power and support to ruin his law practice.

Cormac figured that if his ability to earn a livelihood should end this very day, he'd still survive considerable time in his accustomed style on fortune already amassed. But he wondered how long it might be before he had to divest himself of his plantation and possessions to sustain it. He needed allies to thwart an assault on his business and preserve wealth and standing in Charleston. *But whom can I trust in this God-forsaken town? Have I taken so many for granted that I find myself without friends? Even with the help of friends, what would be the plan?*

It was a riddle he must answer soon before Alexander had a chance to do damage. He furrowed his brow and set his jaw. "What in hell can I do about it?" he mumbled.

Looking to his feet, he sauntered on the rough stone sidewalk and continued muttering. "If the work of my plantation is hampered and my legal practice ruined, where shall I turn?" He came to stand beside the carriage, tapping his forehead with the gold-tipped cane. "A plan, I need a plan."

He climbed up to sit in the one-horse buggy. Pulling the reins from their temporary hold on the seat brace, he tongue-clucked the gentle old horse. It began walking the familiar route back to the plantation just outside town with a lazy clop, clop of hooves. Relaxing the reins, he allowed the animal to have its head. The faithful old horse made the trip so many times it knew the way to Cormac Manor without prompt. It also provided Cormac latitude to put his mind to the task. Unfortunately, every idea crossing his mind ended in destitution. Downsides were numerous. Remedies seemed nonexistent—a slippery slope indeed.

~ * ~

"Is that Charleston?" Little Feather asked.

"Yes. At least I think so." She squinted to discern detail from the cluster of buildings in the distance. "The area is familiar but four years have changed its appearance. It would seem construction did not cease simply because I left town," she snickered.

The two rested on high ground overlooking the city. They munched freshly plucked berries and discussed a plan for an unnoticed entry into town.

Noise from the road at the bottom of the hill quieted them.

"Look," Anne said, "It seems a wagon loaded with spring wool goes to market in town. Let's catch up to it."

Snatching belongings from the ground they ran, sometimes stumbling, down an embankment to the road below. Nearing the wagon that creaked along with every revolution of the solid wood wheels, Anne called out, "Excuse me, sir, is your destination Charleston?"

Startled, the man jerked the reins. The swayback horse whinnied and reared.

"Who goes there?" The man nervously scanned the woods looking for the source of the question. His eyes eventually landed on the two young women. Then he calmed. "Charleston is my destination, yes. Another half hour and I'll be there." He examined them. "It'd appear you've been traveling for some time by the condition of your clothing."

"Yes sir, we have. We were with a group of settlers last year attacked by Catawba warriors beyond the mountains to the west. Save for the two of us, everyone in the pack train was massacred."

"You're Irish, aren't you?"

"Yes. County Cork originally. But it has been a long while."

"The Indian girl…that be your slave?"

"What sort of a bloody..." Anne cut it short. A smile grudgingly returned. She thought on what an unwise choice a temper tantrum would be at the moment, blurting Little Feather as an equal to a narrow-minded colonial farmer. "Oh, you meant servant girl. That's right. She is my servant girl."

Little Feather glanced over but her expression remained neutral.

"You and your Indian are welcome to hop on the wagon and ride into town with me."

"Riding something that's not my feet would be a blessed treat I've not enjoyed for nigh on a year," Anne said, allowing a hint of femininity. "I thank you. My friend thanks you. And our feet most certainly do." She bowed slightly.

The well-worn wagon creaked and rattled along as the girls sat quietly at the rear on the soft pile of shorn wool. Feet dangling, they watched the slowly retreating rutted road appearing inches at a time from beneath the wagon. Inspecting the surroundings, a dense canopy of hardwood trees common to temperate climes enclosed the road they traveled providing near-constant shade. Finally, Anne turned to the man. "Do you know the whereabouts of a man named Cormac...Mister William Cormac?"

"As a matter of fact I do," he said, not divulging anything more, presumably in case shenanigans were in the offing. "How is it you know Mr. Cormac?"

"He's an acquaintance from Ireland where we both hail from."

"Oh, I see." He seemed satisfied with the answer. "Mister Cormac owns a large plantation. As luck would have it, it's just off this very road. We'll be passing by his substantial home within the quarter hour."

The plantation came into view. Anne surveyed the manicured grounds beyond a vine covered split-rail fence at the road, straight enough to shame an arrow. As the wagon rocked past the long rutted path to the house, lined with tall poplars, she leaped from the wagon, urging Little Feather out then said to the old man, "Thank ya kindly, sir. May the saints be with ya."

"Yes and good luck to you." His wagon loaded with wool maintained its slow pace.

She turned her attention to the stately home. "Well, it appears the honorable Mister William Cormac has done quite well for himself."

"Does seeing your father again after such a long absence make you uneasy?" She readjusted the leather roll on her shoulder as she walked behind Anne toward the brick walk to the front door.

"Uneasy? Not a'tal. I am in no way nervous. But I feel old anger wellin' up... old hurts remembered. Staying calm enough to conduct business with the pompous bastard is my only concern."

Stepping up onto the broad veranda near the front door, Anne's step stuttered and she stopped, hand frozen near the brass doorknocker in the shape of a lion's head. She shook off the flash of nervousness and slammed the knocker against the heavy oak door a couple of times before second thoughts had a chance to dictate a different course. She heard the knocks echo inside. *This gaudy house must be cavernous.* Then came the sound of footfalls clopping on a hardwood floor. With a squeak, one side of the double doors opened to reveal an elderly black man.

"We are here to see William Cormac."

"Please wait here. I's get the masser for ya." He turned to walk away then looked back. "What name does ya go by?"

"An... Amber Flanagan."

"Wait here." He seemed disinterested and closed the door behind him.

Little Feather leaned close. "Who is Amber Flanagan?"

"Just a name I remember from my childhood in Ireland. I'm sure my father will recognize me but there's no need to alert others."

Moments later the door opened. Anne looked up into her father's face for the first time in four years. Thick wavy auburn hair that had been oiled and perfectly combed had developed gray at the temples down his bushy sideburns that connected with a mostly gray moustache. He was shocked speechless. The startled look melted to a knowing smile. "So, you're Miss Amber Flanagan?"

"That's right, sir," she said without expression, nodding acknowledgement of his smile.

"Please come in." He looked past her to Little Feather. "And bring your companion with you."

Ill at ease with the lack of conversation, Anne shot glances at the old black man and a servant woman as they were guided down a hall. She remained cognizant of putting forth an appearance of nonchalance as Cormac led them into a parlor.

Cormac closed the door behind them. "Dear Anne, I thought you were dead," he said in a thinly controlled whisper. "Friends of Doctor Radcliffe got word to me that he and a female companion I assumed to be you arrived safely in Norfolk then I was informed he and his lady friend had joined a group of settlers heading west. In just the past month news came to me a massacre had occurred on the trail. I was told no survivors were found among the hundreds killed in a narrow mountain pass. I assumed his 'lady friend' was you, that you'd been killed."

"The information you have is correct, up to the point where we were killed. Little Feather and I were the only survivors."

"Whether you care to believe it or not, my heart swells with joy knowin' you're alive and well and, by God, standin' right before me in my own house." He guffawed then placed hands on each of her shoulders and drank in the sight. "This is a wonderful day indeed." Darting eyes studied four years worth of changes in her face then slid his hands down her arms and pulled her into a full embrace.

His hearty smile wilted as he pulled back and looked again into her eyes. "Is it possible we can put our differences behind us?"

Not returning the affection, Anne let her arms hang limply at her sides, stepping away from his embrace. She pushed him farther away. "I have need of help and by my way of thinkin' all our differences are in the past and should stay there. But it's premature to look upon our relationship as father/daughter."

Ignoring Anne's cold comment, William developed a twinkle in his eyes. "As fate would have it, I have a need, too." He struck a contemplative pose. "The time may be right regardless of our different points of view to collaborate to our mutual benefit."

Still untrusting, Anne didn't respond. She folded her arms over her breasts and wondered if the conversation might be moving forward too fast. She took yet another step back, figuratively and literally. "Your words intrigue me but first things first. What of the warrants for my arrest in Charleston?"

"Ah yes, the warrants," he said, placing a finger over his lips for a second then wagged it at Anne. "The people who sought your capture are either dead or no longer in Charleston. You're still wanted as a matter of record, of course, but maybe not all that recognizable now." He dropped into a chair. "As you remember it was my doing in a fit of rage that those charges were brought against you, but the general population of Charleston paid little attention." His head slumped forward. "For that, I am ashamed and sorry."

The apology came too fast to be sincere. He sprang to his feet and paced away then spun back. "But, as you say, it is all behind us. A wee bit of a disguise will be all that's necessary to conceal your identity."

"Then I shall continue to be Amber Flanagan, the daughter of an old business partner hailing from County Cork, Ireland, and I'll only be usin' me finest Irish brogue in the presence of strangers." She stepped toward Little Feather. "To complete the disguise, she will be my servant girl." She took an aggressive step toward her father. "But know this and know it well, Little Feather is no servant and certainly no slave. She is my best friend in this whole world." She allowed Amber Flanagan to surface. "You best not be forgettin' that, me fine Irish friend."

Anne's words belied feelings. She remained leery of his intentions, head filling with unanswered questions. The fact he paid off the governor of Jamaica for her release, and that he had needs of some sort indicated he might be sincere. *Maybe it's time to trust again. I might as well start with my father.* But a question needing an answer was: How much did he trust her? For now, she saw it as prudent to simply smile, a nonverbal agreement to move forward.

"I feel the sun has just risen on a new day at Cormac Manor," he said with a joyful clap and a scheming glint.

# Chapter Fourteen

Appropriate clothing topped the list of things to acquire in order to start life anew in Charleston. Anne marched to the trash pit at the rear of Cormac Manor House and tossed the mishmash of rags and crudely tanned skins in it. That was the first step. She stood for a time and looked down upon the clothing—a strong reminder of an event-filled year. Shaking her head in disbelief that she and Little Feather had survived, she muttered, "Now, it's time to craft a new life." One slip and it'd be shackles and the hangman's noose. But she also saw promise in what they embarked on.

~ * ~

Cormac, with the help of his unsuspecting maid who only saw it as an additional burden upon her time and the shopkeeper of a local clothier, purchased a number of clothing changes for both girls.

Over three days of grooming, basic hygiene was restored to a necessary standard. A year's worth of grime was removed. Cuts, scrapes, and bruises faded, allowing the ladylike side of Anne Bonny's alias to emerge, that of Amber Flanagan, Irish socialite. A woman known around Charleston as a magician with women's hair was called in. It nearly took a cauldron of the occult to correct the tangled mess that Anne called hair. The woman cut and arranged it in the style of the day. Ringlets framed her face complementing her purported station in life.

Little Feather resisted eliminating all signs of her birthright. Still, she understood the need and allowed her appearance to be altered. Anne gave in easily to one modification she thought insignificant, but not to the girl. Little Feather wore a leather barrette of tribal design adorned with beads that held her long shiny coal-black hair together in the back. What seemed a small compromise was vital to an Iroquois girl as a symbol of who she was and where she came from, a tribal signature.

Sunlight streamed at a severe angle through the second floor bedroom window. Late afternoon shadows crawled across the floor. The ornate wrought-iron rail around the outdoor balcony cast its decorative design in shadow upon the floor as Anne posed in front of an intricately carved full-length mirror. Smoothing its front, she studied the cut and lay of a full red velvet gown. Fingering the scar on her forehead left by the clubbing last year, she feared it might compromise the disguise. She reasoned a lady of means raised in wealth should have no such marks. *My skin should be as smooth as polished marble and appear the color of alabaster.* "I fear there'll be no way to hide this deformity," she told Little Feather.

"Then we will not refer to it as deformity. We'll look upon it as a character mark created by a childhood accident. We'll say you fell from a fast moving carriage at a very young age." She fussed with restrictive white lace-trimmed belting on her plain gray dress. "A story as this might carry the appropriate ring of wealth."

Anne looked at Little Feather with a comfortable smile. She admired the ease with which cleverness flowed from her young mind.

"You look so much like your mother," Cormac said, suddenly appearing at the door. "Your face serves to remind how much I miss her."

Ignoring his comment, "Father, do you know a British sea captain by the name of Peckary?"

"Hmm. I believe so, yes. If memory serves, his name is Telford Peckary. He pilots English trading vessels between the colonies and West Indies. Is this the Peckary you speak of?"

"It is." She spun to face him with a loud rustle of petticoats, surprised by his ready knowledge of the man. She resolutely planted hands upon velvet-enhanced hips in a decidedly unladylike pose. "I have a thought. If all things considered come together, it might blossom into a course of action." She placed finger upon lips. "Michael Radcliffe and I booked passage from Kingston to Norfolk on a trading vessel Peckary commanded. I disguised myself as a man by the name of Andrew and had to pretend no relationship with Michael. Should I have been found out and exposed, I didn't want to endanger his freedom over my problems with Jamaican law. I hired on as Peckary's personal protector and had the opportunity to prove my worth when our ship was boarded by a nefarious bunch of seafaring hooligans."

He fidgeted. "Understood. But where does this tale lead?" He twirled a finger eager for her to get to the point.

Anne ignored the pressure to rush. She turned her back and walked away two steps then stopped. Her head fell forward as she considered a plan. She looked up and gazed through the open French doors across the balcony to the woods beyond.

She faced him. "If your political status remains untarnished in the colonies then a letter by you to Captain Peckary espousing the virtues of Andrew the Protector may net us a letter of marque, commissioned by the King as privateers. Even outside wartime, privateering may have merit as protectors of the British flag within pirate infested waters of the shipping lanes. Don't you think?"

He shrugged as though unsure but nodded anyway. "I think I see where your idea leads."

"Peckary may vouch for me based on our experiences together…backed up, of course, by a glowing letter from you."

Becoming excited, Cormac stabbed the air with a finger, "Yes. I've heard tell that George the First is away from the throne so long at a time that he has named a prime minister to rule in his stead…a fellow by the name of Walpole. Who knows? Maybe he'll be an easier mark than the king." Pacing excitedly to and fro, he continued elaboration of Anne's premise, "I must write a letter on your…I mean Andrew the Protector's behalf, and get it off to Peckary immediately. Of course, it should beg indulgence to be delivered to the prime minister upon his return to England." He paused, tapping his lip. He was clearly convinced the plan was viable. "It's my opinion the current state of affairs in England may net quick approval with little investigation based solely on Peckary's recommendation."

A cunning grin stretched Anne's lips as she lowered herself into a chair watching her father scheme. It was like listening to a poetry reading. She saw no need to interrupt since his thoughts paralleled hers to the finest detail. *Return of plundered English trade goods should fetch handsome commissions—possibly of our choosing.*

Her mind drifted, becoming inattentive to her father's rambling discourse strung together by profit motive. *God help me, I am my father's daughter. His thoughts are mine. That can only mean one thing; he's a wangling bastard for sure.*

"I hear tell," William continued, "the throne believes colonists have grown arrogant, selling trade goods to the highest bidder without giving the crown due prerogative. They may offer a handsome commission to take what they believe is owed them anyway."

Anne only nodded. *It'll take six months, maybe more, to get a reply. But its time I'll be needin' to cultivate my alias, Amber Flanagan, born into great wealth and William Cormac's most important, most prestigious and best paying client.*

She rose and sauntered across the room. Finally, she'd heard enough and interrupted him. "I take it you see wisdom in such a plan. Now I'll see how well you can sell this idea to Peckary then how convincing he'll be with Walpole." She pulled her hair back and held it to appear the lady of means she planned on masquerading as. "I think this plan may have pluck enough to sprout wings."

~ * ~

Anne tentatively made a foray into the streets of Charleston, Little Feather at her side. Unconvinced that anonymity could be assured, it was a well thought out experiment. If successful, each outing would lengthen until the public accepted her as Amber Flanagan. She feared her past might spring forward and ruin everything if she should be recognized as Anne Bonny.

She peered through the display window of a shop and felt staring eyes. She saw the reflection of a man in the glass. A gentleman of obvious breeding touched the brim of his tall hat. "Good morning," he said while looking at the same dress she pretended to admire through the shop window. "Lovely, isn't it?"

"Quite beautiful." She looked back, this time long enough to examine his face. "And good morning to you, too, sir." She quickly looked away as it became clear that his darting gaze studied her face as she did his.

He hesitated for only a moment then walked on. "Well, have a wonderful day."

"To you, too, sir." She kept her gaze fixed on the dress hanging in the shop window and whispered back to Little Feather. "My nerves have been set on edge."

"Look at these people like you *should* have looked at that monstrous bear. They won't eat you if you stop looking like food to them."

Anne tilted her head and chuckled. "Your simple wisdom astounds me."

She walked on, Little Feather one step back. Eye contact with those she passed remained fleeting. *God help me if someone recognizes me. I'll be back in the wilderness and living with Indians which holds no appeal. I should carry a weapon.* She looked down at her dress. *But where would I conceal it?*

Another man tipped his head cordially.

She pulled a lace-trimmed handkerchief and covered her mouth and nose. "Good day, sir." The ruse felt comfortable, offering only a limited view of her face. Hiding the lower portion of her face would be seen as feminine shyness, even appropriate. She noticed more men look her way when she held the handkerchief close to her face. "Humph." *'Tis simple things that work best...I must remember that.* She began receiving exactly what she wanted, attention without fear of recognition.

She felt her allure strengthen along with confidence. Women approached and spoke as she strolled along the crowded street within the heart of the business district of Charleston.

"It seems people are becoming accustomed to your presence," Little Feather observed, continuing to walk a step behind, as is expected of a personal servant.

"Aye, but I must remain aloof. There still may be someone around who knows me."

"No need to tempt fate when royal commissions are possible. Did I say that right?"

Anne smiled once she was reminded what all this was supposed to lead to. "Yes, love, you did."

~ * ~

The daily sojourns into the heart of the busiest shopping area of the city had the desired effect. Invitations to soirees became too numerous to ignore— functions soon to become an integral part of their carefully conceived agenda.

"Miss Flanagan," Francis Alexander said, waving fingers in her direction as he bounded down stairs from the town hall into the street, ample belly bouncing, "Might I have a word with you?"

"You certainly may," she said, holding that handkerchief high, concealing her face. "What is it I might do for you, kind sir?"

"We are having a dinner and dance in my home, Alexander House, this very night. I'd like to extend to you an invitation," he said with a gloating smile, as if believing he favored a lesser human being.

113

Masking anger at such arrogance with a twitching smile, "Would it be improper to make my attendance contingent upon my legal counsel, William Cormac, escorting me? I feel it would not be good etiquette for a lady to arrive unescorted to such a gathering."

His conceited smile dropped so fast his jowls quivered. Yet he continued on in the role of gentleman. "If...that's the price I must pay for your presence then...so be it." He bowed slightly.

"Then it's with great pleasure that I accept your lovely invitation, sir." She walked away with a girlish swish of her long dress and flippant twirl of a parasol.

"What do you make of that reaction when I mentioned my father," Anne whispered to Little Feather from the corner of her mouth.

"There is history there. One we may need to know about."

"Aye, t'is a foul-smellin' wind that blows between those two," Anne said screwing up her nose, "and I want to know the stench's source."

Anne barged through the door of Cormac Manor. "Mr. Cormac, are you about?" She tossed her parasol onto a chair in the foyer then removed her gloves and dropped them beside it. She marched down a hall looking through each open doorway and knocked on the closed ones. "Mr. Cormac?" she called out.

Little Feather followed step for step.

"Mr. Cormac," she repeated, louder still.

"Massa Cormac is on the side porch loungin' with his afternoon brandy," the elderly black man said, appearing through a nearby doorway.

Outside and around the house they went and found him sitting with an open book in his lap. "I want the truth, Father. What is your business with Francis Alexander of Alexander House?"

Lifting his head, as if not hearing the question, he looked to the stately pecan grove beyond the house. He thoughtfully closed the book he'd been reading and set it on a small round pedestal table next to his chair. For a time, he simply allowed his eyes to trace the lines of a tree adorned with Spanish moss like dull gray tinsel on a Christmas tree and chewed on the inside of his cheek. He then swirled his glass of brandy and took a sip. Still, he didn't speak.

"You'll not be avoidin' me on this issue, Father. It might be important to our plans that I know all your conflicts."

"I have no intention of evading your question, dear. It's delicate and must be addressed in the same manner."

Setting the ornate cut crystal brandy glass atop the book on the table at his side, William rose. He walked to the porch rail and leaned against it with widespread hands. After a moment, he straightened and clasped hands together at his back. He made a show of keeping his face turned away from the girls. "Mr. Alexander's wife, Katharine, lost all interest in her husband… some time ago actually. Unfortunately, I found myself in the middle and the object of her distraction—"

"You had an affair with the wife of the most influential man in Charleston?" She tried controlling volume but did so poorly. "Are you a dullard?"

He sighed. "A mistake to be sure, but it cannot be taken back, and I cannot pretend it didn't happen."

"Remember what I told you about English sailing men thinkin' with their jewels?" she asked Little Feather.

The girl showed no emotion, only nodded once.

Anne flipped a thumb toward her father. "It holds true for Irish lawyers as well."

Little Feather showed signs of embarrassment and dropped her eyes to the floor.

"It also seems we stand in the presence of a man-slut," Anne said matter-of-factly, "But I don't think I'll be expoundin' on that observation, considerin' I am the product of a previous lack of attention to consequences by the same man. He may be my father and Mary Brennan my mother but Mary Brennan was not William Cormac's wife at the time of my conception."

"We'll just have to work around it," William said.

"Right you are," Anne said. "We begin tonight."

~ * ~

"Announcing Miss Amber Flanagan and escort, the honorable William Cormac." The stiffly starched butler closed the front door of the opulent mansion behind them.

"Honorable? Humph," Anne mumbled.

They walked in and stopped before taking the three steps down into the main hall where a lavishly dressed crowd of men and women gathered. William helped Anne from her wrap, handing it to the door attendant. Father and daughter surveyed the splendor and vulgar display of wealth spread before them.

"So this is Alexander House, home of the wealthiest man in Charleston," Anne whispered as she lifted her wide blue satin gown to take the short steps down into the ballroom. "Impressive."

Old acquaintances and hopeful new ones began migrating in their direction. "I'll introduce you to all the relevant ones," William whispered.

With a broad smile and air of societal smugness, Anne drew increasing attention. Remaining cool and distant, yet cordial in short bursts, it became the social equivalent of a pool of molasses to flies. Young single men buzzed around as did nosy young wives of Charleston's elite; all trying to figure out who this lovely stranger was, a quietly accepted sport of the wealthy that would inevitably become the gossip. *I must be the prize for the evening.*

Four candle-laden chandeliers sent out golden sparkles from flickering flames giving the ballroom a bejeweled appearance, lending its special magic to Anne's sudden popularity; a new face stood out in the rarified air of snobbish wealth.

As Anne and William worked the floor, the host, Francis Alexander, came into view near the gaudy overbuilt fireplace. His plain-looking wife Katherine stood at his side. Anne was shocked at the woman's appearance. She was ugly; there was no other word for it. Although dressed to match the money in silk, satin, lace, and diamonds, the woman's hawkish nose, sunken cheeks, and eyes too large for their sockets overshadowed the finery. "You could have found better than her if it was only an idle affair you desired," she told her father, whispering behind her handkerchief. "In fact, a few copper coins could have bought better."

Ignoring her, he looked away and nodded a greeting at a passing gentleman then sipped from his champagne glass. He took the latest insult of his admitted affair in stride. "Etiquette dictates I introduce you to the host although you already know him. But I certainly do not relish the task."

The three violinists at the corner of the expansive ballroom began a waltz. The dance floor filled, coming alive and moving with flowing gowns leaving the impression of a colorful spinning bouquet. A channel opened among the dancers, leaving a direct path to the host couple. William scooped up Anne's hand and guided her across the floor. It was time to perform the polite duty. They walked swiftly yet fluidly negotiating the snaking path between waltzing couples.

"Francis, I'd like you to meet—"

"No introduction necessary," he snapped pertly, shoving William aside, reaching for Anne's hand. Then softly, "I have already had the pleasure of meeting the lovely Miss Flanagan." He kissed the back of her outstretched hand, never pulling his eyes from hers.

Clearly expecting such a reception, William waited quietly for Alexander to finish doting then said, "Amber, I'd also like you to meet Mrs. Alexander. This is Katherine."

Still holding Anne's hand, Mr. Alexander shot an angry look at William for presumptuousness of introducing his wife for him.

Forcing her eyes from William only long enough for a glance, Katherine said, "Nice to meet you." Her interest remained with William.

Anne couldn't resist a catty smile. She looked past Mr. Alexander's chubby jowls to her father and saw him as the uncomfortable object of a sexually charged stare by the wife of their host. Feeling her father had suffered long enough, she cut the awkward silence, "It's a beautiful home and plantation you have, Mr. Alexander.

I do admire it all very much."

Pride now pumped, he poked out his lower lip. "Yes, I take great satisfaction in my business savvy." His demeanor softened as he stuck thumbs in the armholes of his vest. Arrogance oozed from him. "Thank you for noticing, my dear. I'm pleased that my efforts have captured your attention. I do indeed work hard but always wonder if it's appreciated." His showy display of modesty was sickeningly transparent.

"Certainly so, sir." She stepped in nearer the fat man to avoid bumping into passing dancers twirling ever closer. "The intricacies of business fascinate me. I fancy the bounty of your annual harvest is tremendous."

"Well," he said, as if telling a secret, "Just this past month I have sent off a trading vessel to France so loaded with cotton and tobacco as to endanger the bulkheads. It has been a good year. I expect the return voyage to carry the gold I expect as payment in full to sustain me for the next year."

Feigning shyness, Anne kept a handkerchief to her mouth, a girlish smile escaping from behind it. "I hope the ship can remain afloat carrying such weighty treasure."

William became increasingly uncomfortable. As the violinists began another melody, he clearly saw it as a duty to offer his daughter an escape from boredom. He took this chance to gracefully depart the tense proximity to Katherine. He reached for Anne's hand and pulled her around to face him. "May I have this dance, Miss Flanagan?"

She smiled, tipping her head politely. Without a word she allowed him to sashay with her off to the smooth strings of the violins. "That man is a disgusting pig," she whispered as she twirled to present her back to their host.

Pulling back, he looked into her eyes. "Does this mean I am forgiven for my indiscretion?"

"Forgiven?" she laughed sarcastically then abruptly changed the subject. "It would be a great pleasure to unburden that ship of its gold, especially since he sold commodities to France. How much commission do you think Prime Minister Walpole might pay to have that gold?"

William didn't comment. They danced around the floor, but Anne's mind had long since left the party. She dreamed of glorious days back at sea, looting and plundering. *This time, as God is my witness, I'll be doin' it right…with the blessin' and protection of King George the First. I'll be gettin' a handsome commission and maybe an extra little cut unknown to the king.*

Anne's longing for success began to align with a strengthening sense that a hopeful future might be coming together. "How much would he pay, indeed." she muttered.

# Chapter Fifteen

Baffled, Anne tossed her hands into the air. "Fate dealt us a strange hand." She laughed bitterly.

Puzzled by the comment after having read it aloud, William dropped the letter and watched it flutter onto a chair. "Aren't you happy? I thought formal announcement of your commission by King George and this letter of marque under his seal would've been greeted quite differently, much more joyfully. What perplexes you?"

She jerked a quick angry glance at her father. "You're still the uncarin' and unnoticin' bastard you've always been. You have no idea what I've been through since we last saw one another and yet only now are you askin'." She retrieved the letter and ran a hand over it, as if a priceless parchment. "But how you think and feel shouldn't be my concern. I'm torn between jubilation and reminded of old hurts at the same time."

She abruptly stiffened and went toe to toe with William waving the letter in his face. "Don't you see? This commission includes the sloop Providence; the same vessel from which Mary, Calico Jack, all the crew, and I were removed from by Lawes, that Jamaican ass of a governor." Her voice rose into a higher range. "And, now it is *my* ship to captain, under the protection of the British Flag? It's an absolutely absurd turn of events. She marched to the opposite side of the parlor. "It would have been joyful news if it were not such a stark reminder of blood that was shed by people I cared for. Now, I look upon it as a tool of my revenge."

120

She folded her arms tightly over her breasts and stomped across the floor, sparring with a confusing mix of swirling emotions. All those feelings finally converged in anger. "The blood of friends still stains the deck of the Providence! I'm sure of it. That…that damned ship!" She slammed a fist against the doorjamb next to the broad veranda at the side of Cormac Manor.

"Leave the past in the past," her father urged. "Look upon this as personal justice. Be satisfied, Anne, please. Don't let it blacken your heart and cloud your judgment."

"Your father speaks wise," Little Feather said, coming to her side. She stroked Anne's shoulder. "You've been smiled upon. We cannot know the reason. But it's a gift, not a curse, to be dealt with."

Anne thought about it. She glided to the window framing the poplar-lined carriageway that led out to the road fronting the plantation property. She came to accept what had been offered while looking for a time at the manicured approach to the house, but what her eyes beheld and where her thoughts lay were separate things.

"Little Feather, you've taught me much about your world. I wouldn't have survived the trip back without you. I would have starved then frozen to death. My skill with rapier and cutlass was worthless in those conditions. Now it's my turn. I have much to teach you beyond defending yourself and pressing your demands through the persuasive use of a blade. Do you fancy a life upon the high seas? Are you willing to face dangers for adventure and the rewards it brings? And…," she turned to face the girl in a calculating way, "…are you prepared to risk your life doing it?"

Softly with eyes downcast, "At your side is where I've grown accustomed. I am a proud Iroquois but distant from my tribe and family. I was once a slave but now enjoy freedom. It is only you that I have to thank for that." She lifted her eyes to meet Anne's. "If it's adventure you seek and dangers you face, this is my quest as well. We shall confront them together."

Anne embraced the girl. She let fingers travel down the knobby lumps of the girl's spine enjoying the feel of Little Feather's lean muscularity. She stroked her gently, lingering at the feel of the girl's slender frame pressed against her own then lightly kissed her ear. Anne pushed her back but continued clutching her shoulders. "Then I declare our plan officially begun." She released the girl and stepped away before lust took root. "Out at sea, on the Providence, I shall be Captain Andrew the Protector. In port, Andrew will vanish and Amber Flanagan will appear."

"I shall be your eyes and ears in Charleston," William said. "All wealth you generate, we share, and will be explained as old family money of yours sent from Ireland."

Anne nodded with a wry grin. "Our first influx of 'old family money from Ireland' shall come to us in the form of gold bound for Francis Alexander. I look upon it as a personal favor I'll be extendin' to that two-legged sausage, Mr. Alexander. He so needs my assistance in pulling that snobbish nose down from the clouds. It should humble him a bit and make him a trifle easier to stomach."

William hoisted a glass of brandy to toast the plan. He did so alone.

~ * ~

Anne's first tentative step onto the deck of the Providence clothed as a man, assuming the disguise of Captain Andrew felt oddly wonderful. It had been a long time since last she stood aboard a ship. And now the circumstances had greatly changed. Hesitation turned to exhilaration as sea air blowing in off the Atlantic filled her nostrils—perfume to a seafarer and a simple pleasure longed for. Gulls squawked and swooped beneath the furled sails, flying here to there looking for a free meal. Every nuance of the life beckoned, imbuing her with renewed strength. Sensations mostly overlooked by others were to Anne Bonny as Samson's hair was to him. She was back in her world.

Little Feather gawked at everything. It amused Anne. The girl wandered about the ship awestruck; placing hands upon everything she strolled by, having only seen them at a distance in the past. The young girl disappeared below deck, presumably to continue exploring.

The day went quickly as Anne spent time one-on-one with her hand-picked crew. Now was the time to become acquainted with strengths and weaknesses, not when times became tense. After a time, she made adjustments to assigned duties of the newly assembled men and issued orders. The group of men dispersed. *I'll be knowin' each and every one of you better.*

She became curious as to the whereabouts of Little Feather and began searching. She went below deck. "Little Feather. Girl, where are you?" She threw open the door to the cramped captain's quarters. There sat Little Feather on the lone bunk, head between her knees. Her deep brown skin, normally with a reddish glow, tinted green. "Are you well? Your color is awful."

"I'm not. I'm sorry. A strange malady has attacked my stomach. It came suddenly...will not go away."

Sizing up the situation, Anne noticed the ship's slow rise and fall as it set anchored in the harbor. "Your malady is not so strange. The motion of the ship causes your illness. If you sit below deck you will remain ill. It's as simple as that, love. It will be to your advantage to spend the first few days at sea topside until your body's rhythm matches that of the ship upon the water."

Little Feather only had time to nod before losing the remainder of the contents of her stomach on Anne's boots. "I pray this will not be a part of what you refer to as adventure," she said haltingly then wiped her mouth and looked up at Anne through heavily veined eyes.

~ * ~

Little Feather could not hold food for the first two days out, spending most of her time at the rail looking down into the water, never knowing when the next heave might come. The attention by the crew was not good—a woman on board was considered bad luck anyway. Grumbling became constant.

"Cap'n Andrew, beggin' your indulgence, sir," the gruff seaman said looking down at Little Feather huddled against the rail. "The men feel that this Indian woman will bring down the will of Satan upon us."

Anne looked up into the big man's eyes. In them, she noticed a look not common to most men who regularly sign on to this type of crew. She believed she saw the light of intelligence backed by heart. She also sensed sincerity behind that bushy black beard and foul body odor—someone trustworthy perhaps? Folding arms over her breasts, she sported a grin. "Those are harsh words, my big hairy friend." She let the comment hang for a moment then shrugged. "Oh well, if you feel that strongly, throw her overboard." She nonchalantly walked away.

"Uh, what was that?"

Anne stopped and turned.

"Are you serious, Cap'n?"

Anne grinned but said nothing, head tilted, arms crossed over her chest.

"You wish me to make the decision?" He babbled. "Is that it? I—I'm not sure I should be doin' that."

"Are you questioning your captain's desire to pacify his crew?"

"No, Sir. Not a'tall." He stroked his bearded cheek. "I mean I don't think so." He pulled his brow down into a deep wrinkle. "Cap'n, are ye givin' us permission to give her the heave ho and feed her to the sharks?"

"It is not permission and it is not an order. I'm telling you to do what you think is right." The smile turned to an icy stare. "That is, if you think you're man enough to get it done."

The big man was in an awkward situation. It was plain upon his face he thought so too, and didn't like it. It was equally clear he didn't want to appear timid to the men. He said slowly, "Aye, Cap'n. I surely think I am man enough to get it done."

He turned and marched to where Little Feather lay near the rail. The big seaman reached and grabbed her by the shirt.

In a flash, his hand felt the sting of the flat side of the girl's cutlass.

He straightened and jumped back, stunned, rubbing his hurting hand. It happened so fast he didn't see it coming. A smile covered his surprise. "So, I must fight for the right to dispose of ya." He pulled a knife from his belt nearly as long as her cutlass. He bore a mischievous look as he stalked Little Feather.

Although still nauseous, Little Feather sprang up and took the fight to him.

The clang of blades quickly attracted a cheering and jeering group of rowdy sailors. Men crowded in a tight circle. Bets were made, none favoring the girl. All wagers down were for how long it would take the big man to dispose of her.

The burly seaman, though strong as a bull, was no match for the Indian girl's speed. He attempted to get in close to immobilize her lightning fast cutlass arm and wrestle her down. He couldn't do it. He wasn't fast enough. Even sick and dizzy, Little Feather masterfully outmaneuvered the big man.

Nevertheless, he continued stalking, but inflicted damage was on him not her. She put a shallow cut on his shoulder then across his belly. The harder he tried, the angrier he became and less in control. Eventually, anger robbed him of good sense. He went into a blind rage, unable to defend against this youngster no taller than his armpit, much less be the aggressor. She now had him defensively backing away.

Anne noticed another sailor standing nearby acting suspicious. He drew a knife from beneath his loose shirt. He must have wagered a sizeable amount of money.

Anne quietly drew her rapier and stepped laterally to him. All other eyes remained on the dual near the ship's rail. She touched his neck with its point. "Uh-uh," she whispered. "Hold steady, mate, right where you are."

He stiffened—his hand still wrapped around the knife's handle.

"Where is your sense of fair play, man? If you desire to use that knife then you'll do it with cold steel through your throat. Now, what shall it be?"

"Sorry Cap'n," he said. His hand fell limp to his side. "I let me desires run wild. Will ye be forgivin' me of such impertinence?"

She smiled and put her rapier back in its scabbard. "I will."

Little Feather allowed the big seaman to back her against the main mast standard then dropped her cutlass to her side. She bore a sweet, girlish smile then opened her arms, inviting him in.

Angered, he obliged and charged. He dropped his shoulder obviously hoping to pin her against the broad base of the spar. As Anne had taught her, she waited until he was upon her then sidestepped, allowing him to knock himself unconscious against the massive timber supporting the main mast.

Little Feather stepped over and straddled him. She held the blade firmly against his throat waiting for his swimming eyes to stabilize. As he became aware, he locked onto the hand holding the cutlass. He wisely chose not move.

"Well, well, well," Anne said. "It appears you owe your life to this fragile and ill young Indian girl who, just moments ago you wished to dispose of with no more care or concern than you'd give a bucket of fish guts."

Little Feather put her cutlass away and helped the man to his feet.

Anne turned a full circle within the crowd of men and in a strong voice, "I pity the man who engages this girl when she is not drunk with sickness." She looked at each of the faces of the gathered men. No one spoke.

Anne stepped in close. "'Tis only a guess but I'm feelin' you'll be havin' no more trouble about womanhood," she told Little Feather with a sly smile and giddy snap of the eyebrows.

Little Feather's eyes brightened. "It's a hard way to defeat an illness but I no longer feel bad." She sniffed then breathed deep. "Has the air always smelled so clean?"

~ * ~

"Ship ahoy off the starboard bow," a crewman called down from atop the mast supporting billowed sail.

Anne put a brass telescope to her eye scanning the horizon and finally locked in on it. "She flies the flag of the French. I'm believin' that's our target." She collapsed the scope with a clickety clack and tossed it into a bucket. "All hands on deck!"

The deck came alive with a hectic rush to follow the order. Men scurried to a point near where Captain Andrew stood. They boisterously crowded, pushing one another about, eager to learn of the plan for the ship.

"Quiet!" she ordered over the chatter of the smelly crowd. "Our prey tacks into the wind. 'Tis to our advantage. We'll be upon it before it can react."

Using her rapier as a pointer she aimed it at the steersman and said to the man at the rudder, "You, Mister Lark, bring us about and a lay in a head-on course." Slinging the point of her weapon to yet another, she barked, "Mister Black, take your men and ready the port guns."

With each order, the assemblage shrank as battle stations were manned and preparations made for a worst-case scenario.

"Make certain your powder is dry, pistols and cannons primed, we cannot be sure yet of resistance." She sprinted to the steps of the quarterdeck and took them up two at a time to watch the unfolding attack. She realized she must be vigilant and remain prepared to modify the plan quickly if necessary. *If we can take gold without losing crew—all the better.*

As the ship came into better view, it became obvious its crew remained unaware of the approaching Providence. Anne saw no activity beyond daily duties of a ship's crew. No hurry. No rush.

As Little Feather joined her, Anne said with cautious excitement, "Look, love. Do you see the possibility? We might board her without a shot fired."

The Providence drifted within shouting distance. Only then did the target ship notice. Anne's threat carried upon the wind across to the men gathered at the starboard rail. "By the order of King George the First of England and with authority of a letter of marque issued by Prime Minister Walpole, I order you to stand down. Prepare to be boarded. Hostile action shall be seen as an act of war and the fires of hell will be brought upon you!"

Seeing no attempt at defense, the men of the Providence threw a series of grappling hooks and snagged the French vessel pulling it in and spilling over onto the deck of the French vessel.

They met no resistance. Men from the Providence herded the other crew into a tight circle. They snarled and hurled insults to intimidate them, preventing any measure of boldness.

Anne, playing her Captain Andrew persona, boarded the vessel and marched to the tightly packed group of seaman who obviously wanted no fight. "Your Captain...where is your Captain?" she barked.

A buzz in French rose up from the group.

"Does anyone amongst you know the King's English?" she said, cutting off the unintelligible cackle.

A weak voice came from inside the tightly packed crew. "I do, sir." The reply was English but the French accent thick."

"Step forward. Be recognized," she said.

From within the crush of men, a slight built older man with stooped shoulders slipped sideways and emerged wearing a grimy apron that may have been white at one time.

"And what is your duty?"

"I am the cook."

Thinking upon their lack in this area, she queried, "Would you consider pledging an allegiance to the English Crown?"

"To what end if I might be so bold?"

"To become cook aboard the Providence, you twit."

The scrawny old man scratched a scruffy gray beard. A smile appeared. His lips parted to reveal the few darkened teeth left in his head. "The offer tempts me beyond control. I'll align with the Crown and gladly be your cook."

"Good choice. Now, where is your Captain?"

"He cowers below deck in his cabin," the grizzled old cook said with contempt. "Knowing his lack of courage, you may find him curled and quivering beneath his bed or any other hiding place that might accommodate that bloated belly."

Without being ordered two crewmen of the Providence retrieved the Captain from below. They dragged him wailing before Captain Andrew. The man lay prostrate babbling something in French.

"Cook, what does he say?"

"He is simply repeating over and over his wish that you not kill him and that a letter of marque authorizing acts of privateering is unlawful outside wartime."

"First of all, tell him he's not worth killing. Then tell him that if goods are sold to a foreign power originating from English colonies without express written consent of King George the First of England, those trade goods, or payment for them, are considered illegal barter and subject to confiscation. That is considered by the crown as provoking an act of war. Tell the fat bastard what I said."

"Before I tell him, sir, I would like to say that it would certainly be okay with me if you changed your mind and chose to kill him." He then humbly looked to his feet just in case offense happened to be taken.

"You take a risk, speaking to me in such a forward manner. What makes you so bold?"

"To save from elaborate explanation, the Captain is a snob, a bore, a bully, and now even you know him as the coward he is."

Anne placed the point of her rapier on the Captain's chest over his heart. *Aye, you have an English twin by the name of Peckary. By the saints, you two must have been separated at birth.* He blubbered and babbled then covered his head with both arms. He fell back. It was obvious he thought his life was about to end at the point of an English privateer's rapier. He rolled over and pressed his face into the roughly sawn deck of the ship and whimpered. "Cook, tell him that such cowardice makes him dead already then ask him where the gold is. If the answer does not come quickly, he shall die twice."

The answer was indeed swift. Men ran below and delivered thirteen small chests topside for Captain Andrew's perusal. "This is much greater booty than I planned on," she said with a surprised glint. She fell to her knees and fondled the contents of an open container. "Surely this can't be all bound for a single plantation owner."

"I know it as fact, Captain, the gold was intended for all the commodities of the Carolinas. The French outbid the English for it," the cook said.

Then I assume the English crown didn't see a need to pay a fair price," she mumbled. *If I didn't think I'd profit handsomely, I'd insist France keep it as a special gift from Anne Bonny.* "This is turning out to be a good day," she finally said. "There's plenty here to pay the King, take a handsome commission, and pay the crew substantially."

As her mouth spoke the words, her thoughts had already moved on, knowing this fortune would be mostly kept and only a small portion sent back to England, just enough to keep the monarchy from suspicion. The influx of wealth would cement the power base of William Cormac and Anne Bonny, alias Amber Flanagan, in Charleston and throughout the Carolinas.

"My lucky star now hangs firmly in the sky. And it's about bloody time."

# Chapter Sixteen

"Your first time out may've carried no consequences but don't expect them all to be without danger. Some could turn deadly," William warned.

"True. Your words are wise, but your paternal concern is grossly misplaced. You're the man who disowned me and sent me away. Could this little show of parental concern be meant to soften my heart for some devious reason? Or, maybe, it's just that you wish to protect your money maker." She made a move to leave him dangling but couldn't let it go so calmly. "Why the hell do you pretend not to remember the ass you were to me? You talk as though you've forgotten. Once upon a time I was dead to you!"

"Anne, listen, I'm not proud of what I did. I was just trying to rid myself of that manipulative leach, James Bonny. Husband or not, I didn't want the conniving weasel around. Even in your best argument you cannot deny that you were impetuously uncooperative when I sought your support. I came to believe you wed the blood-sucking parasite to spite me and still cannot believe that you ever loved him; although, I shouldn't have used you as the excuse to make him go away. Will you ever forgive me for that one selfish indiscretion?"

Off-handedly, "Probably not." She turned away. Then with sarcastic flip, "My beloved James," she mumbled. "Hah!" She spun back. "It took time but my view came to be as yours in the matter of young Mister Bonny." Anne smoothed the front of her fashionable long dress as she sauntered away. *Not only do I never want to see my ex-husband again, I would gladly expunge his memory if I could.* This she did not share with her father. She didn't want to offer additional satisfaction that he obviously felt from the admission. She glanced to see a smile spreading across his face. She refused to allow it latitude beyond that.

He coaxed her to face him so he might refresh her brandy. It occurred to her how often she kept her back to him, still uncomfortable looking her father in the eye. After he filled her glass, she turned her face away so fast, red curls flagged.

He offered some of the brandy to Little Feather. She refused it.

All the while, Anne pretended to check the titles of books lining an eye-level shelf. She didn't want him noticing in her expression that his point was well made.

With a swish of her dress and toss of those springy ringlets in her hair, she kept moving as if she was becoming bored then stopping to study a landscape painting elegantly encircled by a finely carved golden oval frame next to French doors that opened to the side porch. "Can't you simply appreciate the prize I have delivered?" she asked with a dismissive wave. "Let's not bog in sentimentality. It's not genuine anyway. You know it and I know it."

"How can I not appreciate it? You've delivered the means that affords me a lucrative detour on the road to destitution. Francis Alexander has been making good his, so-called, clandestine plan to crush my business, although it's a secret to no one. The arrogant blob can't keep his mouth shut." He gulped brandy. "It may only be whispered within cliques but a secret it's most assuredly not."

His dour look became severe. "Look about you, Anne. Have you not noticed the missing armoire or the empty space where my beloved writing desk had been? Selling those items was to have been the beginning of my financial end."

He stepped close behind her. She paid him no mind and continued inspection of artwork adorning the walls in the parlor. He laughed. "By the way, Mister Alexander's own lifestyle seems to have tempered somewhat; not so lavish since receiving word that payment for commodities has mysteriously disappeared at the hand of nefarious privateers that no one has ever heard of before. That insufferable highbrow hasn't had a single party to show off his wealth since word spread." Offering a quick toast he downed the final swallow. "It looks like turnips and beans at Alexander House for awhile."

Anne thought on the letter of marque she held, legitimizing actions that without sanction would have been punishable by hanging. As it stood, she kept hefty portions of whatever she collected while winning praise from the King of England. It was laughable. She shook her head as she looked to the Oriental rug at her feet. She snickered. She did no differently now than what she did in Jamaica. And for that she was sentenced to death. "Mister Francis Alexander will think twice the next time he feels obliged to sell to anyone other than the English crown."

The morning air set heavy with cool fog. Sounds beyond the porch were easy to distinguish even at great distance. The confining mist created an aura of closeness. The rustle of small animals through fallen leaves—possums, raccoons or armadillos was traced by sound that seemed piped directly to them in this early quietness.

Anne's interest shifted from paintings on the wall to the tranquil real-life scene beyond the doors where only the closest trees remained visible. "The fog shrouding this plantation settles my restless soul, almost as if it protects us from those who wish us harm," she pondered aloud. The creak of grease-starved carriage wheels, the whinny of a horse, and the clip-clop of hooves signaled the passing of an unseen traveler on the road fronting the house. Her eyes followed the sound even though she never saw its source.

"If I did not know you to be fearless, your words might seduce me to believe you're becoming aware of your mortality. Is it possible, sweet daughter, you finally realize you'll not live forever?" Eyes reddening and listing slightly as he walked, he poured another brandy.

She refused to respond but noticed the amount of liquor he consumed. "Drinking your breakfast is not a good habit. Of course, I've never given you much credit for clear judgment even sober."

Having stood quietly, Little Feather now joined Anne at the porch railing. She defended her friend's subtle changes. "Women view immortality differently than men, Mister Cormac. A woman believes it's possible but only through the gift of birth. We cannot forever deny our nature as bearer of children and no amount of denial can keep these thoughts forever from a woman's mind. With each passing cycle of the moon, the body knows it is one more opportunity missed."

Anne didn't reply to, nor otherwise comment on her young Indian friend's assessment. Moments ago she'd been calm and felt secure. Melancholy took that mood away. She absently stroked her flat belly where a baby should have been growing if plans with Michael Radcliffe hadn't been crushed.

She sighed and blew away frustration refusing this maternal leaning to have its way. "Our minds and hearts must stay in the moment. What is it that you have learned of late that might provide us with a new course of action, Father?" She continued looking into the fog.

"Did you happen to notice that young man by the name of Peter Vander Horst while at Alexander House? He's the son of a wealthy Dutch trader, I believe." William stood in the open portal separating veranda and house looking toward the women outside.

"Not that I remember. Why?"

"He saw you and asked to meet you."

"Really?"

"Yes, but you were busy with Mister Alexander. I didn't want to interrupt and now very happy that I didn't. As it turned out that was a very important piece of business."

"Good thinking."

"Vander Horst is up from Norfolk I am told. He's scouting business opportunities for his father, Artur Vander Horst. The father is a man of substantial means as I understand it. He owns three vessels that transport goods to and from the West Indies.

With arched eyebrow and cunning smile, "Well, if Mister Vander Horst so wants to meet me, then who am I to deny him that privilege?" She paced a few steps down the porch then suddenly stopped and turned. "By all means, arrange a dinner party so we might satisfy young Mr. Vander Horst's desire for my company. Affording this pleasure to a visitor of Charleston is the least we can do." She smiled in a girlish way.

~ * ~

It took only a small portion of a week to prepare for the gala. Invitations were sent to all considered important to the plan. The night arrived. It was near perfect for such a gathering, a crisp clear evening. A brilliant blue harvest moon shot beams through trees so bright that shadows couldn't conceal objects under their cloak. The lunar orb guided a stream of carriages, lanterns dangling, up the carriageway to Cormac Manor.

Setting aside all reservations about the evening, William and Anne dressed in their finest. Little Feather acquiesced and dressed to suit her role, dictated by the greater scheme. She wore the plain gray dress of a servant. Anne radiated brilliant charm even in the dimly lighted entry while greeting guests in a royal blue satin gown with high ruffled collar topped by an intricately hand-carved, finely detailed ivory cameo choker. Long lacy material at the sleeve-ends reached past her palms. Her father stood shoulder-to-shoulder with her receiving visitors. Both played parts befitting that rarified class known as the Charleston elite. The gaily lighted interior spilled onto the broad pristine veranda as the trail of guests filed in to Cormac Manor.

Smiles came quickly and easily exchanged, although a look of snobbish insincerity did sneak out from some as if it were their right to attend and not a privilege extended by host, William Cormac.

The first sincere smile Anne noticed came from a young man with a slightly pale but clear complexion and thick black hair, oiled and perfectly groomed with a hint of wave.

He extended a hand and bowed slightly maintaining alluring eye contact. "Miss Flanagan," he said, softly cupping her outstretched hand. He kissed it with closed eyes then resumed that penetrating gaze. "I've eagerly anticipated this moment." He held her hand beyond modest limits.

Anne allowed it with a warm smile then subtly let him know she was interested by dragging her middle finger slowly across his palm as she retrieved her hand.

Her reaction to this man surprised even her. A tingle stunned her into momentary silence. "Call me Amber," she finally said, looking at the most perfect face she'd ever seen but only in short bursts. Heat came up in her cheeks. *God help me, I'm blushing.*

"Pardon my boldness, but I feel that I've known you, possibly in another time or another place." He studied her then added with the suggestion of embarrassment, "Although it's possible your beauty just makes me wish it so." His eyes fell to the floor and added, "Then again, maybe yours is the perfect face that has been in my dreams my whole adult life."

She tried to hold her eyes upon him but couldn't without becoming lost in them. "It is not likely our paths have ever crossed, sir. Unless, of course, you've visited County Cork, Ireland."

"I'm sure the memory is false, born of infatuation."

After a time their conversation was interrupted when the elderly black butler announced dinner. Guests moved into the dining room where a lengthy opulent table had been set, seating carefully arranged. A large reflective chandelier of soft sparkling light enhanced the ambience.

Servant girls, all in starched uniforms, including Little Feather, filed in one by one setting numerous platters of food at various points on the long banquet table. The impressive variety included three roasted ducks, steamed mushrooms, highly seasoned black-eyed peas, and carrots candied with sorghum syrup.

Peter Vander Horst, a quintessential gentleman, seated Anne in her assigned chair next to his. The general buzz, tinkle and clatter of the dinner party, faded into the background as the two created a quiet universe in which only they existed. Time sped by. They became acquainted.

"I hope this is merely our first meeting," Peter whispered."

"It will be our last only if you will it so," she replied, feigning shyness.

Anne allowed Peter to lean in. It was obvious the crowd no longer existed for him. Prying eyes and gossip didn't matter. He seemed lost in her as if contemplating a kiss.

But someone else's eyes captured Anne's attention beyond Peter. Little Feather stood in a doorway watching. Sadness upon the young girl's face jolted Anne. Daubing her lips with a linen napkin, "Would you excuse me for a moment, Peter?"

"Certainly," he said, standing, pulling her chair back.

Anne left the dining hall through a door at the opposite end and walked down a back hall. She approached Little Feather from behind. "What is that look?" she whispered. "Are you not well?"

"I'm having unkind thoughts. I'm sorry." The young girl's eyes wilted to the floor.

Anne didn't need further explanation. "My relationship with Mr. Vander Horst is necessary. I cannot say it will not become intimate. It may. I don't know." She placed a fingertip beneath Little Feather's chin and lifted it. She waited for the Indian girl's eyes to catch up. "But remember you are more than a friend to me." Anne refused to break contact until Little Feather smiled. Finally, she did. It was forced. There was no joy behind it.

# Chapter Seventeen

Sitting at her dressing table, Anne listened to the howling wind outside her bedroom. Mechanically, she brushed rouge on her cheeks allowing her mind to go wherever thoughts took her.

Eagerly encouraging and accepting romantic overtures by Peter Vander Horst, she'd come to enjoy a man's closeness, the game of courtship, and even the pretentious life she now lived. But all it took was a glance at Little Feather to yank her head from the clouds. She had to keep the girlish giddiness in check and remember she was Anne Bonny and not Amber Flanagan.

Anne's desire for family and children fogged her focus on a yet-to-be realized payout. Befuddled, her desires and goals didn't match. She couldn't lose sight of the prize. It became a struggle to keep unobstructed vision. Seduced into enjoying time with Peter, she'd become careless, putting anonymity at risk as she went about the business of learning his business.

She played with a ringlet of hair that refused to retain the proper curl, but her mind wasn't on it.

The schedule of Vander Horst's ships arriving and departing Norfolk was surprisingly easy to obtain. She shied from inquiring about cargo because over-inquisitiveness might fuel suspicion. Peter might raise an eyebrow or get a curious glint. Nevertheless, he offered trust that she too easily accepted.

Sexual attraction created a dangerous distraction. It was unusual to her character that she should overlook it—but she did. Promises to her father and Little Feather that bound her had become tenuous.

*It's a precarious perch where I stand.* She pulled a brush through her hair with fast frustrated strokes. *I'm slung about like a leaf in a gale. What in hell can I do about it?*

Twisting her face this way and that, she checked then rechecked her reflection in the mirror, making sure her appearance was as perfect as she could make it. She stood, stepped back then twirled around craning her neck to see as much of her reflection as possible, back to front and head to toe. She stopped and stared at her image as if that person in the mirror were someone else. "Anne Bonny, what manner of demon is this that you are fast becoming powerless against? You cannot draw a cutlass and slash the enemy. You are the enemy!"

For the moment, remaining reserved was her only defense. Her plan was to meet Peter in town and she must stop mulling and get on with it.

~ * ~

A cold front swept southeastward out of Canada clearing the autumn air. The morning embraced Anne and Peter in a crisp chill. The sharply angled sun cast long shadows. They sat close and snuggled into one another on a bench under a magnificent oak tree that had begun to shed a few leaves but still dressed in dense red and yellow foliage. Chattering squirrels raced about as the tail-flicking critters gathered nuts and acorns, stashing them in the rotted hollow of another nearby tree. Birds crowded a patch of brown grass snatching seeds from drooping heads of the dying plants.

Face-reddening chill had passersby on the street retracting necks into collars. But the sudden change of weather appeared welcomed by most. A general air of cordiality accompanied the seasonal transition. Peter nodded and smiled, bidding a pleasant good morning as people walked past. He touched the brim of his tall felt hat often, as much to keep it from blowing off in the stiff breeze as a show of respect. His main focus was Anne. He looked at her adoringly as she pushed numbing fingers deeper inside a fur-lined muff.

"Do you believe in reincarnation, Amber?"

"There are many things in the heavens and upon the earth that we cannot fathom as real. So, who am I to say that reincarnation does not exist? Why do you ask?"

"I cannot shake this feeling I knew you before I met you at Alexander House. The only plausible explanation is having known you in another life."

She smiled. "Even if it's not so," she said, "the words certainly come together in a poetic way."

"I must know you, Amber Flanagan."

"But I have told you everything about me."

"No. That is not my meaning. I must…know you."

In a flash Anne realized his intention and a dizzying montage of images swirled in her mind, one upon the other. She envisioned a multitude of scenarios resulting from intimacy; from garnering vital information putting her and her crew back on the high seas confiscating yet another treasure for the English Crown, to a quiet anonymous life raising children with Peter, to an overshadowing image of a saddened Little Feather.

Finally, the thought of living a life of deceit snapped her back to reality. Again, it took a conscious self-reminder that she was not her alias. She heaved a sigh. The dream of a domesticated life was an illusion Amber Flanagan might pull off but Anne Bonny never could. Still, there was a job to be done and a game to be played. "Then, Peter, maybe it's time I show you where I spend my nights, because there is much more I'd like to know about you as well." She smiled at the double-entendre.

Standing, she offered her hand, radiating a seductive air that couldn't possibly be confused for anything else. She tugged on his fingertips.

He yielded.

They strolled back to Cormac Manor hand-in-hand, to her bedroom.

~ * ~

"Aye, Little Feather. There is a fair wind that blows." A broad satisfied smile split her face as she sprang to her feet inside the relative privacy of her bedroom. "The Vander Horst trading sloop arrives in Norfolk in two weeks time loaded with rare and valuable spices." She touched her nose with the tip of a finger and whispered excitedly, "But it's not spices that be of interest to me. It's payment they'll be carryin' back to the West Indies." She clapped once and guffawed. She took Little Feather's hands and jubilantly twirled the youngster around.

The Iroquois girl remained expressionless. "Then we should sail to meet the vessel."

Noticing Little Feather's disturbing lack of joy in those clear dark eyes, Anne stopped and cupped the girl's face in her hands. "Look, sweet friend, if this seizure is hefty then maybe finding another before spring, we… you and I, love… can travel to a place I'm unknown and we can live as ourselves. Think about that. No more running, no more hiding. It'll be the last alias we'll ever need. I've thought about the French settlement of New Orleans. Doesn't it sound wonderful, you and I living our lives in wealth and anonymity somewhere near the bayous or in the deltas of French Louisiana Territory? What do you think?"

Little Feather tried to smile. "If that's your wish."

Knowing a relationship with Peter must be maintained for the present, Anne didn't press the girl for reconciliation. Their relationship would be tested again very soon anyhow.

~ * ~

Sending out the word, the crew of the Providence hastily reassembled. Anne arranged a rendezvous at the hidden cove where the ship lay anchored north of Charleston. Donning garb that defined Andrew the Protector, she wore a loose-fitting long white shirt with a black felt vest topping black pantaloons. Upon her head rested a not-so-clean dark brown leather tricorn.

Red hair had been purposely mussed then pulled tight and tied at the rear but the natural curl could not all be stretched from it.

Walking through the shallows of the cove then up the gangplank, her air of authority was complemented by an assortment of weapons about her body—pistols, rapier, cutlass, and various knives.

The grizzled little Frenchman who joined them as cook greeted her with an odd smile. Offering an unusual gesture of humility, his head fell forward. He bowed deeply then backed away. His mouth smiled but his eyes appeared dead. She lingered for a moment but summarily dismissed him and his peculiar greeting. *The French are a strange lot.* She walked on by. Little Feather followed close behind.

The Indian girl passed the burly sailor she fought on the previous voyage who would've thrown her overboard if he could have. He offered a grin and a casual single-finger salute. "It be nice to see ya again ma'am," he said as the young girl passed by him on her way over the gangway, stepping onto the deck of the ship. Untrusting, she didn't take her eyes off him and said nothing, making sure the cutlass slid freely in its scabbard.

Anne ordered sails unfurled and set. "No time to waste, lads. Let's get on with it."

Men scurried to hoist anchor. Forward jibs were unfurled and popped to life as they picked up wind. The Providence responded, coming about. It moved toward the mouth of the lagoon that opened into a narrow passage, providing access to the Atlantic swells beyond. The mains were drawn tight as strong northerly winds blowing in from New Foundland snapped them to full billow. Anne ordered a southerly course set toward the West Indies.

Before the first week was out, every eye searched quadrants of the horizon and all degrees between for a vessel expected to be heading in the same direction, the Vander Horst trading sloop.

Cold blasts of air accompanied choppy seas. Over the course of the day, roughness gave way to calm. Dense fog settled over the Providence. Anne unenthusiastically suspended the search. Nothing could be done until clear vision had been restored and wind again filled sailcloth.

The dark veil of night descended upon them, compounding the problem. As the ship lay dead in the water, it moved only by the gentle tug of current. The occasional lazy lap of water against the hull provided the only sound other than conversations. Lanterns speckled the deck of the Providence but the dim glow did nothing to light the way, each ringed in a white halo of drifting mist. They served only to define extremities of the ship for those topside.

"The only consolation we have is believing the Vander Horst vessel is losing an equal amount of time," Anne told Little Feather. She gripped the rail and wrung it in a frustrated chokehold as she stared into the darkness.

In the dim glow of a nearby lantern, Anne noticed Little Feather cock her head. She then turned her ear in a slow sweep as if determining the dominant ear.

"What is it? What do you hear?"

"I cannot say. It may be a trick of the mind or the cackle of the sea creature you call a dolphin. It sounded like a distant laugh." She kept turning one ear then the other toward the suspected sound.

"I don't hear any—"

Little Feather placed an open palm over Anne's mouth. "There it is again. Can you hear it now?"

Anne listened. Although far away, it became distinct. It was the boisterous laugh of a man. "Go quickly and quietly, Little Feather. Spread the word amongst the men to douse lanterns and make no noise. Sound travels with mystical ease in fog," she warned, now speaking barely above a sigh as she strained to see into the dark.

The crew assembled at the rail. The fizzle of the last flame left it black. Anne reached into darkness and found Little Feather's cheek. She pulled the girl's ear close to her mouth. "Pass the word to hold all weapons securely…no clang no clatter."

Tense seconds became minutes. All hands stood quiet. Even breathing became shallow. Mist settled on the side of Anne's face. It trickled down her cheek. She remained motionless and silent, listening. The first visible sign came with the appearance of a single dull yellow glow. It must have been a lantern suspended at or near the stern because the captain would surely keep it steered in the direction of drift, putting the bow at the other end.

Looking up to the position of the dim light seemed to indicate a larger vessel than the Providence. Anne took it into consideration. The Providence rode higher in the water than what must have been a bulky heavily laden vessel. Her ship drifted faster. The gap closed quickly.

Determining the origin of the ship proved futile. She didn't dwell on it. Anne committed her mind to boarding the vessel, believing they had surprise in their favor. "Pass the word," she whispered, "Prepare grappling hooks. Throw only on my call."

Voices wafted over on the night air. They remained calm and conversational, no hint of having been alerted to the approaching Providence.

"Now!" Anne shouted.

A series of clanks, thunks and bangs followed, as a sailor from the other ship sounded a bell from a central part of the ship, probably the mainmast spar.

The crew used the grappling lines to pull the Providence alongside the taller vessel then shinnied up the ropes. The drift kept the Providence in position. Sailors sought any footing on the side of the still unidentified ship to climb. They spilled onto the deck of the intended target.

"There they are!" Anne heard a crewmember call out. This alert followed a call to arms. Colliding metal blades signaled a battle enjoined. An occasional hiss-boom then smoky flash indicated some used precious single shots from flintlock pistols, presumably before the mist had a chance to dampen powder in the flint pans rendering them useless.

Climbing up the side of the ship, she balanced on the rail and snatched a rope hanging from the rigging above. She swung to the ship's center landing on her feet. Unmoving, she crouched and waited for Little Feather to swing across.

The girl appeared abruptly from the dark. Anne grabbed her loose buckskin legging to halt the girl's forward momentum. "Stay at my side, friend. The dark will make battle confusing."

True to her words, a face bearing a savage look suddenly and without warning appeared within the glow of a nearby lantern. Anne reacted with lightning speed, dispatching the attacker with a fast backslash of her cutlass to his throat. No sooner had she taken him out than another fell against her blind side, already lifeless. She glanced to see Little Feather putting a foot against the twitching man's back to ease withdrawal of her cutlass from his body.

Each aggressor seemed to be replaced by two more. The battle escalated, becoming frenzied. Anne hoped her crew was having more success than she seemed to be. Uniformed men kept coming and she wondered why so many and why the uniforms.

It seemed she and Little Feather stood between her men and this ship's main contingent. If so, what the hell were her men doing?

The amount of gunfire indicated the intended prey were well armed. Had the attackers become the attacked? *Why are there so many well-armed men aboard a trading vessel? Is this the Vander Horst ship? Maybe I have made a mistake and this is not a trading vessel at all.* Each thought was interrupted by a rapier lunging at her or by a gun aimed at her. *Have I stupidly attacked a fully manned warship?*

A momentary lull offered her an opportunity to join her men. As she did, and they came into view, it became clear she fought no more desperately than her crew.

Gunpowder smoke fouled the air with its sharp metallic odor. Gliding along the opposite rail, using it as a guide in the dark, Anne and Little Feather approached the tangle of battling men visible only with great difficulty in the near-useless illumination of a few scattered and flickering lanterns.

Suddenly, bursting from a door beneath the quarterdeck, a portly man bound out upon the deck next to a lantern.

Anne sized up the threat.

He brandished a pistol in each hand, both aimed directly at her. At a glance, she thought she made out two more tucked into his belt.

The first shot went wild. A lead ball sang a single note as it whizzed by her ear.

Little Feather moved aggressively toward him.

Anne saw the pistol in his other hand swing toward the girl. On the way, Little Feather was forced to engage another but rendered that one ineffective with a single slash of her cutlass. Her attention remained on the one she'd bested but he had fallen against her.

The young girl had become the fat man's next target. Anne clearly saw Little Feather had not noticed as she tried pushing the dying man off her.

*Bloody hell, she doesn't see a gun aimed at her.*

Little Feather stood too close to the pistol now being raised. Even a poor marksman could not miss that shot.

Anne dropped her rapier and drew one of her pistols. She leveled it at the man. He stood beside a glowing lantern making an easy mark. "Hey! You fat son of Satan!" she shouted.

He hesitated and looked toward the insult.

She fired.

The ball smashed into his face, spraying blood on Little Feather, sending him reeling back through the door from where he sprang.

She ran to the man and saw that he must be the captain. "Your captain is dead!" she shouted. "Lay down your arms! Do it now!" The clink and clang of metal upon metal indicated the fighting continued. "In the name of King George the First, I order all crew of this vessel to stand down!" she yelled into the dark.

After a moment, it grew relatively quiet.

"By provision of Prime Minister Walpole of England, I, Andrew the Protector, am authorized to confiscate valuables aboard this ship and have them delivered to England, pursuant to a royal decree in a letter of marque I hold in my possession. Safe passage is guaranteed for all who drop their weapons." She waited for indication of compliance. Believing it had not yet occurred. She yelled, "Or face the hangman!"

The sound of all manner of weapons clanked and thudded upon the deck and faces appeared before Anne in the glow of the nearest lantern. "Crew of the Providence, gather lanterns and bring them near."

The carnage became clear as limping and injured men brought the lanterns together illuminating the blood-soaked deck. The piles of twisted bodies and those soon to be dead were strewn, sometimes two-deep, as trickles of blood linked to form a single stream flowing through drainage ports at the base of the ship's rail. It dripped over the side into the dark waters below. Thrashing sound at the water's surface indicated sharks gathered, hoping for a nighttime meal.

Anne moved about the deck in shock. "It's clear that if the element of surprise had not been our ally, we may have been slaughtered." Wandering in amazement, she finally noticed a man whose military garb was better adorned than the others. "You there, step forward."

He didn't move until encouraged to do so at the point of a sailor's pike and came to stand before her.

"Is this a Dutch trading vessel? If so, why would it be manned with so many uniformed fighting men?"

"I swear no allegiance to the English Crown. I will not answer your questions," he replied in perfect English—turning his head to the side, nose bent slightly upward. He quickly added, "It is not wartime and your letter of marque is an abomination of maritime laws and ethics. I see no reason to say a thing." He showed disrespect by turning his head away.

Anne remained calm. "Aye. 'Tis true. You have no obligation to say a thing." She pulled a pistol from her belt, placing the muzzle against his forehead. "Do you see that fat man lying there with his brains sprayed about? He also saw the need to say nothing."

Without moving his head, the man's eyes tilted to connect with the lifeless, bleeding body sprawled in the doorway. He swallowed hard. "You mean Mister Vander Horst?"

Anne Flinched and pressed the muzzle harder against the man's head. "Vander Horst? That is Artur Vander Horst? Why would he be aboard?"

The man's bravery slipped. He sweated profusely and swallowed hard. He closed his eyes as if prepared for the shot to end his life. Still, he refused to speak.

A sharp cutlass at his throat joined the pistol muzzle. "How about I let you bleed a while before I cause your brains to exit the rear of your skull," she growled.

He broke and babbled, "Yes, that is Artur Vander Horst, owner of this vessel."

"Why is this vessel so well armed?" She pulled the cutlass tight into his throat.

"Mister Vander Horst received a warning that an intercept was planned. He felt responsible to see that payment for cargo reached its destination as contracted."

"From what source did his information come?"

"I can't say."

"Oh, yes you can," she hissed into his face, pressing the blade until droplets of blood tracked down his sweaty neck.

"A small older man with a French accent," he blurted, "That's all I can truthfully say."

Thunderstruck, Anne backed away. She muttered to the burly sailor at her side, "Search out gold or other treasures then waste no time in gathering our crew and returning to the Providence. She began walking away. "Little Feather, come with me."

Dropping down the side of the Dutch vessel, she swung back across to the deck of their ship. She hastily entered the small area that served as an open galley on deck and saw the cook stoking a tiny firebox.

He abruptly stopped at the sight of her and stood bolt upright. "Monsieur Andrew. It appears you have been successful. Is that so?" He couldn't conceal astonishment and tried to smile.

Without expression or even slowing her step she walked up to the little man, drew a knife from her belt, and slashed his throat. His eyes widened. The shock of its suddenness locked his knees back, keeping him upright momentarily, long enough for blood to gurgle and hiss from the gash in his neck. He grabbed his throat and collapsed. With his final strength he curled into a fetal ball and twitched twice. The death rattle came quickly.

"Little Feather. Help me drag his worthless carcass to a central point on deck."

As the men returned to a well-lighted deck, those lucky enough to remain uninjured laughed and congratulated one another on their success. But as each saw the bleeding corpse, they fell silent and gathered around.

Anne stood defiant. With calculating coldness, she crossed her arms and spread her legs, planting her feet firmly upon the deck. She announced, "For those of you who may be unaware, I am quick with the rewards of what we do, but let it be known I am equally bloody quick to punish transgressors amongst you!" She kicked the lifeless cook. "For those of you who believe your personal desires are more important than our crew as a whole, be a man and speak up!"

No one did.

"Come on! Step forward. Who among you thinks your better than the rest of us?"

Every head hung humbly.

"Let it be known, from this point forward, if any of you desires to take more than you've earned or choose to trade our lives for your own gain then you'll join your brethren the cook in offering your vulgar hides to the sharks. Have I made myself clear? Is this understood?"

All remained motionless, quiet. No man moved—not one.

# Chapter Eighteen

"Do you remember the name Bufford Moone?" William asked.

Anne stiffened going cold at the mere mention. "How can I forget? It conjures the same sensation as that boil on my rump when I was ten. The pompous lawman gave me nothing but grief as a teenager." She began walking away. "Yes, I remember the name Bufford Moone well but would like to forget it."

"Then you should not be surprised to learn that it was Bufford Moone who wrote the warrant still on the books for your arrest."

Anne stopped her retreat just as the elderly black butler opened the door to the study a crack. "Pardon me, suh," the old man said, "But do you wish a fresh bottle of brandy?"

"We have enough. Thank you. That'll be all."

Anne and William said nothing while the servant was in the room.

The old man had a bland look that never seemed to change. He nodded then withdrew closing the door on his way out. Protecting her identity continued even within Cormac Manor making it necessary to keep their conversations away from potentially curious ears. Anne allowed ample time for the servant to move down the hall, hearing footfalls fade on the wooden floor.

She tilted her head and cracked the vertebrae in her neck then focused on her father. "The fact that Moone wrote the warrant comes as no surprise. It makes sense. He was Chief Constable at the time. But it's the direction and tone of your words that concern me. Why are you mentionin' that arrogant, flatulent swine?"

"Moone is back."

"Back? Explain."

"I mean he has returned to Charleston." He paced across the room. "I heard he'd moved north up the coast looking for land but came to believe he was not a man meant for forging a life in the wilderness." As he spoke, William absently fingered intricate carving centered on the mantle above the fireplace. "The word around town is that he's been offered and accepted his old position as constable. I'm certain he'll be on my doorstep soon, maybe this very day, asking questions about you." He turned to his daughter. "Before you fled Charleston, you had become an obsessive target of his. It galled him when he couldn't locate you, outsmarted by a teenage girl didn't set well with him." William sipped his brandy and grinned.

"This complicates things. Even this disguise," she said, gesturing to her appearance, "cannot protect me from someone so capable of recognizing my face." She wore a lace trimmed flowing burgundy dress, neck and ears adorned with rubies. Her hair meticulously crafted into the style of the day, red ringlets draping her face.

"Yes. We must assume he remembers your face and act accordingly."

Little Feather, who'd been standing away and listening, finally spoke. "When you wear the clothes of Amber Flanagan, your thoughts and speech are that of hers but the answer to your problem does not lie in such trickery." She moved from a distant corner of the room to Anne's side.

"What is your point, love?"

"Allow Anne Bonny to replace Amber for a moment. If the problem is Mister Moone then remove the problem."

Anne nodded, slowly at first. She began to smile. "A wise friend you are." She slipped back into a persona she wore as comfortably as an old shirt. "I fall too deeply into my role at times. We need a plan that comes to that end."

~ * ~

Responding to a commotion at the front door, Little Feather hurried to a partially hidden vantage point near the staircase but out of sight. She stood back in a shadow, watching.

"Please, Mister Moone, come quickly into the house," William said, as cold wind-blown snowflakes swirled in behind the big Scotsman when he stepped over the threshold. William forced the door shut against the hard north wind. "Ah, that's better."

"Thanky, sir. Ye are a true gentleman." The burly law enforcement officer slapped snow from a crudely stitched fur hat upon his thigh.

"Let's get you to a warmer place." William gestured him to the study and to the liquor bottle.

Little Feather approached the two men while still in the hall. She played her role. "May I pour you and your guest a drink, Mister Cormac?"

"That'd be nice. I'm sure Mister Moone will appreciate the warmth on his innards."

As she poured and served drinks, Little Feather studied details of the man picking up clues that might help them rid this obstacle. She then left the room and raced quietly up the stairs to Anne's room.

She rounded the doorjamb to find Anne studying maps. Anne wore a conservative gray dress with modest white trim, yet retained a dash of elegance. Her hair was perfect and nails meticulously manicured using a cutlass as a pointer on maps splayed across a tabletop. The sight was a visual contradiction.

She looked to Little Feather. "Come here. Let me show you somethin' of true beauty." She tapped the map with the dull edge of the broad blade. "See here? We'll sail around the southern tip of the Florida peninsula into the Gulf of Mexico. From there, just a couple of days sailin', with good winds mind ya, and we'll be in New Orleans." She dropped the cutlass with a twang onto the table and twirled as if dancing a waltz. "You and I will reach our goal with enough wealth to make our dreams come true." She held Little Feather's hands and danced the girl in a circle.

Suddenly hesitant to offer bad news while Anne seemed so happy, Little Feather pulled away and stepped back. "Your happiness excites me," she said, "I don't want to spoil this rare moment."

"Aye, 'tis a joy indeed to be plannin' escape and lookin' forward to true freedom to live our lives where I am unknown for my deeds. Deeds that are sometimes outright wicked," she said then laughed.

Little Feather had come to believe that a lifetime of circumstances had given Anne justification for those deeds. By her Iroquois way of thinking, it did not upset the natural order. The girl, even from her earliest days within the tribe, had been taught the sanctity of human life and the connection to all living things upon the earth. A life taken should be done so as a last resort of self-preservation. This maintained the delicate balance of Mother Earth. She didn't see Anne's way of life interfering with that.

Little Feather mused over the concept of amassing wealth in all its various forms. It seemed odd for a person as young as Anne to gather sustenance enough now to last beyond the prime arc of life. It went beyond necessity. On this point she had reservations. But this courageous young woman before her, whom she idolized for saving her from a life of slavery, taught her ways that revolved around adventure and treasures. She loved the life because the one she loved seemed incapable of living any other way.

"We must live life as it comes, right?" Anne asked.

Little Feather nodded.

"What brings you to my bedroom?"

The girl remained silent for a time.

With a smile, "Well...stop staring and start talking. What's on your mind?" She snatched the cutlass up and rested it upon her shoulder.

"The day has come you may not be able to avoid Mister Moone any longer. He is downstairs talking to your father."

Anne's smiled dropped. "I must sneak down and look at him so I will readily recognize him when that day arrives," Anne said.

"I'll go first and guide you so you might remain unseen." The girl's strong intuitive streak fluttered her stomach. It always did when life-threatening situations approached.

She left the bedroom and sneaked down the stairs. She stopped and listened frequently, as a hunter stalking a deer. She glanced at Anne, holding a hand up to keep her at a safe distance. All the while, she massaged her belly where that tingling flutter grew.

~ * ~

"The winter has been long and bitter. Spring flowers cannot bloom soon enough for me," Moone told William.

Eyes cutting frequently to the door, William warily watched in case Anne should burst in unaware. "That's something we surely agree on." He waggled a finger abruptly when an idea struck. "I think it's time for something to chase away winter doldrums, a party perhaps to usher in spring."

"A wonderful idea!" Moone grinned and gulped his drink. But then his mood took a turn. He wiped his lips with the back of his hand and set the empty glass on a table. "Mister Cormac, as you may already know, your daughter escaped from prison in Jamaica. Some say she was seen a few months back in Norfolk in the company of a Doctor Radcliffe. Are you aware of this?"

Taking a defensive posture, "I've heard rumors. What is your point, Mister Moone?"

"Sir, I intend no offense to you personally. I assumed since attempted parricide is one of the crimes she is wanted for, you'd gladly offer information should she happen to be discovered alive and in the vicinity."

"Then you are a wise man. I respect the law and will indeed share such information." William turned to gaze through the window into the dreariness of yet another snowstorm to conceal any expression Moone might pick up on. "Should I ever happen across such information, mind you."

"Yes, yes...I'm sure you would, Mister Cormac." He clapped and rubbed warmth into his palms, cupped them together, and blew warm breath into its well. He then smiled. "I have seen the young Indian girl on many occasions since returning to Charleston," Moone said. "But even after all these weeks, I have yet to enjoy the privilege of meeting the young lady she attends, your house guest Miss Flanagan."

"That might be arranged another time." He faced Moone. "Unfortunately, she woke this morning feeling ill. At last check, she was still in bed. It must be the weather. But soon, I promise."

~ * ~

Now close enough to hear the conversation, Anne tightened her grip on the cutlass she held at her side. She took three quick steps on the tips of her toes down the stairs then stopped, waiting for Little Feather's signal then two more. Having lived in Cormac manor for some time now, Anne had come to know the stair treads that squeaked. Each step down was made softly with even pressure of the foot.

The sound of conversation became clearer as she descended. Reaching the bottom of the stairs, she looked away from the front door and down the hall toward the rear entrance to the study. There Little Feather stood waving her over. High on the tips of her toes, Anne glided fluidly to her side.

Back flat against the wall, Anne craned her head around the open door and peeked in. For a time she watched her father and the constable converse. The man was a sturdily built Scotsman with curly hair almost orange like the color of autumn oak foliage and ample freckles across his fair complexion, some large enough to disappear in one side of a wrinkle in his brow then reappear on the opposite side of the same wrinkle. But the little boy appearance sharply contrasted his girth. He had large square fists and green eyes set firmly beneath an angry brow. She instantly realized the man would be a formidable obstacle if a confrontation developed—a conflict she believed inevitable.

Moone broke wind in a loud vulgar way. Her father remained the gentleman and made no comment. He simply receded two steps to escape the foul odor.

She let the back of her head lean against the wall and looked toward the ceiling. *What a disgusting pig.* Wanting to better inspect him, she slid laterally half a step more, until both eyes could take in the unfolding scenario. She failed to notice the small needlepoint artwork at shoulder level on the wall behind her. She brushed against it. It crashed to the floor.

William's head snapped around. His eyes locked onto Anne.

Anne returned a look, but hers was a gnash of teeth and steely resolve to do whatever necessary—no fear. Her grip tightened further on the cutlass she held out of view at her back.

After an awkward silence, Moone laughed. "You startled us, lass."

Anne snatched a handkerchief from the belt of her dress with a free hand and held it over her mouth and nose. She came all the way in to the study, head bowed in mock shyness. "I apologize for my clumsiness. Little Feather announced your presence. I only wished to meet you."

"Yes, yes," William said, attempting to hide shock. "Mister Bufford Moone was recently reappointed constable of Charleston." William looked to Moone but gestured toward Anne. "I'd like you to meet the daughter of a dear old friend and business partner of mine from Ireland. This is Miss Amber Flanagan."

Boldly approaching, Moone smiled broadly. She actually felt the floor bounce with each of his steps. Yellowed teeth flashed in that smile. "Miss Flanagan—"

Please, Mister Moone, not too close," she said then turned her face totally away for a second. She waved him away with the handkerchief, hoping to halt his approach. She quickly pulled the handkerchief back to her face and held it tight over her mouth and nose. "I may have an illness that can be passed on." The blade she held at her back became one with her hand. *Why don't I just kill this sorry bastard now?*

Obviously fearing she could be right and pass along a sickness, he stopped abruptly. "As you wish," he said. "But it's good to finally meet you. Maybe the next time will be under better and happier circumstances. I dare say if you look this good ill, I'm sure I'd be awed by you in healthier times."

Stepping between them, William said, "I shall follow through on my idea and plan an affair. Then I'll invite you back into my house under more festive circumstances." With a hand upon the big man's shoulder, he pushed Moone to turn and led him into the hall. He politely gestured the Scotsman toward the front door.

Moone snatched his fur cap from the back of a chair, "Then I'll take my leave. Thanky, Mister Cormac, for the brandy and warmth of your fire." Then over his shoulder, "I accept your invitation. I want that known now."

William ushered him through the door into the windy and frigid swirling snow.

Closing the door behind Moone, William's fake smile disappeared. He turned and leaned heavily against it. He took a breath and exhaled pent up fear. He looked to Anne. "You certainly have a way of knocking the breath from my lungs without laying a hand on me," he snapped.

With calm sarcasm, "I believe, dear father, you should be worrying more about carelessly arranging to have me in the same room with the constable for an entire evening."

"I'm not the mindless dolt you believe me to be." He walked briskly to a door beneath the staircase. "You continue to underestimate your father." From a closet, he retrieved a glitter-encrusted mask from a top shelf—shiny black feathers swept out and back from the ends of it. "Your cunning did not spring from thin air. After all, you are your father's daughter."

His manner softened. He placed the mask on Anne's face and pinned it to her hair. "We shall have a masquerade party."

# Chapter Nineteen

Death of the elder Vander Horst by Anne's own hand set off a gnawing sense of accountability to Peter, his son. Anne's affection for him grew, complicating things—clear thinking hampered by contradictions.

She wondered if failure to rid her mind of culpability was love. Little Feather, Jack Rackham, Mary Read, Michael Radcliffe, James Bonny—all had been loves, in a way. But this was different—an emotional potpourri she couldn't sort.

The relationship with her father was easily explained, therefore, easily dismissed. It was mutual need. His selfish desire happened to coincide with her goal. As she pondered those other so-called loves, she came to realize they all had been tinged by personal goals. *What the hell is love?*

Such thoughts plagued her but she couldn't discuss them with Little Feather. That relationship floundered because of Peter. Her feelings toward the young Indian girl were no less complicated. Infatuation with Peter cut deeply into her young Indian friend; Anne saw it in every glance, in every turn of the young girl's head.

Answers remained elusive, just beyond grasp. Intuition told her a pat answer lay somewhere within reach waiting to be discovered but her groping mind couldn't quite pull them out.

A recurring dream showed another side. It played out in fine detail over and over. It seemed so clear—so real. She visualized Peter, a house, children, pets, and genuine happiness only to awaken to reality. Even to hope it was absurd. Each day began by authenticating things as they were, smashing dreams into millions of dusty web-infested pieces then swept away in the light of day.

Anne sank into depression.

This day, before she woke, the fantasy again showed her the contented scenario. She saw Peter. He smiled. Beauty turned ugly as his face metamorphosed into his father's. Her own words, "Hey! You fat son of Satan!" reverberated in her mind as she pulled that trigger yet again. It was the face of Peter shattering from the gunshot.

She sprang upright in bed. Cool clamminess sucked her nightshirt into her breasts. It was saturated. She pulled it away from her skin. The dampness on her face was not perspiration but tears. *Why do I dwell on this so?*

~ * ~

Evening came and the planned party at Cormac Manor was underway.

William called to her, "Miss Flanagan?"

Anne looked about for the source of the question.

The mention of that assumed name from some distance shook her from troubling thoughts. She caught sight of her father. "Are you speaking to me, Mister Cormac?"

"I was saying it's a shame young Peter cannot join us this evening," he said, obviously annoyed at having to repeat the comment. He came to stand in front of her and straightened the mask upon her face.

"Yes, a shame." She sighed and straightened her back into a more formal stance, reassuming the alias. She smiled but it was forced, just a function of the Amber Flanagan alias. "But understandable, considering the loss of his father. That has thrown him into a quandary. He struggles between grief and holding the Vander Horst shipping business together."

She looked away from her father unable to care about exploits or booty yet desiring that her mind be somewhere other than on Peter and his murdered father. She grew weary of obsessive thoughts she couldn't shake. Looking out across the dining hall of Cormac Manor, temporarily transformed into a ballroom, two violins harmonized a waltz from a prominent position at the end of the room.

A wide array of masks ranged from simple black cloth with eye holes cut to elaborate full face masks covered with feathers, glitter and encrusted jewels. Dancing ladies in festive finery appeared as a kaleidoscope of brilliant spinning and flowing colors, moving in unison to the music. All others lined the walls talking or watching the musicians.

Two men, having had too much hard cider, took William aside and monopolized his time with talk of commodity prices and other boring subjects. They bellowed and guffawed boisterously making it impossible to carry on a conversation in close proximity.

Purposely putting distance between them and her, Anne found herself alone.

Little Feather approached with a tray of drinks. "I overheard Mister Moone asking your whereabouts," she whispered into Anne's ear.

Trading a full drink for her empty glass, she said, "Thanks, sweet friend. The moment draws nigh I must take a stand against him." She touched her leg for the reassuring feel of the cutlass scabbard bound to her thigh.

A young man Anne recognized as an employee of the Charleston cotton brokerage house approached. "Miss Flanagan, may I have this waltz?" He bowed.

Setting her drink on a sideboard, she stepped onto the dance floor. "It would be my pleasure," she said, pretending shyness as she offered her hand.

As they twirled across the floor, the soothing strings seemed to touch everyone except Anne. She used the dance as an opportunity to search the room for a large man, fair of face, freckled and topped with curly persimmon colored hair. It was only necessary to waltz around the floor once to pick him out.

He noticed her too.

The music ended and the young man gracefully circled to a stop in time with it.

But Anne took the lead and twirled the young man around one last time. It startled him and threw him off balance but served its purpose. Her back was now presented to Moone. She laughed in a giddy, girlish way, justifying the move.

The young man was so enamored he asked for another dance.

Anne checked the security of her facial covering, fingering the ornate black feathers of the mask that swept back at the sides of her head completing the disguise. She could afford no slip-ups on a crowded floor.

Before she could accept the young man's dance proposal, Moone approached and asked, "Do you mind too much, son, if I have the next dance with the lovely Miss Flanagan?"

"Not at all," he replied and bowed to her. Before yielding, the well-dressed young man kissed Anne's hand and bowed again to Moone.

She smiled innocently at the polite young man. *Damn you for allowing this, you ignorant whelp.* Her smile broadened, acknowledging the transfer with a nearly imperceptible nod.

Roughly, he swung her around in loose time with the music, "I believe under that mask you are, indeed, a lovely young lass," he said.

Anne picked out everything vile about this man—breath that smelled of decaying animal carcasses and not one redeeming physical characteristic. Worst of all, he exuded a manipulative arrogance common to men of authority, enough to cement her resolve. *So help me, if you release gas from that bulging ass of yours, I'll slice your jewels off right here on the dance floor then stomp on them.* She appreciated the mask he wore. It helped her look upon his face without nausea.

"Miss Flanagan, might I offer you a drink in a quieter place, so we might become...better acquainted?" The lusty glint on those bright green eyes was unmistakable.

That wisp of smile below her mask broadened. Things seem to be channeling to her advantage. "Why yes, Mister Moone. That'd be lovely."

The waltz took them from one side of the large room to the other as Bufford Moone directed the course of the dance toward Little Feather, who stood holding a tray of drinks. The music played on but he stopped and picked up two glasses from the young girl's tray. He gave one to Anne.

She winked and nodded at Little Feather.

He guided her by the other hand out of the ballroom down the hall through an open door—away from the crowd. Moone closed the door behind them and turned to her. The glint transformed to naked lust.

"Just how well do you expect to know me by the time this night is over," she said, fingering the rim of her glass. She glanced to another door at her side that led into the back hall to the kitchen.

"It would be a grand thing if we might come to some agreeable arrangement." He gave her a condescending wink then raised a single, self-assured eyebrow.

"No doubt, agreeable only to you." She breathed the words into her upturned glass before taking a sip.

"Excuse me?"

A broad grin stretched her mouth. "It was nothing," she cooed. "If I am expected to yield to your desires then I must insist we move to another room. Down a short hall from the main ballroom just isn't enough privacy."

"Yes, yes," he blurted. His hand shook as he set his glass on a tabletop. He followed Anne through the alternate entry, down the hall, and through the kitchen. She led him past the heavy black iron cook stove out onto the covered porch next to a neatly stacked rick of firewood.

In shimmering moonlight, Anne saw the sparkle in his eyes, not to mention the reflective glimmer of a disgusting droplet of drool forming at the corner of his mouth. The muffled sound of violins and laughter wafted from the opposite side of the large house.

"Your face, I want to see your face," he said, reaching for her mask.

Tilting her head away from his grasp, she avoided his hand. "Oh, but there is something else you must see before my face." She bent at the waist and grabbed the bottom of her gown with both hands.

Expecting a show, he stepped back clearly dumbfounded by his good fortune.

As she slowly lifted the hem, "I want you to see just what I think of you, your questions, your bloody warrants and, aye, the intolerable nasal slime that you truly are," she said, her voice progressively slipping from character into an unearthly low range that was unmistakably Anne Bonny.

His eyes grew large. "By all that's holy, what manner of demon are you?"

"The type that will have your life." She flipped up the dress and withdrew the cutlass from the scabbard lashed to her leg.

"I don't understand. What is it that I have done to anger you so?"

"Nay, it's not what you have done, sir. It is what I shall prevent you from doing."

"It was all to be in fun. You could have declined. I would have been disappointed, but I would have withdrawn. I don't understand."

"You're right, you don't." With calculated evenness, she peeled off the mask.

Without expression, he studied the lines of her face in the dim light of the half moon then with explosive recognition, "You!"

"Have I changed so much in two years?" she asked.

His nostrils flared in anger over having been deceived. "That bastard father of yours lied to me! The harlot and thief Anne Bonny lives and stands before me!" he thundered.

"Well, the conversation didn't have to degrade to such vile language," she said calmly.

Angered beyond good sense, he threw out his hands to strangle her.

Before he could even touch her the cutlass was only a blur as it whooshed across his throat.

The angry look vanished. His lips tried to form words but no sound came, only a rush of bloody bubbles from the gash. He collapsed in a quivering heap. Blood flowed from the open wound in his neck and dripped through the cracks in the planks of the porch floor. He clutched his throat again and again until his fingers went limp.

Standing over him, Anne suddenly experienced a strange rush, a sensation she'd never known. She looked down upon the still-twitching body, detached, as if she witnessed the act of another person and was sickened by such vulgar savagery.

Sinking to a knee, she ran her fingers over his warm face and watched life leave his eyes. The twinge of sadness she felt for him was foreign. *Was he not deserving of the blade? What's happening to me?*

Out of the shadows stepped Little Feather. "I sense your regret."

"Regret?" She mimicked the word as if not understanding it. She pondered significance of the word then attempted to speak but had no more success in doing so than Moone did in his final seconds.

Little Feather took the lead. "We must conceal him and wash the porch until we can bury his body."

"Yes…of course," Anne said blandly, still stroking the cooling skin of Moone's face. His eyes stared but saw nothing.

Suddenly, amassing treasure, life in New Orleans, children, and a permanent home seemed unimportant. From somewhere deep inside, remorse reached the surface and kindled a concept of humanity she never before contemplated.

She massaged a sharp pain in her chest. Even as she hunkered over the corpse confused, the heart already knew what the mind couldn't grasp. The murder of Bufford Moone was by the hand of Anne Bonny, the remorse was Amber Flanagan's. Her personality had divided.

# Chapter Twenty

Troubled, Anne walked the streets of Charleston under the guise of the Irish lady of means, Amber Flanagan, going about the daily diligence of business left purposely ambiguous; forays meant only to spend liberally and make a show of it. If from old money acting the part was integral to success of the plan. Flamboyance was honey to the dealmakers buzzing about.

The charade wasn't as enjoyable as usual. Her heart was heavy.

Thinking and feeling as Amber Flanagan became less a ruse and more genuine daily, often overriding reality. During these episodes, the name Anne Bonny was familiar but nothing more as if Anne were someone she may have run into on the street, an acquaintance perhaps. Or maybe a black sheep cousin she tried to forget. Amber began thinking badly of Anne for the death of Artur Vander Horst.

Today, as in all recent days, she passed the boarding house that Peter Vander Horst called home temporarily while soliciting business for Vander Horst Shipping Company. She hoped to catch his eye—no luck. Her world began revolving around seeing Peter again, all the while becoming culturally confused and muddled, racing headlong toward despondency.

She stopped and walked back to the low gate of the white picket fence fronting the two-story boarding house. As she stood there with her hand on the gate, her head spun with wants, needs, obligations, relationships, and a myriad of things; but no two snippets matched up. A psychosis of confused identities coming from opposite extremes of the same mind threatened sanity.

A neat evenly spaced row of windows lined the lower floor, three on each side of the door. Seven windows lined the top floor. It was a plain structure, void of outstanding features.

Her aching heart washed her mind of common sense. She walked through the gate to the front door before it occurred to her how improper it must appear for a lady to do such a thing. But that was a thought Amber Flanagan would have, not Anne Bonny. "Etiquette be damned," she hissed and rang the small bell suspended from the door.

"Coming," a voice called out from inside. The opening door revealed an elderly woman, strands of hair pulled free from a bun and falling across deeply lined temples. She wiped her red chapped hands on the apron tied around her waist. The hardened look indicated an independent woman who'd stood on her own two legs in life making her way without help from anyone.

Anne looked upon her with admiration.

"May I help you, young lady?" she asked, sharp, no-nonsense.

"Yes, I have business with Mr. Vander Horst. Amber Flanagan calling."

"I'll see if he'll come to the door." She partially turned then whipped back. "But I wouldn't hold your breath."

"Why?"

"Don't know. For three days he's come out only once a day at dinnertime. He spends evenings alone in his room." Shielding her mouth the old lady whispered, "I don't think young Peter has taken the death of his father well at all. He's turned to the drink."

Not waiting for an invitation, "Do you mind if I try to talk to him? Maybe I can help," Anne said, sliding past the old lady.

"That certainly seems to be your plan." The old lady was incensed by Anne's uninvited entrance and glared at her as she marched by. "Oh well," she added pointing to Peter's door, "you'll probably do better than I've done." She left Anne alone to face the closed door.

After a moment's hesitation, she tapped quickly on it before second thoughts spoiled sudden courage.

"If you carry a bottle of strong liquor then come in. If not, go away," was the slurred response.

"I have none and I'll not be going away until we talk."

"Amber? Is that you?"

"Yes Peter. Open the door."

Anne again raised a fist considering a more aggressive knock.

Suddenly, the door flung open whamming into the wall. "Then get in here," he demanded, already turning to walk away. He unsteadily turned and dropped into a chair. His arms hung draped over its armrests, legs splayed wide. Puffy blood red eyes and loose behavior indicated the old woman had told the truth—too much alcohol and not enough sleep. His head lolled to the side.

"I'm swallowing pride by coming to your private quarters. It's certainly not something a lady should do."

"Then by all means, milady, return to the street and I'll not whisper a word that you were ever here." With a sarcastic liquor-soaked grin, he gestured toward the door. He then placed a limp finger to his lips. "Shh...it shall be our sordid little secret."

Her hands rolled into fists at the end of stiffened arms. "You damned bloody fool!" Amber Flanagan vanished and Anne Bonny sprung to life.

A look of sobriety crossed Peter's face. He sat straight. "Pardon me?"

Her look softened. "What I mean to say is, don't you think it's about time to get on with your life. You surely—"

"You know nothing of my life!" He fell back against the chair, again going limp. "Furthermore, you have absolutely no right to tell me when it's time to get on with it!"

"Please, Peter. Let me—"

He slapped his thighs and jumped to his feet then stumbled sideways just as fast. "I'm dreaming of the day I can confront my father's murderer. I'm spending huge sums of money having his killer tracked down. I'll not rest until I have my vengeance," he growled, slobbering. "The heathen will know my wrath!" he barked then dropped back into the chair.

Silence was the only thing Peter seemed willing to listen to. She couldn't find the right combination of words to change that. Playing the role of a soft talking concerned friend was not easy. In the past, she slapped sense into thick drunken heads—effective and much faster. That urge strengthened. *No—no, I must handle it as Amber would.*

Unsuccessful at diverting Peter's desire for vengeance or even generating a desire to sober up, she left him partially conscious and drooling.

The half hour walk back to Cormac Manor was tedious. Even the first few flowers of spring couldn't lighten her mood. Focusing elsewhere was hopeless because it'd come full-circle back to Peter every time. Peter Vander Horst had become the flashpoint for an all-out final battle of good and evil that played only in her troubled mind. Anne knew she held the key to its outcome but had no idea what that key might unlock. Fear of that unknown drove her deeper into depression.

She walked past Little Feather trudging to her bedroom. She sat on the bed. "There are things I must do and cannot keep my mind to the task. I've lost myself. The simplest decisions are beyond reach. All I can see is the dark side of everything." Chin against chest, her head dangled upon her shoulders. "I have been this far down and this confused only one other time." Her voice shot into a higher range. "It's impossible to do battle with my own mind! There's no powder charge strong enough or cutlass sharp enough to defeat hovering demons as this. I'm terrified of an enemy I cannot know or see."

Sitting close, "Your heart is torn," the young girl said, lifting Anne's hand and cupping it between hers. "I am part of that indecision. Plus, the red moon that only a woman knows confuses you more. Until your mind and heart converge and travel upon the same road again, your spirit guide will stand away."

"My spirit guide? I don't understand."

"It is time we go far away from here and practice the ancient rite of the vision quest. I can help you reach into the spirit world to find and retrieve your lost guide."

"You are a good friend, love." She kissed the girl on the cheek lingering over the warm flesh against her lips. Pulling back, she stared into Little Feather's eyes realizing how little attention she'd given her best friend lately. "Let's get on with it. I'm ready to leave this place for awhile." She rose and stepped away then hesitated and looked back. *Can you really help me find myself and what my purpose is upon this earth?*

She smiled warmly at the girl and left the room to prepare.

~ * ~

Ox hides overlaid a pliable willow limb framework that formed a small hut. Smoke curled from the single opening in its top. The Iroquois girl prepared things unknown to an Irish girl. Fascination with the ritual though was jaded, having grown cold to the world around her—no desire to question. Anne's inattentive eyes just watched.

They stopped at a site two days west of Charleston along the banks of a small gurgling creek that rushed over and around colorful smooth stones. It lay at the base of a rocky outcropping in a shady grove of butternut trees. The location was of no importance as long as it was far away from people. Anne's true identity had to remain hidden. Her ability to care had sunk to a new low.

Sitting upon a boulder with knees drawn to her chest, she observed the girl's efforts yet unable to appreciate work done on her behalf.

Squirrels chattered and chased one another. Birds flit about and sang. Temperature and humidity blended perfectly. It should have been inspirational but did nothing for her. Her eyes absently followed Little Feather's preparatory tasks. *I have been set adrift yet again. My mind goes where it will. I have no control. How many times must I endure this?* "I beseech all saints, please show me a signpost," she muttered, pounding a knee with a tight fist.

"It is time," Little Feather called to her.

Listless, she slid from her perch then walked to the hut and stood before Little Feather.

The girl untied the laces holding Anne's shirt together and slipped it off her shoulders. She then unfastened the laces of her breeches, letting them fall, naked as the day she was born and just as vulnerable. Little Feather guided her into the super heated hut and pressed her shoulders, encouraging her to sit upon a soft beaver pelt spread upon the ground. She trickled water on the fire. It sizzled and danced atop red coals. Steam billowed then hovered in the confines of this draft-free enclosure of willow limbs and ox hides.

"You must sing the song of the ancients." Little Feather intoned the rhythm.

Anne picked up on it and followed its rhythm with the sound of her own voice. Her head drifted loose upon her shoulders.

"Your voice will bring the spirits but it will take time. You must not stop because your chant guides them in."

Methodically, Little Feather kept the fire hot and the interior steamy, tirelessly tending to her friend's spiritual needs.

After three hours of chanting, Anne ceased to even notice the girl coming and going.

In the glow of the fire, glistening sweat slickened her body, streaming from the top of her head to her buttocks. Perspiration pooled beneath it. Troubling thoughts faded. She glimpsed formless things in her mind's eye. She tried to discern what her mind conjured.

Another hour passed. She chanted on.

After a time, she couldn't guess how long, it occurred to her she couldn't breathe. The air had been forced from her lungs. Real or not, she gasped for air.

Fear of suffocation popped her eyes open but she didn't see the fire, the hut or anything that had been in front of her moments ago. Instead, she saw the open sea from a vantage point high above it. She had been thrust into a vision; so clear and colorful she thought it might be real. She then realized she was still perspiration soaked and naked watching herself.

She saw herself standing on the starboard yardarm, overlooking the deck of the Providence unconcerned about height or balance.

She swooped in to replace the clothed version of herself and now stood naked high above the ship's deck, having become one with the vision.

The crew scurried about on deck below and seemed to prepare for battle. They rolled out the culverins. She responded to a screech and looked up to see a falcon circling overhead. The crew below paid her no mind, nor the bird. A gull then swooped in—an ordinary seagull. Both birds circled overhead, one following the other. Each appeared to vie for a place upon the yardarm with her, unyielding to the other's threats.

She attempted prioritizing all that she witnessed. Of all the goings-on, it was the birds that held her attention. She didn't understand why that'd be more important than a battle about to begin. She even tried to ignore them in favor of what was about to happen to the Providence.

But the birds drew her eyes away from the action on the ship below.

*Why do they fascinate me so?* She wondered.

She succumbed and watched the aerial dance. Now curious, she wanted to know what these two birds were up to. She observed as though she had the power to alter the scenario if desired, but was compelled to allow the creatures of the sky to have their moment under her watchful eye. Was it to be a ritual of some sort? Combat maybe? Her alter ego studied the falcon with deference; the predator bird would take its rightful place at her side if that's what it wanted—an easy assumption to make even before the feathered battle began.

Smugness vanished in a heartbeat as the gull swooped down then straight up beneath the falcon, driving its beak through its adversary's heart.

Once again, Anne felt as though all the air had been knocked from her lungs. She couldn't breathe and no longer balancing well on the yardarm, certain she was about to fall. She clutched a free-swinging rope while fighting for breath.

It was totally illogical. The unexpected happened. How could that be and more importantly, why?

Stabbing pain in her heart was the same pain of penetration the falcon experienced. Feathers exploded from the impact, drifting in all directions. One settled between her naked legs upon the yardarm. It was a downy soft...tiny...seemingly insignificant...little feather.

"Little Feather! Oh my God! No!" Her voice echoed in the hollow of her head.

"I should have done something," she mumbled. "I should have known and done something...done something...done something."

The light of day slowly penetrated Anne's eyes as she repeated the regret over and over. Muscles of her brow tugged at her eyelids. They opened. Light flooded in. Something cast a shadow, blocking the brightness. Her vision cleared and she saw her young Iroquois friend looking down at her.

The girl knelt and cradled Anne's upper body. Weak and helpless, she could do nothing but let Little Feather hold her head. She glanced down to see her slickened nude body still covered in sweat as she lay on the ground outside the hut.

"It is over. You are back," Little Feather said.

Anne finally forced a swallow. In a raspy, overused voice, "I now understand and know what must be done to put things right."

# Chapter Twenty-one

From the top of the stairs at Cormac Manor, Anne looked down into the foyer. She watched Peter Vander Horst request a visit with her.

"I's has to see if Miss Amber is available, suh," the old black servant told him.

Peter nervously fingered the brim of a tall felt hat he held with both hands.

"It's all right," she called down, "let him in."

He looked above the old man's head to the dark hardwood rail at the top of the stairs and saw her. "Amber, I must speak with you." His head took an apologetic tilt. "But I wouldn't blame you if you turned me away."

She hesitated, uncertain how to handle this situation. She shook it off and quickened her step down the stairs maintaining an air of superiority. Although eager to be at his side, she could not bring herself to relent—not yet. She remained cool and businesslike ushering him into the privacy of a small parlor off the entry and closed the door behind them. Then pertly, "What is your business?" She picked a spot on the wall to his left and stared at it.

He seemed conciliatory and sought eye contact but didn't get it.

"My business, as you call it, is offering an apology for behavior most unbecoming a gentleman at our last meeting."

"An apology?"

"Yes. I want…no, I *must* apologize. My judgment was clouded by lack of sleep and too much liquor. I superimposed my hurt onto you and I'm truly sorry. Regret has multiplied many times over." And then, soft as a sigh, "I now realize that even the depth of my grief is no excuse for acting the overbearing brute."

Even accounting for renewed sense of purpose thanks to the vision quest, Anne couldn't readily set aside feelings. She had come to realize fully that a future with him was impossible, yet hope flickered. She couldn't help it. The manner in which he spoke put a twinkle in her eye. Against better judgment, she was inclined to accept the overture.

Making eye contact, her body relaxed. The defiant pose withered. She was drawn into the blue pools of his gaze. "I shall accept your apology but only if you escort me on a picnic in the country."

A smile disappeared into his dimples. "That's a simple pleasure I can guarantee. I've seen a beautiful place on a grassy hill overlooking the city. Tomorrow at midday I'll return with a carriage. We'll lay claim to it and call that spot our own for the day."

Putting his hat on, he merrily tapped the top of it, spun around, and bounded down the four steps of the front porch then briskly out to his one-horse buggy. As he placed a foot upon the step to board it, he hesitated long enough to drink in another look. "Until tomorrow, Love." He swung into the seat, swatted the horse's rump with the rein and off he went.

She watched and listened to the clop, clop, clop of horse hooves upon the flat stone pavers. The desire in his eyes was her desire too. But it went beyond physical attraction. The familiar vision of a home filled with laughter, love, and children weaseled in. She couldn't douse the dream, but she could now at least differentiate between a dream and reality. To believe otherwise would destroy her plan and a friendship she cherished more than life itself.

For now, she stood dreamily in the memory of his liquid blue eyes—a lusty fascination for sure.

As habit dictated, once she'd returned to her bedroom, she laid out her cutlass to be strapped to her thigh beneath her dress tomorrow. But something inside her whispered a warning—intuition that had saved her life on many occasions. It prompted her to forego the blade in favor of a pistol. She carefully concealed it inside a blanket roll she planned on putting in the picnic basket.

That vision of a sneaky gull fatally surprising the favored falcon suddenly burned bright. The falcon, she came to believe, represented Little Feather or maybe her relationship with the young Indian girl. The gull she had no idea about. It could be anything or anybody that should attempt tearing them apart. *That will bloody well never happen!*

~ * ~

Picnic day dawned perfect. A breeze stirred leaves upon trees under a cloudless sky. All the foliage and grasses wore the brightest hues of spring greens. Try as she might to remain aloof, Anne let anticipation build. She looked forward to this outing with Peter and was pleased with his punctuality.

The horse pulling his buggy trotted up to a point near the front door of Cormac Manor. He arrived to pick her up about midday as promised. As they sat comfortably close in the carriage, it rolled along at an easy pace to match the feel of the day. Anne watched the horse's tail swishing side to side as the animal plodded along, drawing them up a winding road. Less than a mile from Cormac manor, Peter turned the horse's head northward onto a seldom used trail.

About a hundred feet above the road, Peter pulled the reins. "Whoa, boy." He tied them to the whip stand. "What do you think, Amber? Good enough for a picnic on this lovely day?" He spread his arms wide, introducing the view.

Chills coursed her spine. Anne felt as though an omen had been handed to her. This was the exact location where she and Little Feather rested and looked out over Charleston when they first arrived. *Sweet Lord, it must be more than coincidence. Of all the places, why this one?* She turned and looked to the overview of Charleston in the distance. "It's...lovely, Peter," was all she could think to say.

Blanket spread, the spot offered a beautiful view. But Anne appreciated it less now than when she first stumbled upon it with Little Feather. She was sure his decision to picnic here had deeper meaning than happenstance would allow. It seemed as if a hand guided her on this day.

After a time, the clean clear spring air crisply outlining even distant images melted apprehension away. She sat with Peter's head in her lap, feeling a rare sense of warmth. Few words were shared. Conversation wasn't necessary.

A butterfly settled upon her fingers as she twirled strands of his hair between them. She admired it for a moment. It walked up a finger to the back of her hand. She slowly lifted it and gently blew it into the air. It fluttered away looking for a calmer place to light. Her sense of femininity had never been greater.

He sighed. "Perfect...absolutely perfect."

Her gaze shifted from his eyes to his mouth. In that instant, it occurred to her why she had not strapped the cutlass to her leg. She smiled but it wasn't for Peter's benefit. Now, no reason existed to restrain her desires. She was drawn to his mouth and sucked his lower lip between hers, the first step toward the inevitable union.

Afterwards, they satisfied hunger and the mood altering effect of the wine faded along with the sexually charged atmosphere.

Peter talked of his father and the business. His behavior took a dark turn, regressing to a place where words of revenge seemed to offer solace. He remained close to Anne yet no longer intimate. He aggressively flicked blades of grass—his face reddened, his nostrils flared. Anger ratcheted up. "There is one other time in my life I have vowed vengeance, and to this very day it is still unfulfilled."

"When was that?"

"It was when my father paid that scoundrel James Bonny for information leading to the capture of a thieving band of buccaneers intent on robbing our vessels. But that swill-slurping weasel committed the same crime for which he was paid handsomely to help avoid. This time my vow of revenge will have its day. I swear it!" He slammed a fist into his open palm.

"Do you love me?" She continued staring at the city below.

Shocked by the sudden question, Peter settled. "Of course I do."

"Then I must ask, what if you should discover something of my past that you considered wrong, terribly wrong by your standard? Is your love for me strong enough to overcome it?"

"There is nothing that could change my feelings for you. Why do you ask?"

Slipping her hand into the basket at her side, away from his view, she retrieved the pistol and slid it beneath the fan of her dress splayed upon the blanket. "Then it's time I risk sharing a secret. Where you stand on it is vital. I must know your reaction."

After an awkward silence, "Speak. Surely it can't be all that bad."

"Peter," she said, her eyes dragging up to meet his, "that man you've sworn vengeance against was, at one time, my husband."

"But that would make you..." He leaped to his feet, as shock of recognition hardened his features. "The scar on the forehead, the fine clothes, the clean face, the hair neatly made, all these things are what camouflaged your identity." His face was a mishmash of expressions from anger to confusion to bland then back again. "That is why you looked so familiar at our first meeting. You were at that wretch's side when my father paid him for the information."

Anne said no more. She waited for the information to have its way with Peter. She had to know when once his emotions settled, which one would be left. Anger? Forgiveness? She waited.

Uncertain how to take the revelation, he paced in choppy abbreviated steps back and forth. "I thought you had been hanged at St. Jago de la Vega, Jamaica. When I heard, it was most assuredly welcome news. I can tell you that."

"Peter, can my past be set aside and we start anew?"

"You are a wanted woman, a known pirate and murderer!"

Again she tried, "Peter, your love for me. Where does it stand? I am the same person I was a moment ago, unclothed and beneath your naked body. It's only the name that has changed. Tell me, where does your heart lie?"

"Love and devotion is one thing but casting my lot with a known criminal would be... well, hell, it would be selling my soul. You're not just another woman. You're the heathen murderess, Anne Bonny!" He rose to stand stiffly defiant. "That would be nothing short of dancing with the devil himself!"

She had her answer.

Without expression, tears welled and spilled from her eyes, streaming down her face. Her accent digressed. "Do you realize how privileged you are? Aye, you are witnessin' somethin' no other man has ever seen." Her voice broke into a squeak as she choked off a sob. She rolled over and fluidly rose to her feet presenting her back to him while she stared up the hill into the forest. Her eyes swept across the view as if she might see an alternative. But all she saw were swirls of tears blurring her vision. In those seconds of searching, she came to realize that if he couldn't accept her identity as Anne Bonny then her other alias of Andrew the Protector and murderer of his father would most assuredly doom her should it ever be revealed. Either way all was lost.

*I am such a fool for havin' believed otherwise.*

Clutching the pistol in both hands to her front, she cocked it.

"Privileged?" he snarled. "How can a swine like you tell me that I am privileged? You know nothing of the word. I see no advantage in having been duped by a criminal."

With shaky hand, her back still to him, Anne hurriedly wiped tears from her eyes with her free hand to sharpen her vision. "Aye, love, you are a privileged man for sure. You've seen me cry. No man has ever seen it before. That makes you honored by my reckonin'. The problem, as I be seein' it now, granted this honor and all, is that it sadly must end with you." She turned and raised the pistol. "No one can ever know that you were so privileged."

The bead on the barrel of the pistol covered the bridge of his nose.

It was the last view she had of Peter Vander Horst alive.

# Chapter Twenty-two

Daring the curves in Peter's one-horse buggy, she drove the animal to its limit. Now thinking clearly, Anne was again goal driven and quite narrowly so. The last obstacle lay dead on a hillside above Charleston. Her future would turn bleak should her deeds be discovered. Those standing near would go down with her. She was on a collision course with destiny.

The Irish lady of means, Amber Flanagan, from County Cork, Ireland died on that hillside with Peter Vander Horst. Discovery as a murderess was now reduced to a matter of time. Working faster than the flow of information in Charleston was the only way. Even in death, Peter and Bufford Moone would point at her from beyond the grave. She whipped the lathered horse for more speed to Cormac Manor House.

*The last grains of sand are clearin' the hourglass at this very moment.* The full dress and petticoats flagged just as the horse's tail did. Twice the slobbering beast almost stumbled. Still, she whipped its flanks to maintain the pace. *By God, I'll not be facin' the hangman's noose twice.* Anne Bonny was back.

Bursting through the door at Cormac Manor, she saw Little Feather. "Make haste. Get your things together. We must leave this plantation, Charleston, and all the Carolinas as soon as possible." She scarcely slowed before sprinting up the stairs.

She abruptly stopped halfway and whirled around. "Take the fastest horse we have and assemble Providence's crew. Once I've taken care of details here I'll ride up the coast and meet you at the ship."

Anne's sudden order came as no surprise to Little Feather. Like Anne, the girl knew this day would eventually come. Accepting the instructions with a simple nod, she began preparing.

The black butler appeared from behind a door down the hallway. Anne reversed and bounded back down the stairs. "Where is Mr. Cormac?"

Before he could answer, William appeared from behind an opening door. "What's all the commotion?" He stepped into the hall holding a book. His finger marked the page.

Racing to where he stood, she pushed him into the room he appeared from and slammed the door behind her. "I must put the Providence out to sea and not come back," she said, pulling pins from her hair shaking it loose. She was removing her dress as she asked, "The gold, Father, I must have my share. Where is it?"

"I've been meaning to talk to you about that. We've grown so comfortable with one another that I assumed you wished to maintain your alias and stay. I took most of the gold and purchased another piece of property to extend our real estate holdings and make a nice addition to the plantation so that we might share and operate it together. I assumed—"

"You assumed!" she exploded. Snatching up a china vase, she hurled it, purposely missing him by inches. "You bloody arrogant Irish scum," she growled then began stalking him.

Backing against the wall as Anne was losing control, he chattered, "I did it for you. Don't you understand? It was to have been a nice surprise for us to co-own and live peacefully *together*. Don't you see? It was not a selfish act. I promise. I wanted us to stay together as father and daughter, as a family."

Undeterred, she ground her teeth so tight the gnash of enamel squawked in her mouth. "I'll not be allowin' ya to dance your damn waltz around me. Save your tripe for the gullible." She grabbed his half-full brandy glass and hurled it at him hitting him squarely in the chest soaking him in liquor then smashing to the floor. "If my cutlass had been within reach, you'd already be dead!"

Moving laterally, without taking his eyes from her, he stepped over a small rug near the fireplace and fell to a knee. He yanked it aside revealing a hinged door covering a cutout in the floor about a foot-square. He pried it open and retrieved a small canvas bag. "Take what's left."

"I intend to!" She ripped the two remaining buttons off the burgundy velvet dress, stepped out of it and tossed it in his face. In the same motion, she snatched the bag from his outstretched hand. "You've always used words of a parent but the intentions were never born of love. I've always been just another mark, a bloody source of income!"

Whirling around she marched to the door but once her hand held the handle, she looked back and held an icy penetrating stare. Heaving a deep sigh, she reeled in rage and in a controlled voice, she said, "I shall not see you again in this lifetime. If heaven is to be your destination, I look forward to hell."

~ * ~

With one foot in sparse grass at the water's edge and the other perched on a moss-slickened stone at the base of the gangplank, Anne stood watch over provisions carried aboard the Providence. She still fumed over the final encounter with her only living relative, conflicted, wondering if she should've killed him too. William Cormac was the only person alive in Charleston who knew her true identity. *Would my own father turn me in for a few gold coins? Could he? Aye, I think he could. The man is Judas Iscariot reincarnated?* Her budding sense of humanity prevented her from taking his life, even if it meant her eventual demise.

Amber Flanagan was the last person to be seen with either Moone or Vander Horst. People would be putting that together soon. Leaving the Carolinas and the entire eastern seaboard forever was the only way. Law enforcement would be searching for an Irish socialite, not Anne Bonny or even Andrew the Protector, unless her cowardly father should give her up. But he'd implicate himself if he did. There was some comfort in that.

All angles considered it was time to go. It should be done while the choice was hers to make.

The final sack of salted meat made its way up the narrow plank on the back of one of her crew. She followed him up and called for the crew to assemble. Taking a head count, she saw that all twenty-eight men were present. She and Little Feather rounded that number to thirty. "Lads," she said, assuming her Andrew the Protector persona, "you must know that this voyage we are about to embark on will take us north, searching out vessels of trade so that we might lighten their load. But now I must give you the option not to go along. I have two reasons..."

The men whispered among themselves.

Even Little Feather looked confused.

"...The first is that we'll not be returning to Charleston...ever."

Three men made their apologies and stood aside from the rest.

"Now," she continued, "for the most important reason. We may fly the Union Jack as a ploy, but what we take will be under the banner of the skull and crossed sabers." She paused, paced, and continued, "Know ye well, we'll be operatin' outside established laws. The rewards will be great but risks could very well be greater. Be takin' your leave now if this is not somethin' you want to be part of."

Looking about, she waited for a response then added in a somber tone, "Make no mistake, the hangman's noose will be tight around your neck if you choose to stay and we should be captured. But if we strike and move quickly, we all can be set for a lifetime as long as we agree not to become overly greedy and know when to stop and disappear from the high seas. What say ye?"

Without hesitation, Little Feather moved to Anne's side.

The men mumbled, questioning one another. From the center of the group, the burly sailor with an attitude—the one that attempted to toss Little Feather overboard—stepped up almost as quickly as the Indian girl.

Looking up at him, the young girl said, "Are you sure you want to be on the same ship with an Indian, even worse, a girl? It's bad luck...or so I was told by a big hairy-faced seaman that looks like you."

"Ya fight almost as well as Cap'n Andrew. So, it seems to me that twixt your two cutlasses and my roar, we should be able to scare the gold right out of some of the traders sailing the Atlantic." He grinned and showed his gapped, crooked, and off-color teeth through an unruly beard that blended with the hair of his head.

"From this day forward, I will know you by your roar and the hairiest of all faces and call you Bear," Little Feather said, not at all displeased. Still, she bore no expression of pleasure.

Having heard Little Feather's nickname, Anne said, "Who will join Bear on the adventure of a lifetime? Who else among you will risk it all to have it all?"

Twenty-one hardy, adventuresome souls stepped forward to stand alongside Bear, leaving behind six who couldn't justify the risk. They gathered their things and bid farewell.

The wind proved adequate as sails were unfurled and set. The sloop moved away from the heavily wooded cove toward the open Atlantic, leaving behind security of this hidden inlet.

"Set a course south," Anne announced to the steersman.

"Don't you mean north," Bear said.

"The men who did not join us may be tempted by a few gold guineas to turn us in once word gets back of our exploits. It's better they be believin' we've sailed north. It might be the edge we need. Set a tack south."

"Aye, Cap'n Andrew. South it is," Bear said with an air of pride in her cleverness.

Brisk southerly winds brushed her face. The Providence sliced east-southeastward tacking into the wind. The fresh smell of salt air hit her nostrils like a potent drug. That old euphoric sense of adventure returned as she stood straight and walked to the bow. The plan to amass wealth then end this risky career of piracy at the French port of New Orleans as soon as possible was underway. New Orleans meant salvation, last chance at settling down, and living a life that did not include stealing or killing. She saw no contradiction in plundering ships and killing if it meant a life in which neither was ever necessary again.

Looking over the rail, the ship rose and fell with the swells revealing marine worm damage on the hull; one more reason the race she embarked on must finish in a timely manner. The hourglass of this voyage had been turned, sand running fast and free. All things had to run according to that timekeeping device if they were to survive and prosper.

Glancing back, Charleston shrank away.

# Chapter Twenty-three

The Providence followed the coastline of southeastern America tediously tacking into an endless southwesterly wind. Otherwise, the weather was good—breezes cool. Summer heat hadn't yet taken hold. Only the occasional cotton boll cloud marred the blue expanse as it disappeared over the curve in the distance.

Anne held a collapsible scope to her eye, searching for a sailing vessel. Even the tip of a mast on the horizon would have excited her but, so far, nothing. Standing at the base of the bowsprit, she propped against the waist high rail in the hunt for booty-laden prey. "Steady as she goes, Mister Lark," she said to the steersman. "Maintain a sharp eye. If luck is to be ours, lad, we must be vigilant."

The bow of the Providence rose and fell rhythmically as it cut through angled swells, the scope fixed over her right eye. Suddenly, she was struck with unusual queasiness and pulled the scope from her eye. She flushed and swallowed. She took a stomach-settling breath then shook off the anomaly.

Never the sort to think on failure, she wondered what might be a better way to seek out trading vessels she knew to travel these waters. Their departure from Charleston three weeks ago left them no time to gather information on shipping schedules out of England, Spain, or any of the Dutch companies. In her haste she put them in position of depending entirely on chance. She could think of no way to hasten the process. Sailing the known corridor and keeping an eye out was the best she could do.

"Cap'n Andrew," Bear said.

Still looking across the open ocean, "State your business."

"Water seeps into the cargo hold behind the aft bulkhead, Sir."

"Damn!" Anne grimaced and dropped the scope to her side. "'Tis a thing I've been fearin'. Marine worms are cuttin' into the plankin'." She collapsed the scope and shoved it in her waist belt then paced by the big seaman.

She abruptly stopped and again faced him, head tilting in thought. "Our choices are few…maybe nil. I don't know. We have but one cask of pitch and must now put it to use. Assign a man to pack the leaks with hemp and daub them. Find others with nothin' better to do and form a bucket line to bail the hold. Then, my big hairy friend, we look to the saints for a blessin'. If ya know some words of prayer, now would be a good time to be sayin' 'em." She smiled. "I hear God favors people as ugly as you." She pulled the scope, snapped it long, and continued her search of the horizon.

A westward tack brought the Providence to within sight of the Florida peninsula. Still, no other vessel had been spotted. It had turned into a daily ritual of swallowing apprehension before going about her business. Today it hung in her throat. She questioned what to do should it become necessary to abandon the Providence if it deteriorated beyond repair or they simply ran out of material to patch it with. Indications were becoming clear that that is exactly what would happen—just a matter of time. From the day she pulled the trigger on the pistol taking Peter Vander Horst's life, time turned against her.

Seeing no other way, she took the scope from her belt, pulled it to length, and put it to her eye.

Hours rolled by.

Even seemingly insignificant details were not passed over lightly— everything pondered. She labored to find advantage to anything that didn't quite fit—a gull that oddly flew alone and too far from shore, or the dolphin chattering a greeting that lingered a bit too long.

And then came a sweet call, "Mast off the port stern," a seaman yelled from overhead in the rigging.

Whirling around, Anne desperately scanned that clean line where water and sky came together at the edge of the earth and saw the tip of a mast and occasionally, the yardarm, as rolling swells permitted. "Drop sails," she shouted. "We must not be seen. It might be our only advantage."

Bear took the order and barked out distribution of duties to the crew.

Little Feather joined Anne.

The limp sails flapped lazily, pushed by a bare breeze. The Providence ceased moving and began bobbing and drifting with the slow rise and fall of a near-placid ocean.

She turned to Little Feather. "We are between it and the setting sun. They'll not be burnin' their eyes by lookin' into the glare." She smiled for the first time in days and shook the girl's arm. "By the saints, I believe we may go unseen." She then whirled around to see Bear below the quarterdeck. "Bring us about." She put the scope back to her eye. "We must pace ahead of them. I see no square riggin'. It appears to be a schooner but our sloop should be faster if they are laden."

Sails were again brought to standard but undulated to the erratic breeze. Finally, each popped and filled with light wind. The Providence responded and came about. The northward race to stay ahead and out of sight began.

Anne kept a close eye on the mark and made sure the tip of the mainmast spar of that distant ship remained visible, but little else. *If I can see more than that small part of their vessel, then they can see us too.*

The light of day dimmed. As darkness set in, Anne ordered a correction taking the Providence northeasterly on an intercept course by dawn.

Below deck, the men took turns patching ever-increasing leaks in the hull. Endless oak buckets of water were hauled up and dumped overboard.

Anne ordered this process accelerated to keep the ship riding high in the water insuring speed and maneuverability.

Anne looked sympathetically to the exhausted bucket brigade. "Lads, if I could trade my pinky finger for a bilge pump right now, you know that I would. But we *must* keep the Providence drafting shallow."

A tired voice from one of the crew, "We'll be fine Cap'n, nothing a few pints of ale or a crock of rum wouldn't fix."

The comment brought laughs but the timbre lacked enthusiasm.

Anne chuckled then turned away. *This had better work or that tired laughter will turn to mutiny.*

The night brought about a period of waiting. Anne couldn't be sure the course they'd set would intercept the target as planned. She wondered about weaponry and manpower of the vessel pursued. She called the crew together. "Men, as I told you at the onset, the risks are great. Hopefully the rewards will be greater. The fact of this matter is, we've only a guess at what we are about to get ourselves into. We have no knowledge of that ship's cargo, the number of fighting men aboard, or the depth of the ship's armaments. As you can see, our crew is small by any ship's standard."

Grinning broadly, "Aye. What you say merits consideration, Cap'n Andrew, but ye be forgettin' the Indian wench's cutlass and my roar," Bear said.

The comment elicited hoots and hollers. The men began dancing about on deck proclaiming support. "Dangers be damned!" one shouted.

That started an impromptu primal ritual of courage mustering. They shouted obscenities and blasphemed Lady Luck as a whore of the rich becoming intoxicated by the thought of glittering riches—careless words of general contempt irreverently tossed about. They shoved one another like kids at play.

Waving them to silence, "Then tomorrow morning at daybreak," she said, "we sail to glory or death…maybe both. For now, lads, eat hardy then find your place upon the deck to rest. You'll need to be alert and focused to prosper and, maybe, just to survive."

~ * ~

The first dim ribbon of light appeared upon the eastern horizon. Anne already scoped it with the glass. She had the full double mast of a schooner in sight. *We should intercept it within the hour if we can go unseen a while longer. If she happens to be English or an ally of the crown, it may buy time when they notice our Union Jack.*

Another quarter hour passed. The entire ship, now fully visible, treaded low in the water—loaded with something of considerable weight. There was no way of knowing what but Anne suspected what it might be.

The gap narrowed.

The crew of the other vessel noticed and began gathering at the port rail waving.

She collapsed the glass with a clickety-clack, "Aha! Whoever they are, they're not fearin' our flag."

"Bear, once we hit the point of no-goin'-back, hoist the skull and crossed sabers," she shouted. "We may approach under false pretense but we shall board her honorably, our intentions known."

The big sailor, hoisting a hairy arm, pointed to one of the crew and relayed the order. The crewman hooked the banner of the skull and crossed sabers and winched it to the top.

The squeak of the wooden pulley brought Anne back around. "Not yet, you fool! Take it down! It's too soon!"

Glancing forward, she saw the crew of the other ship scurry about. Flaps opened, revealing cannons along the gunwale.

The gap between ships began closing.

"Set a course for collision!" she shouted. "We must be head-on to make as small a target as possible. If we ram her, so be it."

A massive gray cloud appeared at the side of the ship, followed a split second later by a thunderous boom. The first volley whistled over the Providence landing with a tall splash but harmless.

Another cloud and another boom sent whistling their direction.

This time Providence's rail and part of the forward rigging took the ball as splintered debris flew across the deck into the water over the side of the ship.

"Get away from the bow!" she yelled. "Prepare for impact!" *I pray we ram the ship before it has a chance to get off another shot.* She pounded her hip with doubled fist.

Lady Luck must have heard the brash seaman that labeled her a whore of the rich, because now she stood away. A deafening boom sent its destructive force directly into the mainmast spar. It shattered the support pole and sent dangerous splinters flying like daggers. The sails collapsed. Rigging toppled backwards.

"Protect yourselves!" Anne shouted. She looked around for Little Feather and caught sight of the girl slithering beneath a small pinnacle on its side strapped to the stern rail.

The timber and all its attachments crashed to the deck. A rigging block swung wildly and hit Anne on the shoulder. It sent her stumbling and wailing in agony. Even before she lost footing, the Providence rammed the ship and reversed her direction. Her whole body slammed the deck, face first.

She fought for breath but couldn't claim enough time for even that. She leaped to her feet grimacing and reaching for the injured shoulder.

The first of her crew began boarding the target vessel.

She had no time for the pain. "All hands to your feet! Let's board her and see what our destiny holds!"

As was her way, she felt advantage would come in a fast offensive. They charged and climbed up the side of the larger ship and spilled over onto its deck by any means possible. Pistols emptied in both directions and before the Providence drifted away, its entire crew scrambled up and over the railing to the other ship, engaging adversaries as they went.

The clang of colliding blades rang out. Anne ran for the rail of the Providence and balanced atop it, preparing to climb up to the deck of the other ship. She thought she was the last to do so and struggled to get up and over the rail of the taller ship. Use of her numbed right arm limited movement but she refused to relinquish a hold on her cutlass in the other, even for the briefest time.

She felt two hands against the bottoms of her feet. It was Little Feather giving her a boost. "Whatever awaits us, sweet friend, we must believe it is preordained and our destiny."

Little Feather shoved hard against the bottoms of Anne's feet.

Anne tumbled onto the deck. The Indian girl followed close behind.

A nauseating stench assaulted them. "As I thought," Anne said, "This ship carries slaves. Judging by the smell, the holds below deck are loaded."

The words no sooner left her lips then an attacker descended upon her from the rigging above, slashing as he fell.

He missed his planned target but Anne's trademark left-handed slash, left to right, blade forward did not.

He fell and rolled, holding his midsection in a futile attempt to prevent his insides from spilling out. He squealed like a young pig looking for a teat.

Struggling to use the injured right arm, she clumsily unsheathed her rapier but it was of little use in a hand without feeling. *Maybe if I keep it clutched in my fist it can provide distraction so the cutlass in my left hand can do the work.*

Little Feather engaged two at a time.

They became separated.

Anne's hands were full with another big sailor in front of her. She made use of a small advantage by backing up to the steps leading up to the quarterdeck. It provided cover at her back.

Little Feather was not so fortunate. Another assailant charged her rear. He was bent on skewering her with an outstretch sword.

"Behind you!" Anne yelled.

Then from her side came a roar worthy of a young maned lion. It distracted the charging seaman long enough for Bear to tackle him and smash his head against the deck. Snatching up the sword spinning across the deck, Bear fought savagely to protect Little Feather's back.

As Anne disposed of a toothless sailor, she finally had the chance to notice a well-dressed man. He looked the part of a cavalier, with a neatly trimmed pencil-thin moustache and goatee, wearing a felt hat with a broad brim that drooped into his face. It sported a red plumed feather from its band.

Figuring the fight would continue until that man was stopped, she fought her way in his direction. As she neared, it became obvious the limited use of her right arm—her dominant, would certainly play a major role in the confrontation.

Four of her crewman lay bleeding at his feet. As she approached, he thrust that ornate sword through the gut of another. His speed was formidable; he knew swordsmanship.

Shying away would accomplish nothing. Now committed, Anne had but one choice; engage him or watch as he systematically shredded the remainder of her crew. Even if she retreated, she'd eventually have to confront him anyway as a matter of survival. *Better now while it's my choice.* "Face me, you bloody demon!"

He whirled around and squared to her. As a gentleman swordsman might, he placed his left hand on his hip and began to parry her advances and thrusts. He went on the offensive.

She blocked with the rapier in her injured right hand, but only once.

He twirled his sword around hers and slung it from her numbed hand and thrust again.

She slapped his blade aside with the shorter cutlass at the last possible instant before the tip found its mark into her heart.

Taking the fight to him, she slashed upward and across with her left hand. He jumped back. It was clearly an odd move from the off side he was not accustomed to. She got respect and breathing space.

192

He continued backing away. Then abruptly he stopped. He roared in anger at having been bested even on a single move.

He charged and put her on the defensive with his longer blade.

She retreated. Back stepping, she worked at keeping his weapon from piercing her flesh at the expense of watching where her feet were. In an instant the situation turned desperate.

She stumbled and fell over a lifeless body.

Her back slammed the deck followed by her elbow.

The cutlass flew from her grasp.

As a satisfied look crossed his face, she glanced, cringed and steeled her body for the final thrust that would end her life.

But that smug expression vanished—wiped clean, replaced by surprise. He fell sideways, unconscious before he hit the deck.

As he crumpled away, she saw Bear standing over him with a barrel stave gripped tightly in both hands—a weapon of opportunity.

Anne shot him a quick smile. "I thought it was your habit to roar."

"Pardon me, Cap'n. I was busy. I forgot."

Leaping to her feet, she retrieved the cutlass and held the man's head up by the hair with the blade at his throat. "Call your men off!" she shouted, struggling with the lack of strength in her right hand to maintain control of his head.

Groggy and slow to come around, he finally regained a grasp of the situation. With grit teeth he snarled, "Call them off yourself," he said in English but with a strong French accent.

"All right. I will," she said. "The last of you holding a weapon," she yelled, "shall be held accountable for the removal of your captain's head. Then I shall leave you to your crewmates to determine your fate."

She pushed her face close to his and whispered, "We shall see just how loved you are."

The metallic sound of falling weapons clanked across the ship.

Providence's crew herded the surrendering men to a spot near where Anne had the captain pinned.

"The stench tells me this is a slave ship. Am I right? Or could it be that your crew just smells that bad?"

With a blade still at his throat, he hissed, "Yes. A slaver."

"Where do you hail from?"

"The Gold Coast."

"Are you fully laden?"

"No, we sold a portion to the governor of Jamaica and were sailing for the Virginias."

"Lawes. Do you speak of Governor Lawes?"

"Yes."

"Then you have payment aboard?"

After several persuasive attempts, it finally took a light cut on the throat and a trickle of blood to convince the captain to give up its whereabouts.

Two men scampered to retrieve the booty.

"Little Feather, go below, take a headcount and find out if any of the slaves speak English." Anne began counting gold pieces and jewels, placing them in neat stacks in a sunny area on deck.

Little Feather reappeared with a small man, skin so black it glistened with blue highlights in the morning sun. His smell arrived before him. "This one speaks English."

"How is it you know our language?" Anne asked him, holding her hand over her nose.

"I am a teacher. I also speak French and Dutch," he said matter-of-factly.

Believing it incredible, "I can't imagine a man of your intelligence being sold into simple menial service."

"The men of this ship care little about how we think, what we know, or what we have to say. They only care if our backs are strong."

"What is your name?"

"I am Nantumbo Abaké."

"Too long," she said. "I'll call you Nani. You'll be my translator. Is this fair with you?"

Uncertain how to take this brash, fast-talking fair skinned and freckled little man who'd be his liberator, he hesitantly nodded approval.

"Go release your people then all of you bathe, for God's sake."

The men of the Providence bound the captain and surviving crew. Anne rose from the small pile of treasure and surveyed her surroundings. She held the limp right arm. "I think it's time we traded up. Don't you agree, lads?"

There was no disagreement as the slaver crew was herded onto the ailing Providence, provisions and weapons were brought aboard the newly won vessel.

As the disabled ship drifted away, the French captain and his remaining men crowded the ship's rail watching as the commandeered slaver pulled in the mainsheets to capture the wind.

"Bear, tell Mister Lark to set a course south." She and the big man at her side kept an eye on the receding Providence.

"Aye, cap'n."

The defeated Frenchman yelled across at Anne, "You and I will meet again! I swear it before God that I'll have your life as payment for this deed!"

"You'll be waiting in line for quite some time, I wager," she shouted back.

The Providence drifted away carried by the Gulf Stream. Anne figured it would drift ashore within the week if it didn't sink first—plenty of time to round the Florida Strait into the Gulf of Mexico with no fear of pursuit. She turned her back to it and her mind away from that situation. But even before a sigh of relief could clear her lips, she faced another.

A crowd of black slaves, young, old, male and female streamed from the dark holding area below deck into blinding light. Shielding eyes, they strained to get a look at the one who now held the key to their lives.

The sight was no great surprise. The foul odor of death, feces, and unwashed bodies was repugnant but expected, gagging and staggering the crew. Anne stood back with folded arms. She studied black faces huddled together. Those healthy enough to be expressive showed fear. Apparently they believed they'd be thrown to the sharks. Others offered bland looks, presumably a result of disease or hunger.

# Chapter Twenty-four

With the addition of culverins from the Providence, battlements along the gunwale of the confiscated schooner contained two per port behind four closed flaps capable of resisting or overtaking almost any adversary. Anne renamed the now formidable fighting vessel Windsong's Freedom in honor of a fallen friend. But the name carried weight beyond a simple honorarium; it was the means to an end—freedom from life on the run. Anne Bonny sought it desperately.

Even after a week of near-constant scrubbing with seawater, a lingering putrid odor remained below deck. The smell saturated every beam, bag, and barrel. Now that the blacks had been privileged to breathe clean air perfumed by the sea, they could barely stomach it. Just days ago, they all had been drenched in the vilest smells known to man. But, with sixty-two men, women and children aboard, not including the remaining crew, these same holds, regardless of disquieting aroma, must serve as sleeping quarters. Space was premium.

In a ritualistic ceremony, Nani ordered his people to bring shackles and chains to a point near the stern rail. They placed black iron hardware in a heap with astonishing gentility then backed away as if, somehow, they revered what had bound them into slavery.

Anne's respect for Nantumbo Abaké, Nani as she called him, grew. He was intelligent, fair, and passionate. She valued his opinion on the blacks but had also come to listen to philosophical things he spoke of. He had a knack for simplifying complicated situations.

In the case of the shackles that lay piled on deck, it was clear he knew the importance of putting a face to evil then disposing of it—symbolic yet tangible. His people danced and chanted in their native tongue. Appearing as kelp reacting to the sea's current, black arms flailed to the sky rhythmically. They took turns spitting on the wrought iron heap. Then they shoved it all into the sea.

Anne marveled how the simple ceremony put smiles on the faces of the healthiest. It boosted morale—a joyful end to the brutality of enslavement. No longer would they be subjected to such dehumanizing treatment. They could look to a future that didn't include devices of bondage and enjoy the most basic of freedoms, the right to choose their destiny.

*Aye, if it is within my power you'll always be a free people.* Then she mumbled aloud, "Just as I wish to be."

Nani backed away from his people to join Anne. "It is a fine thing you do, Captain Andrew. We will not forget that you are the one who set us free."

"Your freedom may be comin' at a rather high price." She glanced at him. "It's not something I foresee, mind ya. But I certainly fear it possible."

Anne presented her back and stepped away so her thoughts would not be affected by questioning eyes. "We sail for the port of New Orleans in French held territory. But we must try to up our wealth in a dangerously short period of time. The only way to get that done is take it from unsuspecting vessels of trade. We have no choice. We have to finance our future or live destitute."

She paused, sighed, then again faced the little man about her height. "Are ya willin' to help me train your people to fight? Can you and your people look past whatever your beliefs are about life and death to take by force that which is not yours? Most importantly, are ya willin' to take human lives to get it done...if that be the case?"

"The choice you offer is an easy decision." He drew a comfortable smile. "Our freedom was taken from us. In that, we had no choice. It's our nature as humans to seek justice in reciprocity. We are in your service. But, with all respect due you, I'm compelled to ask what would become of us if I should have said no?"

"Only a learned man debates his heart and questions his conviction." She looked away from him and gazed across the open sea. "You and your people would be allowed to disembark at the nearest landfall and given freedom to make it on your own."

Finding new thoughts in those words, she held up a finger for Nani to withhold comment. Having been given a philosophical point of consideration, she paced in a tight circle before the small black man drumming her lips with fingertips then abruptly stopped. With measured ease she faced him. "Let me go on to say, when we arrive in New Orleans, my plan is to make a major life's course correction, leavin' the high seas forever. When that day comes, this ship will no longer be of value to my goals. Therefore, treasures we take and claim as our own, I'll share with you and your people. In turn, you may offer your share in payment to my crew for safe passage to your homeland."

Continuing the pace for a moment longer, she finally stopped and looked sideways at him. She squared to him placing hands upon hips. "What say ye to such an offer?"

"Even without sweetening, the answer would still have been yes. We'll fight at your side as compensation for our freedom. But your offer will add amazing ferocity. This I promise." As a sign of respect and sincerity, Nani put his hands together and bowed deeply.

The former slaves were a mishmash of farmers, merchants and simple people. There were several different tribes represented; none had ever been in combat. Having dealt with slavers for her father in her younger days in Charleston, Anne knew traders specifically sought people strong and healthy yet docile, displaying a temperament better suited for loosely supervised manual labor. People from warrior-like tribes were prone to violent resistance and might possess the wherewithal to succeed.

Little Feather worked with the women and teens. She educated them on survival skills with swords, cutlasses, rapiers, and throwing knives. She taught moves to surprise and defeat with weapons of opportunity, anything on deck that might be used as clubs. At times training turned comical. Some seemed more a threat to themselves than anyone else.

Nani took an active role, although he, too, possessed no such skills.

Anne looked on in satisfaction as the small, articulate black man stood among larger and less literate men, chastising them, throwing orders in their native language, determined to forge a fighting force Captain Andrew would look upon with pride. Anne need not understand the language to know he was not accepting *I can't* or *I don't know how* as acceptable responses. The little man was relentless. Nani knew the best way to become proficient with a weapon was to teach the use of it. Ability with the ornate sword taken from the French captain improved with each lesson. Like her, he must compensate for lack of size with speed.

~ * ~

A week of fair winds in the Gulf of Mexico took them west of the Florida Strait. Sailing was smooth. Southeasterly wind filled and kept sails billowed. Windsong's Freedom slashed the water at a satisfying clip over gentle swells.

Anne couldn't hide concern.

Little Feather approached.

Anne held a fixed gaze upon the keel slicing swells, mesmerized by the rhythmic regularity. She stood at the base of the bowsprit as she had for more than an hour staring into the water.

"Are you well?" the young girl asked.

"'Well'?" Anne asked, mulling the correct response. "That would depend on what you mean by the word."

"Are you ill? Sick?"

"Not at the moment, but it will come soon enough."

"How can you know such a thing?"

Looking about first, she leaned into Little Feather and whispered, "I think I'm with child."

Little Feather's shock drove her to brief silence. "If so, we have reason to accomplish our goals with all haste." The girl quickly looked away.

Anne saw dismay and confusion beyond Little Feather's concern. The stunning revelation clearly had thoughts whirling that the young Iroquois in love with Anne couldn't sort. She continued glancing in short bursts, hoping to read the girl's thoughts. But even as she did, Anne was unwilling to burden her friend with potential problems that might complicate the situation even more.

She turned her gaze back to Gulf waters regressing into her own thoughts. She struggled to piece together a life's course from this point forward. A troubling possibility dogged her.

Once upon a time she'd been pregnant with Calico Jack Rackham's baby and left on an island to bear the child with the aid of locals. The baby did not survive. To complicate matters, she grew depressed, even contemplated suicide. It might have happened if Jack had waited longer to return. She couldn't be sure even now if she would have killed herself if left a day longer on that island. Losing control seemed to be connected to pregnancy. Could it happen again? If so, could she control its course? How could she command a ship if she couldn't control her own mind? Furthermore, could she continue in command once the men discovered she was Anne Bonny and not Andrew the Protector?

Changes in her body were on the verge of becoming obvious. She pondered possibilities, ruing the fact that such things happened to women. She pounded the ship's rail with a clenched fist. The day fast approached that her disguise as Captain Andrew no longer would work. That would be an interesting day indeed. It was in God's hands now, the loose thread that could unravel her life. What might provoke him to pull it?

~ * ~

The six weeks Nani's people spent chained in darkness took an irreversible toll. A few that survived to be liberated succumbed to diseases and infections. As Windsong's Freedom swung southwestward toward Yucatan to skirt the eastern Mexican coastline in search of plunder, the ranks of the blacks shrank, the weakest dying.

Anne spotted one of the youngest standing at the starboard rail—a pitiful sight. The boy was shirtless, shoeless, and wore a ragged pair of canvas pantaloons tattered above the knee, tears drying in white streaks on his dark face. He was the son of a woman who'd just died of a leg infection—buried at sea this very morning. Remaining family was thousands of miles away. She looked upon him with pity, born of a maternal leaning growing stronger by the day. Tears filled her eyes. She hid her face. Normal calm aloofness took sudden leave. In fast nervous swipes, she cleared watery eyes.

After a moment to recompose, she called Nani to her side and approached the child at the rail. "Nani, tell the boy I'm sorry for the loss of his mother."

Nani pulled the boy's head up to face him. "Captain Andrew wishes to convey his sympathy for the passing of your mother," he told the child in their native language.

The youngster attempted a brave face, lips tight and quivering yet he did not openly weep.

Suddenly awash with emotion, she took his hand and pulled him to her. The head of the child mashed against her bosom. She hugged the child. Her eyes uncontrollably filled with tears.

The soft protrusion of breasts beneath the loose-fitting shirt pushed in to the side of his face. He pulled away. The look of sorrow turned to surprise.

It was obvious he realized her gender. At the moment she didn't care. Holding the child close, Anne smiled and dropped to sit on her heels. "I know what you have discovered and it will stay our secret. What is your name?" Looking to her translator, "Tell the boy what I said and ask him his name, Nani."

Although understanding the words, relevance eluded Nani. He looked quizzically at Captain Andrew then translated the ambiguous message.

"My name is Ladosamé Nabé," the boy replied after Nani translated the question.

"Nani, tell him I'll call him Laddy." She smiled at the boy but kept on addressing the older man. "It's just that the names of your people are cumbersome and the name Laddy comes fast and natural to me." She finally looked to Nani. "If you'll indulge a whim for me, please teach him some English."

Leaving Nani and Laddy standing, Anne walked away and resumed her position near the bowsprit. She scanned the horizon, glancing at intervals back to the boy. She wondered how much longer she'd be able to conceal the fact that she was not a man. She held one of those glimpses and gazed at the boy for a lingering moment and wondered if Laddy would be able to keep the secret. For some inexplicable reason, she trusted him and thought no more on it.

# Chapter Twenty-five

It could've been disappointment but, then again, it might have been the pregnancy knotting Anne's gut. Problems were numerous and all vied for the top of the priority list.

Remaining determined to finance living in obscurity, she sailed within sight of the Mexican coast. As she did, another problem reared its head; the crew was restless. Idle talk took on threatening tones and was difficult to ignore.

Anne spent hours looking for opportunities, examining the seeable horizon. Fatigue pulled her down. No sign of promising targets, not even shuttle sloops making short freight excursions between Mexican ports—nothing.

Bear quelled another dispute. It was a fist fight and only the addition of his big square fists on both heads put an end to it. Extreme physical violence remained contained. So far, nothing beyond bloodied lips, noses, head lacerations, and broken knuckles. Angry outbursts were increasing though. The men were illiterate. Pack mentality came easy to them. All it'd take is one negative shout about Captain Andrew and all out mutiny would follow.

Nani had his own problems. The difference between the blacks' frustrations and that of the crew was the difference between fear and violence. The former slaves watched the sailors with cautious glances and worried looks.

Laddy followed Nani everywhere the small man went, sometimes at the little man's insistence. True to his promise, he taught the child English. Anne allowed the boy to approach and practice his new language any time. Fondness deepened, maternal instincts sharpened.

Anne arranged a training session. It served two purposes; to keep the men sharp for battle and reduce idle time. The exhausting routine of techniques with the blade and wrestling matches provided a diversion from the monotony of sailing and searching. Still, the crew was mouthy about everything.

Anne had the distinct sense sharks were circling. She cast a wary eye to the freed slaves, too. They whispered. It didn't require language skills to know they questioned their future.

Stores of meats and dried fruits dwindled. Anne's timetable for accomplishing her mission tightened. Hungry mouths depleted food supplies to a dangerous point. Her attention shifted from financial acquisition to food replenishment. She searched the coastline for a place to dock that might satisfy the need.

It came in the form of a promising inlet near the village of Campeche on the Yucatan Peninsula. Taking advantage of the opportunity she ordered mainsails furled, leaving forward jibs taut to steer into the narrow passage between high cliffs.

Lazily rounding the lead precipice, the sight of an English Galleon greeted them, careened to its side on the beach. Its crew had apparently taken advantage of low tide to patch the hull. Carpenters scurried about in shallow water, hauling boards, timbers, and tools. There was quickness to their actions. They worked fast while receded water permitted.

"Bear, hoist the Union Jack."

Wooden pulleys squawked as the English flag went up.

"Little Feather, retrieve my letter from Governor Walpole." She never took her eyes from the much larger vessel as they closed in. "It's a warship. We are woefully ill-equipped to take it on in a heads-up battle, but maybe we can find opportunity while discovering its purpose and cargo."

The carpenters noticed them. They came to a standstill watching

Windsong's Freedom ease into the lagoon. Others climbed the severely tilting deck of the warship crowding the rail to see what was going on.

"Bear, have the men drop the pinnace and pick out two hardy lads to man the oars. I shall be greetin' them properly by payin' a personal visit since the water is too shallow to ease alongside."

Pulling her hair tight, she retied the rawhide strip securing her ponytail. She adjusted the soiled leather tricorn hat she wore, putting on her best Captain Andrew face for the unknown captain of the English galleon.

A sudden hot-flash gave her pause. She rubbed her baby bump beneath the loose fitting linen shirt. She took a breath and blew it out between rounded lips; a reminder that time was no friend. She followed her men into the small boat.

As the men rowed by the carpenters, all standing in waist deep water, she noticed they seemed friendly enough, shouting words of welcome, some making lighthearted gaffs as well. One shouted, "If ya be bringin' a few crocks of rum then ye be welcome…otherwise go away." He then let out a bellowing laugh.

Arriving onshore, her two mates beached the boat. Anne led the way walking toward the galleon. They marched up the plank stopping at the gangway. She marveled at its size compared to her ship, Windsong's Freedom, a schooner that began life as a slaver.

Her ego suddenly deflated, realizing she'd never have the chance to command such a vessel. Not wishing to belittle the blessing of the galleon's presence, she dispelled the notion as something to be pondered another day. Had it not been beached and under repair, the galleon itself might have been the biggest prize of all.

Cupping her mouth, she shouted, "Captain Andrew the Protector, hailin' from Windsong's Freedom under private letter of provision issued by Governor Walpole and stamped by King George wishes to have an audience with the Captain of this vessel."

"Aye Cap'n," a bare-chested sailor replied as he climbed the gangplank behind them. "I'll fetch Cap'n Peckary. He walked past them to the cabins below the substantial aft quarterdeck.

"Peckary?" Anne muttered. "Is it possible? Have the saints blessed me so richly?"

Her question was answered in a flash as her former employer and the one that dubbed her 'The Protector', bounded from a short narrow stairwell at the stern bouncing unsteadily off a wall, fighting for footing along the listing ship's slanted surface. "Andrew, my boy," he shouted, gleefully clapping his hands. "What a marvelous surprise!"

Anne glanced skyward. In a breathy whisper, "Thanks be to ya blessed Virgin."

Excitedly, "Wait right there," he said from near the door he appeared from, "I'll fetch a bottle of French Cognac. We'll find a flatter surface on the beach and share a drink."

Joining Anne at the gangway, Captain Peckary, bottle and glasses in hand, led the way down to the beach. Passing her pinnace, she left orders for the men to stand-by then joined the Captain at a small table and chairs set up on the sand.

More as a question, "It would seem piloting English trading vessels from the West Indies to England and the Colonies is no longer your duty."

Pulling the cork from the cut-crystal decanter, he filled two dainty glasses. In this environment, the delicate glassware seemed odd.

He handed her one. "I've been commissioned by the King to sail the Gulf and the Caribbean protecting English trading vessels. I've been charged with seeking out then destroying all pirate and privateering ships not flying an English flag. Piracy has become so rampant that cargo, or payment for it, hardly ever arrives at its destination. It's become nothing but luck." He took a swallow then quickly added, "If it happens at all, I mean."

She smiled then took a sip. "'Tis a necessary and noble thing you do. What successes can you boast?" Her smile was more a show of thanks for happening on potential good fortune than pleasure of talking to the droopy-jowled overweight Peckary.

"First, I must say that you are a major reason for my good fortune of gaining command of this ship. You see, all that gold you sent back to England taken from that Dutch trading vessel so enamored King George with my recommendation of you, he promoted me."

Anne was just given another reason to be thankful. She held her glass out to toast Peckary's commission. It was also to toast selfish desires that took shape. *How can I capitalize on this?* As Peckary rattled, the wheels of her mind spun.

Peckary withheld nothing. He trusted Andrew twice before—both times to his great advantage, and now obviously saw no reason not to trust the small fancy man he called The Protector. "We've successfully retrieved stolen cargo and treasure from two pirate sloops sailing out of Kingston and sunk them," he said smugly, his nose turning upward.

Anne moved to the edge of her chair.

"We were in pursuit of another when we had to delay because of ripped planking along the hull from an accidental encounter with a shallow reef. But we'll soon be repaired and underway again." Turning up his glass he downed the liquor.

"Then I suspect you'll be sailing for England soon to return the recovered goods."

"Eventually...but after we take care of that other floating den of heathen French Corsairs then I must deliver payroll coin for the English garrisons in the Carolinas and Virginias. A mundane task for sure but it must be done."

Anne fought away giddiness at the news. "Then I should allow you to get back to the task of preparing your galleon to sail. Your fighting men must be eager to get on with the chase."

"Yes, all two-hundred-twelve of them. Andrew, we won't be seaworthy for at least three, maybe four days. That said would you care to join me this evening? We shall dine together. How about it?"

She nodded. "A splendid idea. I gladly accept."

~ * ~

Aboard Windsong's Freedom she put her crew to the business of replenishing food stores while she devoted time to planning. *Shrewdly and to the letter is how it must be handled. My crew is no match for two hundred soldiers. But, as God is my witness, we can sure as hell outrun them.*

Clutching the ship's rail, knuckles whitening, she gazed into the placid water of the lagoon. Her focus narrowed to only the plan—every step critical. Glancing to the hodgepodge assemblage making up her crew, she muttered, "If I handle this badly, it'll be a bloody slaughter."

"Do we fight soon?" Laddy babbled in broken English.

"Fight?" she repeated as if the word had sparked a notion. Clasping her hands, she tapped her mouth with combined fists, declaring, "Yes. Yes, that's it."

Laddy looked puzzled. "We make ready to fight…yes?"

"Yes, we make ready to fight. But not with blades, pistols or cannon." She knelt and placed hands upon the boy's shoulders. "Sometimes, Laddy, battles are won or lost here." She pecked the boy's temple with a fingertip. "It appears the backdoor is the perfect place to enter this battle. We might do this without firing a shot or drawing a cutlass." She grinned big and winked at him. "And that would be a grand thing. Don't ya think, little man?"

He nodded slowly, still not grasping it. "Do our people get the chance to prove themselves?"

Little Feather stepped to Anne's side and addressed his question. "Maybe not. Not this time anyway. Be silent now and let the Captain lay out the plan for us."

Anne rose. "Bear…Nani, come close. We need to talk."

The four exchanged ideas. A plan came together. It must be quiet and in the dark of night. An armed confrontation would be last resort only. Success lay in no confrontation at all. Should it fall short of impeccable, it was further agreed, all would be swept away like a teetering frond hut in a gale.

~ * ~

"There are advantages in being landlocked for a time..." Anne said..."Fresh meat for example." She clamped teeth onto a chunk of wild boar served by Peckary's cook. She tore a strip from it. Juices glistened on her fingers in the combined flickering candlelight and dying flames of the cook fire. It trickled down her chin. The fire crackled sending sparks up past the skewered carcass. The cook basted and rotated it over low flames. The fire illuminating the table set up on the beach as well as gently lapping waves at the shore a few feet away provided a soothing ambience. She noticed shadows cast by the fire magnified Peckary's bulbous nose.

"Andrew, it's such a wonderful break in the monotony to see you again. Where do you sail from here?"

Not wanting to reveal anything near the truth, or offer information he might use later, she said, "We'll be sailing east to the West Indies." She licked pig fat from her fingers then gulped a swallow of wine. *I wonder if the child in my belly is responsible for this voracious appetite.* "This is the best dinner I've had in weeks." She gestured to the cook for more meat.

Looking beyond the cook toward Windsong's Freedom, she wondered if their carefully conceived plan was underway. She kept a tuned ear to the beached galleon listening for telltale sounds, all the while ravenously consuming roast pork. Glancing down the narrow beach over Peckary's shoulder, campfires dotted the sand between a tropical jungle and the waters of the lagoon. Most of the galleon's crew had disembarked for the night because the ship listed to an uncomfortable angle. Only a few remained aboard as guards. That suited Anne's plan nicely. She couldn't see or hear anything from the galleon which might or might not be a good sign. She couldn't be sure.

After a time, hunger satisfied and belly full, she prolonged dinner as long as possible and slowed eating to occasional picking. She indulged Peckary in conversation that disinterested her greatly. "What do you hear of news from England, Captain?"

"Ah, news from home," he said, "I do miss it. The last I have of import was as I departed, nigh seven months ago. It concerned growing unrest that King George may be leaving too much control in the hands of Walpole. I fear this may swell into a problem if it hasn't already."

Quizzing Peckary further on the subject, Anne noticed the glimmer in his eyes. He relished conversations about politics and happenings in England. She prodded him to keep talking as long as he liked. The hours passed and the portly little red-faced man eventually yawned. "Oh my, it seems I have spent far too long and encumbered your time beyond courteous limits."

She laughed. "Nonsense, we don't have to call it a night yet. It's not like we have to prepare to sail at first light."

Thinking on it, "Humph. You're right."

Anne returned to asking well-planned questions and Peckary talked on into the wee hours.

Believing a sufficient amount of time had passed, Anne jumped to her feet and said, "Well, the weight of my eyelids and the fire within them tells me it is now time to take my leave."

Peckary followed at her heels chattering.

The time to pretend interest passed. Once she arrived at the pinnace, she helped the two oarsmen push it into the water interrupting the captain in mid-sentence. "Well, good night, sir. Thank you for the excellent meal. Maybe we'll meet again someday."

Disappearing beyond the firelight into the lagoon, the last thing Anne heard was Peckary saying, "Yes, good night to you too. I bid you fair winds and good fortune. I am in need of sleep as well... right after I check the ship."

"Put your backs into those oars, lads," she whispered. "The game may be over but now the running begins. It *is* over...right?"

"That it is," one of the oarsmen said through darkness.

Another voice topped his from some distance. "You scoundrel!" came a yell from the galleon. "You bloody scoundrel! No one takes advantage of Telford Peckary or the English crown and lives."

Flashes and booms from muskets fired along the beach were the only response made and a futile one at that. The distance was just too great.

Peckary continued issuing threats but the intensity lessened as distance increased. The small boat closed in on Windsong's Freedom.

The warship leaned away from the lagoon into the shore rendering the cannons useless.

Obviously hoping to catch them before an evening breeze filled the sails, Anne heard Peckary barking orders for all available longboats be put in. In dim starlight, Anne saw at least four of them pushed into the water. She heard splashes as oars dashed the water furiously.

Shouting toward the deck of Windsong's Freedom from several hundred feet away, "Set full sails. Get 'er done and turn that little darlin' about. Quickly lads! Quickly! We must shoot the passage out of the lagoon fast as possible. Caution be damned!"

The soldiers giving chase had six oars in the water in each of their boats. They found their rhythm and closed the gap fast. A muzzle flash, followed by a throaty boom, sent a musket ball whizzing past Anne. "Their muskets are within range! Row faster!  It's now our very lives at stake."

Loud fwump-pops signaled that the main sails of Windsong's Freedom caught the night breeze. She saw the bow respond to filled canvas as Bear shouted orders to weigh anchor. "Quit your groaning and get that anchor out of the water!" she heard him yell.

She feared timing might be off. The ship started moving as quickly as their small boat moved through the water. Squinting into the darkness, she saw a tiny figure at the port rail. "Throw us a rope, Laddy boy! We won't be catchin' up with oars alone."

The two oarsmen huffed, fighting to keep up but the ship displayed more of its stern as it began pulling away.

Musket balls whizzed close enough to spray seawater on them. One smashed into the stern plate sending splinters flying. The ball sang off at a sharp angle.

Anne and the two men ducked low, offering no clear shot.

She saw then heard the rope thrown from the deck above fall short with a splat into the water just ahead of them. "Try again," she shouted.

A much larger figure raced up to the side of the boy, pulled in the rope, coiled it, and with a mighty heave sent it sailing over their tiny boat into the water behind them. Anne fished it out, and as the men rowed she added the strength of her arms, pulling them forward, closing the gap on Windsong's Freedom.

By the time she began shinnying up the rope, the lead boat loaded with fighting men from the warship smashed into theirs, knocking it from beneath her feet.

She swung free, struggling to gain a footing on the side of the ship.

She glanced down. Her men swung oars as weapons, landing blows wherever and whenever possible.

Given circumstances, getting up the rope quickly to allow her men the same opportunity was the most pressing priority.

Reaching the hinge of a closed gunwale flap, it provided footing to vault up and over the rail.

She fell face forward onto the rough, splintery deck of Windsong's Freedom, just as a hiss-boom rang out.

On hands and knees, she crawled and looked down between rail balusters to see one of her men clutch his belly.

He wilted then fell into the water.

Leaping to her feet, she yanked a musket from the grasp of a crewman, cocked the hammer. and aimed.

She fired.

It hit the shooter squarely in the chest, knocking him backward into the water. "Send the rest of them to be bottom of the lagoon! Leave no one standing!"

A volley rang out. Every shot found a mark. The attacking boat now floated empty, save for one man screaming in agony.

The surviving oarsman from Anne's pinnace climbed to the deck of Windsong's Freedom.

Another English long boat approached then another and another. They closed in and appeared near enough to get it done. Anne ordered her crew to hold fire. Although a couple of the boats came close enough to kiss their hull, Windsong's Freedom had achieved speed enough to begin pulling away.

Soldiers squeezed off parting shots but found no targets.

Within seconds, Anne and her crew were leaving their would-be executioners behind.

Thanks to the expert work of the steersman, Windsong's Freedom threaded the narrow passage putting it in open waters of the Gulf of Mexico picking up headier winds beyond the lagoon.

It was only then Anne saw by lantern light the immense pile of booty scattered about the deck. The fragrance of cinnamon bark, pepper, and all manner of spices filled the air. She sucked in the satisfying aroma. "This is a far cry better than the stench of human waste and decaying flesh that still reeks below." She laughed.

Little Feather joined her. Together they inspected all they'd laid claim to. Eight chests of varying sizes loaded with gold coin. Spices Peckary's warship confiscated from the pirate sloops, she suspected, would fetch as much gold as they already had seized, maybe more.

Although satisfying, the victory provided no lasting comfort. She could not relax; not yet. Peckary would not give up until Andrew the Protector was hung by the neck from the yardarm of that galleon and left to rot—one more reason life in the disguise of Andrew must come to an end.

Massaging the small swell in her belly, she smiled at the absurdity. Soon, masquerading as a man by any name would be impossible. She belched and fondly remembered good wine and good food.

# Chapter Twenty-six

Sailing north out of Campeche Bay, Anne realized Peckary's warship couldn't sail from that lagoon in Yucatan for at least one more day. And that was only if he ordered all hands to the task of repairing the galleon's ripped hull.

Anne's fears of mutiny withered. The crew's bitter murmurings stopped. A light, jovial mood spread throughout Windsong's Freedom once the men understood how substantial each share of the prize was.

At the end of the first long hard day under full sail, the sun dropped below the horizon in the western sky. Anne gave her blessing to a celebration then encouraged it. A well-deserved party made good use of Peckary's confiscated private supply of liquor. She ordered rotating watches and duties at the helm so everyone had the chance to enjoy food and drink. Merriment became spirited, filled with raucous shouts and crude jokes. Sobriety took general leave along with the light of day.

Nani and his people held back and watched. It was clear the former slaves looked upon the sailors as untrustworthy. Dwindling inhibitions and rough, wild-eyed fun put an edge to that lack of trust as the men eyed the black women with lusty glints.

Although working for a common cause toward individual goals, Nani approached and whispered to Anne that it appeared the crew steered clear of them only as a courtesy to Captain Andrew. He shared with her the contempt he saw and felt from the crew even while sober. Now drunk and carefree, that wariness stole away any chance of a good time for the former slaves.

Needing no prompt from Nani on the matter, she nodded agreement. She, too, noticed prejudicial looks and unkind acts like shoving someone aside for no reason. Each gulp of the spirits escalated a black and white division. If the collective mood were anything other than jovial, she'd be concerned. If this had been the night before an encounter with Peckary's war ship, it would be different. In that scenario she had no doubt she'd be pitched overboard with the blacks if she lifted a finger to defend them. It was that pack mentality of illiterate men. These seamen would be frightfully easy to work into a murderous frenzy. But this night, she viewed it as releasing pent up tension. It was vital they did.

She, Little Feather, and Laddy relaxed in a small corner at the stern, letting the men have their way. Gazing into the night sky, she pulled Laddy close. "See the halo around the rising moon? 'Tis a bad omen to a seafarer. Did ya know that?"

The boy searched for the right English words to give his question a voice. He did so haltingly. "Father once told me it was a sign of good crops. Isn't that good?"

Smiling down at the lad, she jostled his hair. It was long, unruly, and nappy, appearing as dusty black smoke puffed from a cannon blast then frozen in time. "I suppose if you're a farmer that might be true." A solemn look replaced the smile. "But along with life-giving rain comes life-threatening storms, possibly the worst, hurricanes. I'm afraid of no man but options are limited when storms of this magnitude overtake a sailing vessel."

Feeling the sudden impact of the words, a chill raced up her back. Hair rose on her neck. Her eyes fell away from the young teen and wondered aloud, "Only a fool would stay upon the water and not consider alternatives. Am I that fool or just that desperate?"

A loud string of obscenities by a drunken sailor jarred her from thought. It'd be the last thing he said this night, crumpling to the deck in a drunken heap. She ignored it and returned to mulling contingencies while gazing at that hazy ring around the moon.

She decided to stay the course under full sail through the night, pushing Windsong's Freedom to make use of all wind while it blew at a favorable speed. They steered north.

After a time, raucous noise died down. With Laddy's head in her lap, she looked to Little Feather lying on her side next to her. The girl made good use of a rope coil as a pillow. Anne stroked the young girl's buttocks then used it as her pillow. She dozed.

Anne opened her eyes. The sun was breaking the horizon. Its light glowed blood red emerging off the starboard bow—an ominous sight. A rush fluttered her stomach. The rising sun appeared to boil the ocean at the edge of the earth. It cast an eerie glow. *It portends things to come—dangerous and uncontrollable things.*

First light was a warning, unlike the friendly yellow sun of promise. The air turned heavy overnight. The smell of a storm was in it. Wind increased and blew sporadically, gusting occasionally to flag-popping speeds.

Within an hour of sunrise, Sol disappeared. Dimming shadowless light was all that was allowed by a thickening blanket of gray clouds hanging low and bulging on their bottoms.

The crew of Windsong's Freedom was quiet and as somber as the morning. Hangovers played a part but only a small one as they woke to the threat of nature's fury. Seeds of fear sprouted in well-tilled minds—no laughing, no loud talk, all retreating into the worried recesses of their own heads.

Windsong's Freedom maintained a northward course. Inconsistent wind kept the crew busy. It shifted from southwest to southeast and sometime directly from the west. Swinging jibs pushed them generally northward.

Little Feather started toward Anne then quickened.

Anne, thus far, successfully concealed the pregnancy and its complications but only from the crew. The Indian girl could not be fooled. Little Feather followed as Anne bolted below deck out of sight and heaved the contents of her stomach. It wasn't the sea; it was the child growing in her womb. The changes in her body were now almost impossible to hide.

Through pale green complexion and reddened eyes, "I'll teach you a new word, Little Feather." She wiped her mouth with the back of her hand while stifling another gag. "It is *enigma*. It's something you're watching me deal with now. I sit before you sick like a helpless child and cannot let the crew know." She turned her head up and forced a swallow like a bird taking a worm then fell forward to rest elbows on knees. "On the one hand, if I say it's seasickness, I lose respect as a seafarer; control of the crew will go with it. In the other hand I hold truth. Sharing it would result in the same outcome. There ya have it. Two answers and no advantage in either; now I must choose one. This is the enigma. Time is running out on secrecy as an option. What to do?"

She rose unsteadily, maintaining balance clutching a low-hanging beam overhead as the ship rose, fell, and rolled with increasing Gulf swells. "The way I see it," she said, wiping her mouth with a rag, "the only way is to keep ignorin' it, hopin' the crew doesn't notice." An attempted smile vanished as she choked back another heave.

Little Feather did not respond. Anne looked into the girl's beautiful dark eyes above high cheeks. They softened and grew tender. In that look, Anne saw that the girl shared the dilemma remaining close and helping best she knew how.

"Ship off the port bow!" came a shouted report.

"Well," Anne said, "Solution at the ready or not…and stomach churning or not, I must be Captain Andrew and go command this ship." She swallowed repeatedly, hoping the gag reflex would find its way back to the bottom of her stomach and out of her throat. Taking cleansing breaths, she pinched and slapped color into her cheeks. She straightened and climbed the ladder up through the hatch and joined the crew on deck. "The situation, Bear…what is it?"

"It be a demasted caravel sitting dead in the water, Cap'n."

Anne directed her eyes to where he pointed. "Aye. It be rollin' mightily in these swells. When the waves grow taller, it'll capsize." She ordered the sails of Windsong's Freedom released. Topsails dropped so they might take time to check the situation. Adjusting course, she approached slowly and saw about a dozen men waving wildly. As they drifted closer, she heard pleas above the noisy wind. "Help us! We are stranded and adrift!"

Fearing an old pirate's trick she had employed in the past, Anne cautiously maintained distance. "Why are you without sails?" she shouted through cupped hands. "Where is your canvas?"

"We were surprised and attacked by well-armed French Corsairs. We've been robbed and left to perish."

Windsong's Freedom slowly closed the gap between the two vessels and Anne heard a familiarity in the voice of the spokesman. The news of particularly ruthless Frenchmen was unsettling. She paced the rail. "Yes, we've heard news of those buccaneers. Apparently they're a savage lot."

"Yes. Yes they are. Can you help us?"

The two ships came together.

Anne finally saw the man plainly. She recoiled with recognition. "James Bonny? Why in the name of Lucifer are you here?" Only after the name cleared her lips did it occur to her what a mistake it was to say it aloud. She glanced side to side as inquisitive faces of her men came into peripheral view. The crew began to crowd close, all curious.

Taken aback, James stuttered, "But who...how...I don't understand." Leaning far forward over the rail of the disabled ship, nearly to the point of going overboard, he studied her appearance for a moment as she attempted to cover the lower half of her face with an arm but too late.

"Anne? Is that you?" he asked haltingly. "My lovely Anne?"

Bear looked at Anne for a moment, studying her and the situation. "Would ye like for me to be killin' him now, Cap'n Andrew...you know, for insultin' ya like that?"

Weakened by a churning stomach, Anne managed only a quick headshake. Another heave welled from her gut. It was out of control. She vomited over the rail into the swells below.

Now, Nani's people began tightening a semi-circle behind her, wanting to know what was going on, crowding in for a better look. She had neither desire nor inclination to look them in the eyes just yet, keeping her head down over the rail as vomit drool strung from her slack mouth.

Everyone was silent and staring.

An unbearable situation had suddenly been thrust upon her. She did not know what to do or say. No longer was she the imposing Captain Andrew the Protector. Instead, a flash of nausea transformed her into a small frail woman whose identity had been blurted for all to hear.

James clapped his hands and laughed. "It *is* you." But the joy went away as fast as it came. Anne had threatened to kill him if she ever saw him again. It was clear on his face he just remembered that. He held long, windswept hair over his ears in frustration. "Of all the ships and all the people sailing Gulf waters, how could I have been so unlucky as to be granted your presence before all others? Am I already dead and simply unaware? Is this my last stop before hurled into the pit of Hades?"

Staring into the rolling swells beneath her, she muttered, "French Corsairs plundering a West Indian caravel…itself bent on thievery." Suddenly nothing made sense. She continued shaking her head and mumbling. "Windsong's Freedom also looks for treasures to take. We would have ransacked that caravel had the French not beaten us to it." With a disgusted clench of teeth she spoke louder. "When pirates plunder pirates then I'm certain it's time to quit." Louder yet, "It's like eatin' my own bloody foot to survive! What the hell has it come to?"

Unwilling to address the situation with her ex-husband until she brought the tense situation aboard Windsong's Freedom to conclusion, she turned away from him. Her crew deserved the truth. The time had come.

Weakened, she supported her limp self on the rail. Illness was laced with resignation. She removed the leather tricorn from her head. With a listless flip, she dropped it to the deck. She pulled the rawhide strip from her hair and shook out her long tangled red tresses.

"What's goin' on Cap'n Andrew?" Bear asked.

Looking to Bear but purposely speaking loud enough for everyone to hear, "My name is not Andrew. It's Anne...Anne Bonny."

Gasps of quickly drawn breaths came from the crush of men.

"For these months we have been together you have been under the command of...a woman."

Shock electrified the crew. Tension thickened the air. Surprise washed every face.

Nani whispered the translation to his people. But only the black men showed surprise. The four women among them were clearly not surprised.

A general buzz of whispered voices spread across the deck of Windsong's Freedom.

The situation reached an explosive crossroads.

Little Feather pushed through the shoulder-to-shoulder throng and broke through the tightening crowd to join Anne at her side.

Laddy followed sporting a faint grin, having known Anne's secret all along.

Unable to endure speechless scrutiny any longer, she stepped boldly up to Bear and stood toe-to-toe with the big man. She had to look straight up to connect with his eyes. "Well, what is your thought, you big ape? Do you wish to throw me overboard?"

"Beggin' your pardon, Cap'n, but I prefer havin' a word with the men before I answer, if that's agreeable, sir... er, m'am?"

He didn't wait for permission. He herded the crew to a distant corner of the ship. A heated discussion ensued. Angry words were hissed but not plain enough for Anne to know what was said.

A slight built, yet well-muscled young man, naked from the waist up, flailed sinewy angry arms.

Bear told him something.

The boy ignored it and continued ranting.

Bear allowed the boy to have his say. The big man again said something, this time accompanied by a gentle gesture with a relaxed arm.

It didn't quell the young man's anger. The boy stopped addressing Bear and was now taking the debate directly to the crew.

After listening to his ramblings a few more seconds, Bear suddenly threw a massive fist and connected with the boy's jaw, sending him reeling across the deck, flopping prone on his stomach. He made a single attempt to get up but groaned, collapsed to his knees, and fell over unconscious.

Bear returned to face Anne. "We've talked it over. Here's what we agree: You've commanded this ship disguised as Cap'n Andrew and during that time have made us wealthy with your guidance. If I'd known in the beginnin' you were a woman then…yes, I'd likely have favored feedin' you to the sharks. But now, be you a man or be you a woman makes no difference. We shall just call you Cap'n Anne and go on from here." A grin spread across the big man's face. "Besides ma'am, we've seen you in action with a cutlass and rapier. It's not somethin' we care to test."

Maternal tears welled more quickly. She had little control but dropped her head anyway, hiding sentimentality. She turned away to face the crippled caravel and James Bonny. "Then I shall do now what I must do as the captain of Windsong's Freedom. I'm sure it's what any good captain would do."

Hearing a moan by the young man just then regaining consciousness a few feet away, the crew turned to see him sit upright. "By the way, Cap'n Anne," Bear blurted, "We did have one naysayer. But I don't think ya need to be worryin' 'bout him."

The crew broke into boisterous laughter. The last vestige of tension released. Again, the crew had become one under the guidance of the same captain now known for who she actually was—the lady pirate, Anne Bonny.

Now comfortable in giving full attention to the problem at hand, Anne believed she knew the best course of action. "Though you'll probably deny it, James, I know that it was you who gave the position of the Providence to Governor Lawes' men off that Jamaican coast. It led to my capture. By that same cowardly act, I have likely lost my dear friends Mary Read and Calico Jack Rackham to the hangman. I don't know. But even if not, you are responsible for their suffering. I further believe money is your god, gold your mistress, and power your seducer. Your heart has no room for love beyond that. You're a manipulative snake and cannot be trusted. Therefore, the choice was made before I found you today. I'm just giving it a voice."

James quietly listened to Anne's rambling, clearly knowing she was his only possible way out of this dilemma. Therefore, he heard her words but acceptance of them was not on his face. Still, he did not throw an accelerant on an already fiery situation by speaking his mind, but his grip on the rail and the quivering lip told of dwindling hope and growing anger.

"Furthermore, James Bonny, had I not escaped that stinkin' Jamaican prison at St. Jago, I would have hanged too, sharin' the likely fate of my friends. You set me adrift, thinkin' I'd die by someone else's hand so you could be rid of me yet keep the blood off your own filthy hands. Doesn't matter. You *are* guilty of murder. I'm an eyewitness to that intent. Now that I've rendered judgment, I shall pass sentence—"

"But Anne, I love you!" he shouted.

Her bland expression didn't waver. "And I you…once upon a time."

Pacing to a fro for a moment, she then announced for all to hear, "It appears passing sentence may be unnecessary, as the saints have apparently already done so. You, James Bonny, are to continue your journey unimpeded, set adrift, and I prefer to believe that it was preordained; a sentence handed you, not by me, but by omnipotent forces for your evil deeds, using French pirates as a divine tool. I further believe the saints blessed me with this opportunity for closure so that I might have the chance of ridding you from my head forever. Therefore, I shall not interfere.

"Anne, you can't do this—"

Your men should not have to accept the same fate that results from your cruel stupidity. They are welcome to join us on Windsong's Freedom. And then you shall be free to continue your one-way voyage to hell...alone." She turned her back on him. "I think I've said quite enough on the subject."

Upon hearing the news the men from the caravel, using all means at their disposal poured over onto Windsong's Freedom. Some swung across on ropes. Some jumped. All cheered.

Looking beyond the bobbing and rolling caravel as its crew came aboard, Anne observed that the sky had turned more ominous. Raindrops began to leave darkened spots on the deck. Wind gusts increased. Although early in the afternoon, the light dimmed to a dusk-like appearance.

"Raise top sails. Draw in the rest. Let's fill them with wind, lads and move on before we share James Bonny's fate."

Anne ignored his pitiful pleas as sobbing words faded in the distance. James Bonny had become just one more nightmare that needed to be forgotten. She bid him farewell and all the bad dreams born of his actions.

Looking north, in the direction of their still-distant destination, she realized outrunning a hurricane that moved west but northeast of their position was a slim chance indeed. Skies darkened as did their immediate future. But turning inland and racing west to search for a sheltered beach along the Mexican coast was not an option. It would give Peckary's warship time to catch up. A battle seemed inevitable whether it be from a well-heeled English war galleon from behind or head-on into a raging storm. Chances for surviving either weren't good.

Security for those under her command and the future of her unborn child suddenly seemed quite far beyond her grasp. She needed a magician's wand.

# Chapter Twenty-seven

The storm had yet to overtake Windsong's Freedom although its outer bands announced that it'd soon be upon them. Swells were rolling mountains lifting the vessel to each peak then dropping it into valleys between, obliterating views of anything but water. Even the sky presented roiling clouds that did not appear any drier than the Gulf waters. Anne wrenched her hands over the rail partly afraid and partly to maintain balance. Control of the ship was becoming tenuous. *God have mercy. We're sailing directly into a giant watery cocoon. This vessel will be no sturdier than a floating leaf in such turbulence.*

Shouting over gusting wind, "Bear, steer in line with the swells, let's go against that roll. Keep the bow into the waves. We're at their mercy and will go wherever the waves take us lest we capsize."

The warning scarcely had cleared her lips when gusts became difficult to stand against. Forced to set aside her race for New Orleans, she and the crew now stood against a foe they couldn't defeat, and it would be lucky if they outlived it. She set her jaw and resisted flickering desire to give up. *It's only a temporary inconvenience. We'll make it.*

"Aye, Cap'n," Bear yelled. "Into the wind we go."

Mr. Lark struggled at the wheel against yet another rudder shift, an ongoing problem in erratic and powerful currents.

Bear ran to lend support, giving a mighty shove to a long oak pole at the stern. The added leverage assisted the helmsman. The big man had rigged it directly to the rudder shaft that extended up the rear of the ship. One man simply couldn't control the stern rudder against the uncontrollable power of the waves.

A single forward jib, narrowest of three, was all the canvas left aloft to facilitate steering. It strained against the gale, the rigging squawked and groaned. All other canvas had been removed and stowed. The ship responded to the correction but reluctantly. The bow rose high with an enormous swell moving beneath them.

The crew stumbled and fell backwards until the giant wave rolled the length of Windsong's Freedom, giving steep rise to the stern pitching them forward like toddlers learning to walk. As the bow dipped water sprayed from bowsprit to stern.

The spray alone was difficult to stand against. Just standing topside became dangerous without an anchoring handhold at all times. A sudden unexpected wave could sweep the deck clean of crew like so much debris.

As biggest and strongest, Bear took responsibility as steersman, strapping himself to the rudder arm with a length of rope. Holding or changing course would take every bit of power he possessed in addition to Mr. Lark at the wheel up on the quarterdeck. Any one of the monstrous waves had the potential of rolling Windsong's Freedom over and sending it to the bottom.

Little Feather held a lantern out from a hatch below deck.

"Stay below deck!" Anne yelled. "The brunt of this storm hasn't reached us. There'll be no time to be fishin' people from the water if swept overboard. Use rags, ropes, or whatever you can find to stuff cracks around hatches and portholes—anyplace water might seep. Seal yourself in."

"But Anne—"

"Do as I say, girl! Seal it up tight! It's for all our safety, not just yours and those below. The ship must be kept light. No water in the holds. We must remain high in the water. Do you understand?"

Little Feather disappeared below the closing hatch. Light around the edge of it disappeared as material was stuffed into the cracks.

Staring at the darkening hatch, *I pray I'll see you in the morning, love.* The wind blew her hair straight. The sea spray intensified. It stung her face like gravel from beneath a bolting horse's hoof.

She couldn't take a single step without first replacing one handhold with another. It was no longer just the waves; wind alone could blow a grown man off the ship.

"Cap'n!" Bear shouted, "It might be wise if you be joinin' the others below deck!"

"You bloody big ape! Just because you now know me as a woman doesn't mean you can speak to me as anyone other than your captain."

Through a watery mass of beard and hair, the big man showed all his off-color teeth in an ear-to-ear grin in the dim light of a lantern just before it was blown from its hook, leaving the deck black as pitch.

Pulling a knife from her belt, she cut a length of rope, wrapped it around her waist, and tied herself to the rigging. "You just hold this little darlin' on course and don't let us go broadside! Ya hear me?" A harsh spray slammed her face. She spit seawater.

"Yes, Cap'n. I hear ya."

"If it happens, Windsong's Freedom will roll for sure." She grinned but knew he couldn't see it then shouted a jest anyway, "As ugly as you are, I'd still like to see you alive in the morning."

Bear howled with laughter.

She checked the knot of the rope that held her fast. "Everyone, find a length of rope. Tie yourselves to something. I don't want to lose a single one of you. I've grown accustomed to all your ugly faces."

She heard voices indicating compliance, but she could only hope they actually followed through. She couldn't see.

Although others were on deck, the darkness brought a strange loneliness. It quickly became easy to feel like the last person on earth and this could be death's transition to the afterlife. The only navigational tool left was the feel of the waves. They might as well be confined inside a cavern shaken by Satan himself. Darkness had become absolute.

"All hands," Anne shouted, "count aloud so we know you're still at your posts."

Voices called out from various points on deck. It was helpful, placing reference to physical boundaries of the ship. "Good," she yelled, "Keep it up." It was a comfort to hear the shouts. In such darkness it quelled loneliness.

Roar of wind and the drone of men counting ground on for several hours.

Then a voice called her name—a young voice. She searched the darkness. "Laddy, is that you?" she called out then spit seawater pulling saturated hair from her mouth.

"Captain Anne, where are you?"

"I'm at the center of the ship," she yelled above the roar of the wind. "Don't try to get here. Stay where you are!"

Words of warning came too late as a shrill young voice shrieked a second after a wave broke over the top of the ship.

It came from somewhere beyond the deck of the schooner.

Cutting the rope that bound her, she felt her way to the location of an empty oak barrel she remembered lashed to the rail. She fought to keep from joining him overboard, crawling, unable to stand. A simultaneous wave and roll of the ship slammed her into the rail. Her ribs depressed her lungs knocking the wind from her. She grimaced and clutched her side. Then, with renewed resolve, *Discomforts be damned.* "Laddy," she screamed, "I'll throw you a barrel. Find it and hang on. We'll come back for you. Do you hear me?"

There was no discernible reply.

"Laddy!"

She listened but heard nothing. Having no idea whether he heard her or not, or even if he remained on the surface, she still did what she could to give the boy a chance, desperately sawing through the rope binding of the barrel with her knife. Then, with one hand remaining on the rail, she pushed the barrel up and over it.

"Find the barrel, Laddy! Find it! We'll be back! I swear it!"

Still, she detected no response—nothing, aside from the roar of wind and water.

Clutching the rail against waves breaking over the ship into her, she strained to see but darkness was black upon black.

Suddenly, what seemed like a distant human voice pierced gale force wind, but it was impossible to be sure. Still, it was hope.

Anne lay fully prone, stretched out against the rail. She haphazardly retied the rope around her waist and a rail baluster then looked into the darkest night she'd ever seen. She held tight and let it all out. The pain of life crashed in upon her and she cried.

Water slammed into her back and kept her pinned to the rail, but there was no advantage to being anywhere else. She sobbed uncontrollably, convinced that to show favor was the same as sentencing that person to death. The urge to curse God was strong but a smidgen of faith prevented such blasphemy. Water hammered her. Disturbing images filled her head with visions of those she loved that had died. In each case it came as a result of a close association with her. Whether a death happened by her hand or indirectly didn't matter. *God, why do you damn me so? Would you rather I lie in Satan's bed?* She bawled.

At twenty-three, Anne had had a belly full of adventure and intrigue. She experienced more than most people do in a lifetime. The sanctity of life had finally found its place in her.

Every person that had ever been felled by her hand flashed before her. A dagger through the heart could cause no more pain. Shame washed over her along with the next wave. She lay baffled—confused that she remained alive while many she'd known did not. *Is pregnancy creating this strain upon my heart? Or do divine forces deliver messages I should be heeding?* For hours she struggled with the riddle of life. Strength leached away. Fatigue overwhelmed her. Wind, waves, and the passage of time became moot.

~ * ~

Awakening, she saw light beyond the turned rail spindles, her face poked between two of them. She forced swollen eyes to open wider. She moved then remembered a rope bound her body to the balusters. She noticed that somehow during the night, the rope had been securely retied. She had no memory of doing it. She couldn't be certain if she'd fallen asleep from exhaustion or if she might have been knocked unconscious. Pain and lumps on her head indicated the latter to be likely.

Movement was painful, but she had to see what the light of day revealed of her ship and crew. She twisted around and saw Bear asleep, his massive arm slung over the makeshift leverage pole attached to the rudder arm, and she glimpsed, in rapid succession, other members of the crew still lashed to rails, masts, balusters, or anything else they were able to find. All slept. Bear was no longer tied to the rudder arm he manned. It occurred to her he had endangered himself making sure she had been safely lashed to the rail.

The forward jib, the only canvas left up, was tattered and flapping impotently. But it must have done its job and provided that all-important small measure of maneuverability that helped Bear and the boys keep the ship into the waves. Swells were still larger than normal but not breaking anymore. The vessel rose and fell. The wind subsided, now only a stiff breeze.

Loosening the knot on her rope binding, she slipped it off and began the painful process of standing. Stiff joints crackled. She felt twice her age. After a quick body check for injuries, she took a moment to massage the swell in her belly. She mumbled, "Sorry for the rough night, my little darlin'."

She then headed straight for the hatch to the cargo hold below. Throwing it open, she saw the dim glow of a lantern still burning but no one seemed to care. Bodies were strewn all about. Everyone slept. She stared at the only face of a different color, Little Feather's. Heart-wrenching thoughts of the night before came back to her, and once again she pondered her purpose upon the earth, and figured the only way to guarantee Little Feather a long life was to get away and stay away from the girl so she might have the chance to grow to adulthood. *It's only a matter of time before you die simply because I call you friend.*

"We made it, didn't we Cap'n?"

Startled, Anne jerked her head around to see Bear hovering over her. She smiled. "Yes, my big hairy friend. We did."

"It would seem we caught the outside edge of the storm 'cuz we didn't go through the eye."

"It may have been our salvation. What's your reckonin' on our position?"

"I can only go with my gut." He looked around. "I believe we may be three days out, 'stead of the one. I think we may have to sail east by northeast for up to two days just to get back to where we were."

She pushed out her lower lip. "T'is a reasonable assessment, but there's a risk I'm compelled to take. We sail southeast for a day first. I must find Laddy."

"As you wish, Cap'n."

"Rouse the men, replace the jib sheet, check for damage then pull all canvas from the holds. We set full sails. Let's get on with it."

Odds were against finding the boy, but she followed her heart and put Windsong's Freedom at risk of capture by Peckary and his warship, or attacked by French Corsairs she now knew roamed these waters. Looking across the bowsprit, she thought, *Out there somewhere is my destiny.*

# Chapter Twenty-eight

Wind filled the sails and Anne went directly to a position at the bow. For fifteen hours, she scanned the water for signs of a boy, a barrel, or both. She kept the glass to her reddened eye refusing to stop even to quench thirst ignoring discomfort. Maintaining the vigil was all-important. Darkness had been the only reason she called off the search the night before. At first light, she resumed examining every square inch of the seeable Gulf surface. Precious hours ground by.

Little Feather joined her at the bow. "At what point do you accept that he is gone?"

Dark circles framed vein-laced eyes. "It draws close, I'm afraid." She collapsed the spyglass with a clickety-clack and returned it to the pouch on her belt. She turned to the young Iroquois and cupped her face in her palms. She watched the ends of her long, straight coal-black hair dance with each puff of sea breeze. She lovingly cleared the girl's face of errant strands with a sweeping finger. "You've been the wind fillin' my own sails and the reason I am here today. You are the sparkle that makes gems precious."

The young girl nervously looked about. "You cannot speak this way while the men are so close. You'll lose respect." She whispered with a hiss of harshness.

Unperturbed, "Maybe, but my heart is holdin' the question: What difference would it make in the grander scheme?" She rubbed the swelling lump in her belly.

Little Feather took Anne's hands and pushed them down to her sides. "There'll be time for such talk once we are in that French city you hold dear, but not yet. You have given voice to exhaustion. It does not fit in this time and place." Glancing about, Little Feather sought curious eyes. "You must give up this search and order Bear to turn us around. Time grows short."

The glassy eyes and dreamy look covering Anne's face persisted.

Little Feather whispered through clenched teeth, "Please, Anne, let's not invite darker times in trade for a single moment."

Gaze darting back and forth, Anne's lids fluttered. She began to understand the gravity of their dilemma. "Yes, yes. We must be headin' north," she finally said but it was halting. She looked across the deck spotting the big man laughing with another. "Bear, bring us about and lay in a course north. The time for searching is past. The time for New Orleans is upon us."

"Aye, Cap'n." He cupped his mouth and barked orders. "You heard the lady, Mr. Lark, turn us about."

Wooden pulleys squealed and ropes squawked against wood, the crew scurrying to fulfill Bear's order. Windsong's Freedom's bow responded. The ship began a sweeping arc until the sprit pointed due north.

Still, Anne couldn't let it go. She walked to the stern and visually combed open water as they distanced themselves from areas Laddy might have drifted should he have survived.

Something did catch her eye but it wasn't what she wanted to see and an unwelcome sight it was. A fast-moving sloop skimmed along at a pace common to the smaller more maneuverable vessel. Straining to see without the scope, she surmised it could be those French Corsairs.

Often she'd stalked ships upon the seas and now she must face the same situation but from a defensive standpoint. "Let no sheet go slack!" she yelled to the crew. "We'll not face them in battle if it's not necessary. It's certainly not in our best interests."

Watching the smaller and faster ship, she noted her timetable changed again and not for the better. *It's as if a noose tightens around our necks.*

"Bear," she shouted, "have the men roll out all cannon and reload with dry powder. Load all backups at their sides. We might be needin' them if that's the corsairs we've heard about." Running from man to man, she continued issuing orders, "All hands check your pistols and your muskets. Have blades in hand. Keep your powder dry, lads, and the slow matches burnin' and at the ready. I have a feeling you'll need every grain of that powder before the day's over."

Nani approached Anne. "It looks as though my vow to you will soon be tested."

"What vow?" she replied, eyes and mind focused on the approaching sloop.

"My promise to you. I'll not forget who freed us even in the heat of battle. We will fight ferociously to protect you and your interests."

"I shall not take time to explain," she told him, "but your promise of friendship does not bode well for you." She snapped a glance at the little black man. "That is, if you plan to live a long time."

"Possibly true," he said, obviously not baffled by the comment, "But I shall live and live loudly, all the way to the end." The warmth of his smile did not fit this situation, but it was a comfort. She returned the smile.

All the freed slaves gathered in a tight group. They began a melodic chant, presumably a tribal muster of courage. They swayed and pranced in unison, waving swords and clubs. Nani backed away from Anne, bowed to her, and joined them.

The battle ritual was picked up by the rest of the crew. They added a European twist to the chant; a bawdy barrage of insults aimed at the sloop, waving blades in a show of defiance.

Anne stood with hands firmly upon widening hips—Little Feather on one side, Bear on the other. She looked at the battle-ready group then shifted her gaze to the sloop that moved too fast to outrun. Shaking her head, "I'd prefer a peaceful sail to New Orleans with no more blood on my hands, but it doesn't appear that'll happen."

Bear," she said calmly, "give the order to drop sails and bring us about broadside. No use puttin' off the inevitable. Keep culverins at the ready, lads."

Little Feather pulled the cutlass from the scabbard slung around her neck hanging at her back. She sliced the air with practice swings.

"Take no unnecessary risks, sweet friend."

"Your fate is also mine," the girl replied.

"Run up the Union Jack," Anne yelled across the deck, "Let's see what attention that might bring. They surely won't respect it, but maybe they'll fear it."

From a distance of some two hundred yards, the sloop ruddered hard right, throwing the mainmast to a near forty-five degree angle. Once it settled, Anne got her answer with a muzzle flash and puff of thick gray smoke followed by a throaty boom and a whistling cannon ball. "Everyone down!" she yelled then fell to her face. The ball hit the forward spar. It shattered and left sails impotently limp and dangling.

She leaped to her feet. "They spoil for a fight. By God, we'll respond to their bloody invitation! Cannoneers, let's answer their call. Penetrate their forward hull if you can."

Timing the rocking motion of the ship, the first cannon fired a fraction of a second late. The ball fell short, splashing impotently.

The sloop moved to within a hundred yards and kept closing. It responded with two more cannon shots. The first high, whizzing over Windsong's Freedom hitting the water far beyond with a kerplunk and spray, but the second came in lower and struck just above a forward cannon port.

A powder keg exploded.

Men screamed in agony and dove through the jagged hole into the water for quick relief from fiery pain.

The sloop began an evasive maneuver. It appeared to aim the bow head-on at them.

"Aha, trying to make a small target of yourself, are ye?" Anne muttered then yelled, "Fire all cannons now before they have a chance to come around.

Then roll out the four spares and fire them as well. We must do damage and do it now!"

Six cannons fired near-simultaneously, throwing up a thick blanket of grayish-white smoke. Before smoke cleared, Anne shouted, "Fire the spares!"

Spent cannon retracted and four primed culverins rolled into position. They fired as quickly as they hit the chocks. Smoke billowed.

The acidic cloud prevented a quick assessment of accuracy.

When it cleared, she saw the sloop had successfully come about and on a collision course. "Bloody hell, we may be done for." Then she noticed something else—a hole in the forward hull. It was above the waterline, but water rushed through it when the sloop dipped between swells.

"She's takin' on water, lads! Prepare to be rammed!"

"Bear, try to get us around enough so it might glance away!"

Bear yelled the order to the helmsman then manned the makeshift rudder arm that aided them during the hurricane. As the helmsman turned the wheel as fast as possible, Bear lived up to his nickname and roared as he shoved the rudder arm with both hands, using all his weight. His strength overpowered the helmsman and threw him away from the fast spinning wheel.

Windsong's Freedom shuddered a response but agonizingly slow.

Anne clung to hope that the maneuver might prevent being rammed and sunk.

Windsong's Freedom now exposed a three-quarters forward posture.

A wave lifted the bow of the attacking sloop just as it made impact, but the bowsprit of Windsong's Freedom took a lucky dip at the same time. It gored the hull of the aggressor as it rebounded.

Planking from the sloop broke and splintered off into the water. The lower portion of the exposed area was below the waterline. The ship of the French Corsairs now had a gaping hole in the hull. Water rushed through it.

Armed men came spilling over the front of the sloop onto the deck of Windsong's Freedom.

The blacks were the first line of defense. Nani shouted orders in their native language. He personally took on the first to set foot on the deck of the ship they were honor-bound to defend.

The impact caused the sterns of both ships to come together quickly and men leaped across. Anne's crew took the defensive posture. They fought to keep aggressors from coming over onto Windsong's Freedom and then to keep those that did from advancing across the deck. The line of resistance held.

Fighting was savage and bloody. The corsairs showed no mercy, taking scalps and ears as souvenirs.

Strangely, they seemed to be avoiding killing blacks. Instead they clubbed them unconscious whenever possible. The white crew they skewered and hacked to death. But they underestimated the ferocity unleashed in the blacks.

Seeing the bloody rampage reeling out of control, Anne back-slashed the belly of one nearest and yelled, "Little Feather, do you see someone who looks like a leader?"

Equally busy, Little Feather ducked a wild swing by a sword and fell on her buttocks. As the attacker prepared to run her through, she hacked his ankle with a short chopping motion. He screamed and bent at the waist to grab for it. She slashed his throat.

"Over there," she shouted wiping a spray of blood from her face. "That man with the red scarf, curly black hair, three men at his back."

The Indian girl had no more time to talk as another would-be killer charged. She leaped to her feet and engaged him.

Anne turned her back on her friend and slashed her way through the crush of fighting men. Smoke filled the air. Muskets and pistols fired in all directions.

Bear wielded a club longer than his arm in one hand and a sword in the other. If he couldn't cut them, he crushed their skulls. Anne didn't worry about his ability to survive and kept her eye on the clean-shaven man with the red scarf covering his head.

Nausea swarmed her. Her face flushed. "Not now," she growled. "Bloody hell, I don't have time to be sick."

A screaming wild-eyed man lunged at her.

She sidestepped him.

He stumbled forward going down.

She hacked the back of his neck, narrowly missing the point of his sword.

She tripped and fell.

Having always been sure-footed, the awkward bobble surprised her—even frightened her. She jumped to her feet, panicked. She heard a grunt from behind and whirled around to block a downward slash by a sword whooshing through the air.

She looked directly into the eyes of the man she sought.

The clash and clang of blades was fast, furious, and nonstop.

His speed matched hers, plus he was larger and stronger.

She couldn't advance and yielded, stepping back. She drew on all gumption but physical reserves dwindled. She had no time to send out a single aggressive move.

Dangerous swipes came at her quicker, faster than she could handle.

She stepped backward with every thrust and slash.

She tripped on a pulley block and fell.

Making peace with God crossed her mind.

She glanced up, desperately seeking where the point of his sword was.

One final defensive move was all she wanted.

The blinding sun over his shoulder washed out everything except a blackened silhouette.

Finally, the glint of steel caught the sun and flashed in her eyes.

It was overhead and pointed at her chest.

Raised high, he clutched it with both hands.

As it came down, she rolled left and heard a thwack as the point stuck in the deck near her.

Suddenly, a banshee-like yell was followed by the sound of metal against bone and Anne looked to see her would-be killer standing motionless. She rolled back in time to see his hands fall away from the sword. It remained stuck in the deck next to her arm.

From the sword her eyes went up. She saw his head tumble from his shoulders. Blood pumped in a stream from the stump of his neck. The body collapsed onto her. She shoved it off in revulsion and rolled away.

She froze, looking directly into the dying eyes of the detached head. The mouth still moved.

A much too feminine reaction overtook her. She dug her heels into the deck and pushed away on her butt, sliding away squealing and grating across the rough surface of the deck just to get away from the horror. She whimpered.

She looked to see if Bear had again come to her rescue—but no. Standing before her was a small black man with a very large sword. Nani had made good his vow. "Are you okay?" he said in a voice raised above the din of battle.

"Yes. Go. Protect yourself."

Crawling on hands and knees she retrieved her cutlass but did not stand to join the battle. She couldn't. She crawled into a corner, partially hidden by a small rowboat lashed to the rail. She made a tiny ball of her body and cried, terrified, totally without control.

Watching the battle from her hiding place, she flinched and whined each time another man fell.

The corsairs were a ruthless lot. The loss of their captain seemed to have little impact on how barbarously they fought. Nonetheless, the tide of the battle turned in favor of Windsong's Freedom.

Anne saw Little Feather looking about frantically before finally spotting her.

She ran to Anne and dropped to a knee, scooping her mentor and lover's head into her hands. "Anne, are you injured?" She swept her hands all over Anne's body for blood or puncture wounds.

"I must depend on you now more than ever. Not only does my body change but my mind changes too. I cannot control my fear. I'm suddenly too aware of my own mortality."

Realizing Anne's predicament, Little Feather took Anne's cutlass as well as her own and rejoined the battle. She fought tenaciously to protect her fallen friend, shielding Anne from all comers.

One by one, the blacks and the crew of Windsong's Freedom took out the attackers. But the French Corsairs had lived up to their reputation as a ruthless lot. Every last one had to be killed. Even the final man standing refused to lay down his sword and pike. The blacks swarmed him and shoved his body overboard.

The Frenchmen had been trained to fight to the death, and they did.

Bear jogged to where Anne lay. "Cap'n Anne, are you hurt?"

Little Feather intercepted him, planting her hands on his chest, "She'll be okay. Captain Anne just took a hard blow to the head—knocked senseless."

As the crew dragged bodies to the port rail, throwing them into the water, Anne made her way starboard, watching the French sloop drift off. The bow rode low with the weight of water filling the area beyond the forward bulkhead.

"Should we try to salvage anything, Cap'n?" Bear asked.

With no enthusiasm, "Just let her sink to hell where she belongs."

As she turned her back to it, she heard an unintelligible human voice from the sinking ship.

Spinning back to see the stern rising high, she again heard it—a young voice in broken English. "Laddy!" she screamed.

Anne fumbled with her belt and scabbards, dropping them to the deck and dove into the water. Swimming hard, she saw through water-filled eyes the ship had begun to list to its side. It was beginning a roll before going down bow first.

"Hang on Laddy! I'm coming," she shouted, sputtering through seawater.

Reaching the partially submerged deck, she sought hand and foot holds struggling against severe inclination as the ship began a downward dive. "Laddy, where are you?"

"Here, Anne. Up here."

Snapping her head toward the call, she saw him, hands to his back tied to a stair baluster, now hanging at a grotesque angle that would surely wrench his shoulders from their sockets. Struggling to climb the steeply inclined deck, she finally made it but his legs dangled free and were already sinking into the water as the ship began its dive. It sank as fast as she climbed.

Pulling a knife from her pantaloons, she cut his bindings.

He fell free.

"Swim away Laddy, quickly, before the ship sucks you down." With one hand on his tattered shirt collar, she paddled furiously with the other.

Bear rowed toward them in a small boat. Water churned at its sides. He made the distance quickly.

He reached into the water and with one hand pulled the young black boy into the boat by the waist of his shredded canvas pants.

Seconds later, Anne was helped into the boat as well. She collapsed, sprawled, huffing for breath.

Laddy cried and apologized repeatedly, but she couldn't understand why. She sat upright. "Slow down, boy. Tell me your story."

Sniffing, "They spotted me holding on to a barrel in the water and picked me up. I told them I had fallen overboard from a slave schooner in the storm. When they spotted this ship I told them it was the slave ship. I'm sorry. Please don't kill me!" His little body convulsed with sobs.

She was astonished he'd even think such a thing. "Kill you?" You told the truth. This is a slave ship and you did fall overboard. Besides, you planted seeds of overconfidence in them that this would be a poorly armed slaver. It likely gave us a much-needed edge in battle. We would have been engaged regardless of what you said." She pulled him to her breast and hugged him.

He looked up at her. "They were going to take this ship and sell us in New Orleans," he said, still sniffing. He again buried his face in her chest.

*If they fought that savagely with such bloodthirsty abandon just for slaves, God only knows what they would have done for the real treasure aboard.*

As Bear rowed back to Windsong's Freedom, Anne sat behind him and stared at muscles working in his back. With considerable trepidation she wondered: *How might you react if you should find out about my emotional instability, big man? You may appear the gentle giant but I know you control the hearts and minds of the crew. A pregnant woman and an Indian girl would not stand a chance.*

Sitting straight, pointing her chin in a staunchly dignified pose, "Bear, you and the men fought valiantly today. I shall not forget your aggressive tenacity against formidable odds." She glanced over her shoulder up to the deck of Windsong's Freedom. "Sadly, we are left with barely enough crew to sail the ship, much less engage anyone else in battle."

"Aye. 'Tis my life and treasure I fought for. One without the other is pointless," he said with a shrug. "Besides I fancy a quieter life somewhere. I'm not getting any younger, ya know."

"You are wiser than you appear," she said with a much-relieved wink and smile.

# Chapter Twenty-nine

Thinking back, Anne marveled at how fast it happened. Sailing from the Carolina coast southward then southwest to hug the northern tip of Yucatan, eventually turning north to Louisiana territory had been a remarkably quick sail.

*Maybe I regret ending my days upon the seas that makes this time seem short? I should be thankful.* Every adventure played out in fine detail in her mind. Mumbling a quick prayer, she gave thanks that Little Feather remained alive and Laddy had been successfully brought back into the fold.

The voyage netted substantial treasure, despite bloodthirsty corsairs and a hurricane. Her world continued to change color. Every day how she looked upon problems and possibilities took on hues previously unknown due to her changing physical condition. *Until the baby is born, my thoughts are my enemies. They crush courage. That could get me killed.*

Land came into view. For the moment, she stood satisfied. The Promised Land had just appeared.

Now within sight of the port of New Orleans, Anne ordered sails disengaged and dropped. At a central point on deck she knelt—total spoils splayed in piles in front of her. Standing over her, to her left, were Nani and the sixteen surviving freed slaves, to her right, Bear and the remaining twelve members of the crew. Little Feather and Laddy stood behind her.

Taking a moment to look the tattered assemblage over, "We are a raggedy group, aren't we?" she said then drew a broad grin.

Nani translated and a young black woman laughed aloud then slapped her mouth, cutting it off abruptly.

But Anne gave her cause to smile again when she, too, laughed.

They all joined in.

Mirth provided a soft introduction to a serious subject. Anne let them have this moment.

Destiny waited.

When laughter died, seriousness was the phoenix that rose from its ashes.

"It's not without sadness we mark our departure, but let it be known that you…everyone of you have earned my deepest respect and can depend on me in the future should you need my assistance. I'll tiptoe through hell, past Satan and his minions if necessary, to be at your side."

She rose and placed hands upon Nani's shoulders, "Tell your people, my friend, they are free and now have enough money to secure that freedom in America if they wish to stay. If not, that's equally fine. It is their choice as free people and may seek to buy passage home if that is what they choose."

She turned her attention to Bear. "And you, you big ape, have earned a place as my lifelong friend. I hope that is not a death sentence for you."

He roared with laughter.

"As far as I'm concerned," she told him, "the ship is yours to command…or not. It's your decision."

"What I've said before I meant." The big sailor's head dangled humbly upon his shoulders. "I'll be disembarkin' in New Orleans. I have no intention of returnin' to seafarin' ways, ma'am. I'm feelin' father time in my joints…the bastard. Now that I be havin' the means, I fancy a calmer life. If Windsong's Freedom is now mine, then I'll be givin' it to my men, along with me wish for clear sailin' forever."

"Really," she said then thoughtfully pursed her lips. "What would your thought be on growing cotton, gathering pecans, and planting sweet potatoes in a fertile piece of bottom land?"

Surprise brought his drifting head to attention. "Be a farmer!" Are you daft?"

"I think you know the answer to that question, but it's no answer to mine." She paused. "A simple farmer is not what I had in mind. I'm speakin' of a full partnership in a plantation; the largest, most magnificent piece of real estate we can be securin' with our combined wealth." She patted his belly, "And don't ya worry none. We'll hire a staff to handle the hard work."

Anne turned to the gathering. "As a matter of pure fact, I offer this same proposition to anyone here. I'll give you time to think about it."

She sat and began dividing the substantial purse. The crew became a hiss of whispered voices as did the black contingent. After a time there still was no answer.

"Let me add if it's a wonder you have, each one of you has means to be an equal partner. I'd welcome that kinship."

Nani jabbered the translation of what Anne had said. A buzz went up among the blacks.

"It sounds like an amazing adventure," he said and then put his palms together in a gesture of reverence. "But I believe the only chance of a real future my people back home have is through education. It's a difficult decision I make but I must regretfully decline so that I might return there and teach."

"A noble cause indeed," Anne said, eyes still on divvying the valuables.

He listened a moment longer to his native language being bandied about then spoke for them too. "My people agree, but no two reasons are the same, save one—this land is foreign. They just want to go home."

Laddy dropped down and knelt with her to be eye to eye. "What about me? Am I old enough to have a say?"

"With all you've been through?" She stopped treasure sorting and chuckled. "How could we not include you? Of course you have an equal say and share of all this." She fanned her arms wide at the wealth spread before them. "You have every right to dictate your own future and money enough to be makin' it happen."

Giddy, he clapped his hands and squealed. "Then I want to stay. I have no family. You are my family." He hugged Anne so hard she nearly toppled from her haunches.

"As do I," said Little Feather. "You are my family and my life. I only say this for their ears. You've known it all along."

Bear alternately chewed then pursed his lips. He scratched his beard, brow furrowed.

Anne noticed. *Had he looked that way when I first met him, I'd have wagered large sums it was not intelligence I was seein'.* "Well, ya big ape…what'll it be? Your face tells me you're thinkin' about it."

"'Tis a harder decision than I imagined."

"While you think on it, tell me what your real name is?"

He boyishly swept the deck with the point of his toe. "Horatio Marple, ma'am. My friends used to call me Hory. At least I think they were my friends."

"I'll make you a deal, Horatio Marple. Join us and you'll never hear me call you by such a disgusting nickname as Hory. Otherwise, I'll make you no guarantees."

Tight knitted brow relaxed.

"I see wisdom on that hairy face of yours. You hesitate but I dare say an intelligent answer is about come from that mouth nearly hidden by whiskers."

"If stayin' at your side is what ye mean by an intelligent choice then, yes, I suppose it is."

He decided to join Anne, Little Feather, and Laddy, giving up piracy while his head still rested upon his shoulders and his neck unbroken by the hangman's noose. The big guy only appeared dim-witted. Anne had come to realize the man was amazingly analytical, clearly understanding the odds stacked against his chances of survival if he remained in a pirate's life. Now he bet that the day for being captured or killed awaited if he chose otherwise and not that far in the future either.

The remainder of the crew needed no more time to think. Being younger, they were not quite ready to give up the adventurous life. They struck a bargain with the blacks to return them to their African homeland for a sizeable sum from their share of the wealth.

All things now agreed and debts settled Anne took leave to stand at the bow. Wind blew her hair away from her face. She'd ceased hiding femininity under scarves and tricorns, allowing long curly red hair to play upon the wind. She looked to her version of paradise, New Orleans.

She then looked down to her protruding belly. She placed a hand on it and patted then whispered, "We're almost home, little one."

~ * ~

The search for a plantation site proved quick and simple. The eclectic family found eight hundred acres a quick jump north of New Orleans, mostly fertile bottomland set in a broad picturesque delta. The enticing piece of ground was dotted with massive moss-strewn oak and pecan trees—a picture of tranquility. It drew Anne as a moth to a flame. *No other place will do. This is it.*

She needn't have worried about a consensus; it was unanimous—an enthusiastic meeting of the minds. They pooled money and made the purchase.

Construction of a house befitting such a fine plantation-to-be and all outbuildings began the same day papers were signed. If weather conditions proved favorable over the fall and winter, they'd move in to a spacious new home by spring.

The boardinghouse they temporarily called home was tense at times. The crotchety old lady who owned it had a deep prejudice against an Indian and a black living there. The old hag didn't seem too keen on Bear either. Anne employed subtle intimidation to keep the old lady quiet about stupid prejudices. The boardinghouse was cramped but homey and would keep them warm and dry until the new house was finished.

Little Feather, with Anne's help, convinced Bear that shaving his face, getting a haircut, and taking a bath is actually a good thing and not at all unmanly. It took time to turn his head on the subject. Bear did almost anything Little Feather asked of him.

"'Tis infatuation, I tell ya," Anne told her with a wink.

Anne seized the philosophical approach to his hygienic pursuits or lack thereof. His mindset had certainly been cut from a different bolt, having lived life by rules many did not understand. She did. Anne understood well that turn of mind. Persuading the big man remained gentle but relentless.

Eventually the hairy seafarer consented to losing some of that hair. He sat in a chair in the boardinghouse as Little Feather stood in front of him, waiting for a decision. He was so big that sitting was the only way Little Feather could look him directly in the face. And she did with admiration.

He cast an adoring eye to her. "I suppose amendin' me look won't be hurtin' anythin'." He fingered a beard that nearly hid his entire fist. "If, of course, that's what you think I should be doin'?" When he spoke to Little Feather, he was humble to a fault, stammering. That afternoon was dedicated to the barber.

Sporting new clothes to complement grooming, the former pirate who once appeared more primate than man, now boasted sophistication Anne could not have imagined as long as he kept his mouth shut and didn't show his teeth.

On the day Anne exposed her pregnancy to the big guy, she worried he might fly into a rage over having been duped. It didn't happen.

He spoke of how best to raise a child in a communal family situation. He looked upon himself as an uncle becoming. He included himself in a division of duties concerning care for the child.

The one Anne often called the big ape had a gentle side he seemed more than ready to show.

Anne credited Little Feather entirely. Bear and the Iroquois girl became inseparable. *There'll come a day those two will be making the same plans with their own child.* She felt strange about that—exhilarated yet tinged with jealousy.

Each passing day her belly swelled.

The life Anne left behind grew distant; some days imagining it had all been a bad dream. Now confronted with a different future, it was like remembering a nightmare she had no desire to revisit.

One last alias could not be avoided. She became known to New Orleans as Anne Hebert, transforming into an Irish widow of a wealthy French landowner hailing from a plantation near Biloxi. She hoped she could forget it as an alias, carrying the name Anne Hebert to the grave and allow Anne Bonny to rest in peace.

Laddy followed his surrogate mother everywhere. He catered to her, leaping at every request. As pregnancy began to restrict activities, he joyfully did what she couldn't. He now spoke English with only a hint of accent but also had begun to pick up some of Anne's Irish brogue. Anne admired his tenacity and loved him as her own. His thirteenth birthday was coming. She intended to celebrate it.

In the first week of the eighth month of her pregnancy, she began this day as usual. "Come on, Laddy. Let's ride out to check the progress of the carpenters."

She climbed into the seat of a one-horse buggy in front of the boarding house and waited. She loved seeing the latest improvements made on their new home. "Laddy, come on. Don't be dawdlin', boy."

He burst from the front door, ran then leaped into the buggy beside her.

"Those craftsmen have a tendency to be sittin' idle without frequent prompts from the one holdin' the purse strings ya know."

Bear and Little Feather stayed behind in town, locating and securing services from other construction experts, hoping to accelerate the timetable, maybe even move up the day they could get out of that cramped boardinghouse.

It was the fifth day of November, the morning foggy. Buggy wheels creaked, rattling over stones and depressions in the road. Anne kept the pace slow and comfortable, at peace and excited about the future.

"It'd be better if the house were finished. The baby deserves more comfortable quarters," Laddy told her.

"Aye, little man. T'is a fact. The boardin' house is cramped but the appropriate time must be taken so we have the best home possible for the baby…for the rest of us too, I might add." She smiled and stroked his shiny black cheek. "Nothing shoddy for us, right?"

"Yes, Mistress Anne…only the best."

The construction site appeared out of the fog. Anne reined the horse up close to the two-story skeletal frame. She heaved a sigh, the sight satisfying. It was a visible marker separating the new life from the old.

They strolled around a huge pecan tree decorated with dangling Spanish moss, moisture from the dense morning fog dripped from its tips. They approached the construction site admiring what would eventually be their home, tiptoeing around grassless muddy patches.

Men walked about on narrow planks high above the ground unperturbed by precarious footing. The rasp of saws and pound of hammers harmonized, echoing back from the dense fog. The smell of fresh-cut wood filled the wet air. She saw the hazy outline of men going about their business in the mist. They worked hard. She'd given them a deadline of having the house closed to the weather before heavier winter rain set in. That could be weeks or only days away. Much remained to be done.

Walking the length of the house, she dodged piles of building materials and scraps. "Our home, Laddy, that's what this will be…our home. It fills my heart with pride and joy" She sighed.

Laddy now stood as tall as she. He hung on every word.

Without warning a heavy wet log butt, trimmed from a beam, fell from the framework overhead.

"Look out below!" a worker shouted.

It struck Anne in the lower back. The heavy beam stump drove her to the ground and slammed her hard against other waste lying strewn about. Air rushed from her lungs as did water from between her legs. The ground slapped her unconscious.

She woke having no knowledge of how long she had been out. Her head lolled to the side. Somehow, she'd made it back to her bed in the boardinghouse.

A painful cramp replaced bewilderment.

She bolted upright and screamed. Shooting pain in her back offset the contraction.

Little Feather sat at her side and gently pushed her down. "You have been badly injured. You must control your breathing."

The young Iroquois's admonition convinced Anne the cramp was indeed labor and coupled with the injury to her back, agony squeezed perspiration from her face. It was excruciating. Drawing a full breath was impossible. She panted like an overworked sheepdog.

The young girl wiped Anne's forehead with a cool damp rag. "Your labor is premature."

Between breaths, "If there comes a choice between my life and the baby, save the child." She gasped and pressed her head back into the pillow.

Little Feather nodded agreement.

Anne wondered why the girl didn't argue.

The labor didn't feel normal. She felt as if her body attempted expelling a foreign object, not at all like her first pregnancy.

Anne gnashed teeth, creating an amplified squawk from between retracted lips.

Little Feather had her bite into a leather patch then ordered, "Push!"

Anne gave it her best then relaxed as the contraction subsided. "It must be alive. Why else would it try so hard to stay inside?"

A forming smile was cut short by another contraction.

She came up, squealing, and pushing.

"If the baby cannot be pushed out and is without life, you'll die too. I won't let that happen." Little Feather snaked her hand inside Anne to find the infant's head.

Anne raised up, suspending on elbows; her knees wide apart, sweat streamed dripping from her nose and chin. Tangled red hair matted to her forehead.

Another contraction hit.

She took two quick breaths then held it.

She pushed.

She screamed and fell back.

Another vise-like pain gripped her.

"Again!" Little Feather ordered.

Jaw muscles bulging, veins stood proud on Anne's neck. She came off the bed and repeated the push. Breath escaped as a squeal but she didn't stop pushing.

"I've got it," Little Feather said.

Anne felt and heard a gush issuing from her body and fell back. She swallowed repeatedly unable to speak. But the lack of a cry made her force it. "The baby...alive?"

Fighting her way to her elbows she looked between her knees just as Little Feather rolled the slick, shiny infant over. It was a boy, a face the color of midnight blue, head misshapen. It was dead.

Saying nothing, Little Feather wrapped the lifeless little thing in a sheet and carried it away.

Bear and Laddy stood at the door and watched as the girl walked by. They stepped into the bedroom but hesitatingly so.

A mournful wail came from deep inside Anne as her heart broke. Pain, physical and emotional, poured out. The once hardened lady pirate shouted in anguish, "I have offended the saints with my life! They punish me by denying me a family!" She bawled for a baby that could not cry for itself. She covered her face with both hands.

Bear leaned over and gently placed a large square hand on her shoulder. He rubbed it in soft circles. He sat next to her. "You most certainly do have a family," he said in a deep yet childlike voice.

Little Feather walked back into the room and draped an arm around Laddy's shoulders. The boy cried for Anne.

"Look at us," Bear said, "we are your family. We'll always be at your back whether the enemy be a man, a bad feelin', or the tricks of your own mind...at your back, always. The words may not mean much right now, but they will."

Laddy sniffed. "Forever and always, Mistress Anne."

As had been the case so many times, just as the night became darkest and hope seemed to stand away, one door slammed shut just as another cracked open. The big man's words were like music but, for a while, wouldn't be enough. She rolled over, not wanting to look upon them. Sadness could not be talked away. Not yet.

# Chapter Thirty

After a cramped winter at the boarding house in New Orleans, spring and move-in day finally arrived. The concept of home and hearth was fast becoming more than a sought after dream for the family of rebel misfits, Anne Bonny as head mistress.

She used the word *misfit* often to describe herself, disbelieving she belonged anywhere, having to make her own space in the world and usually by force. The word was not a derogatory reference, just something four people of very different backgrounds had in common.

Anne and her family prepared to move into the new home they agreed to christen Windsong. The name meant something different to each one of them; to Anne and Little Feather it epitomized friendship, to Bear it was wealth, and to Laddy, freedom.

Anne took in the sight. The centerpiece of the plantation was this magnificent structure that stood imposingly before them now, a testament to local craftsmen and detail Anne refused to compromise on.

A broad veranda had newly constructed rockers and tables beckoning to a lifestyle of pristine comfort. The house boasted private bedrooms for each family member. Additionally, the second floor had been sectioned into quarters and dedicated to individual needs. All common areas were on the first floor and whether the need be for privacy, space, or both, it was available.

The four stood outside and looked upon the front elevation in reverential admiration hesitating to take that first step. It didn't matter that they'd all been inside many times. Today was different. Symbolism ran deep—far beyond wood, stone, and iron. This structure represented home—a powerful bend of mind for them all.

Little Feather, Bear, and Laddy looked to Anne to make the first move. She smiled but couldn't hold it long. "The only way this day could have been improved upon would have been if my baby boy were snuggled at my breast."

She sought no response nor did she receive one.

They listened to chirping birds darting about carrying bits of grass and straw to build spring nests. A myriad of early season wildflowers crowded their feet. Huge pecan trees were dressed in emerging lime green foliage, the most brilliant greens they'd wear all year. Spanish moss hung in dense tufts from them. The natural adornment added a festive appearance as the morning sun beamed warm. It struck the dew gathering on the hairy clumps and sparkled like gray crystals. The musty smell of rich damp earth added to the spectacular ambience.

Walking abreast, slowly at first, they chose to allow the spell of shared enchantment to linger. Each step brought a new view and a pause. They must know it from all perspectives—still unable to comprehend that this opulent home was their own.

Young and impulsive, Laddy could not contain enthusiasm. He pranced about and pulled on her arm. "Come on, Mistress Anne. Why do we move so slowly? Let's enjoy the view from *inside*."

Stepping through the front door of Windsong marked their entrance into a new life.

~ * ~

Busy days turned into busy weeks, an industrious and happy time. Setting up a planting and growing operation was the first order of business. Bear gladly accepted the title of foreman although his knowledge of what he oversaw was nonexistent. He went about hiring a crew versed in such specialized pursuits. He found help searching out healthy livestock.

Although offers came repeatedly and prices attractive, Anne refused to purchase slaves for Windsong—all workers were fairly paid. She never passed up a chance to call slave traders scum to their faces.

As on the ship, everyone looked to Anne as the final word on contentious issues. She listened to arguments but it was not to stand in judgment. It was to develop consensus. She possessed no more knowledge about what they did than Bear. She knew people but she had to learn the business. A small thing like ignorance did not stand in their way. For Anne it never did.

Stress sparked subtlety at work within Anne. She felt it but was powerless to prevent it. Her maternal nurturing side withered. She reverted to a cynical and abrupt creature given to outbursts and fits of anger. Tolerance of talkative strangers and dull witted people had narrow bounds. She offered no leeway for sluggish thinking. When negotiating, she regressed to intimidation if clever banter failed. The Anne Bonny of old reemerged.

She became aware of her growing reputation in the area, hearing the gossip come back to her. It spread throughout New Orleans that Anne Hebert of that new plantation north of the city, Windsong, had a fiery temper and should be avoided. A joke passed back to her was that if the scar on her forehead matched her red hair, it might be time to turn tail and run.

She exercised restraint but mainly at home. She never spoke badly about any of her family of misfits. But if truly angered, she'd fume for days and stay to herself. She feared loss of self-control around those she loved.

Taking the buggy into New Orleans on a late autumn day, Anne intended purchasing a bolt of cloth and sewing notions for a black family Bear hired in the spring. She planned on fulfilling a simple promise to Laddy. The boy was infatuated with their prepubescent daughter. He wanted her to have the gift of a new dress. It would be her first. Anne saw it as worthy and wanted to support such benevolence by the boy.

With little chitchat, she told the proprietor of the small general merchandise store of her needs. She waited impatiently for the order to be filled.

A man strolled through the door.

She glanced casually, disinterested. But while fingering a small stack of handkerchiefs, something struck her as familiar about him. She glanced again. The wheels of her mind began to grind. *I've seen that face...but where?*

The wife of the store proprietor approached the man offering assistance. In English but with a heavy French accent, he replied, "It is not merchandise I desire but information. I will pay handsomely if it is good information."

The accent and sound of his voice sparked an image of an angry French captain drifting away on the disabled Providence, yelling, "You and I will meet again! And I will have your life for this deed!"

The memory's abruptness jerked her head up.

She looked again.

It was him.

Angered merely by his presence, she believed the Frenchman to be one more manifestation of God's curse on her life.

A little voice in her head told her to remain calm, cautious, and quiet. She well remembered his talent with the blade—fast and strength enough to make speed count. Had it not been for Bear smashing a barrel stave into his head, he would've killed her; a strong reason to remain quiet. He was well heeled. She was unarmed.

It occurred to her she was staring at him. She quickly turned away, pretending interest in the proprietor's choice of merchandise to fill her order. She moved to keep her back to the Frenchman.

Having noticed Anne glancing in his direction before she turned away, he mistook that sudden jerk of the head as a gesture of disgust at his lack of manners. Removing his hat, he bowed slightly. "Good morning, mademoiselle."

She moved her head only slightly. "Good morning to you, sir." She refused him a profile view of her face.

He craned his head for a better look and studied her appearance. "Have we met somewhere before?"

"Not likely," she said, using words sparingly in a contrived southern accent. She dropped the Irish brogue best she could.

The wife of the proprietor offering assistance to the Frenchman became impatient, "Sir I have work to do. What is the information you seek?"

Pulling his eyes reluctantly from Anne, he said, "Yes. Yes, I'm sorry. I have forgotten my manners. I am Christian DeMornét. I am in search of a small fancy man, usually armed with cutlass, rapier, and pistols and well versed in their use. I believe he goes by the name Andrew. Some call him The Protector."

The woman appeared to give it thought. She looked to her husband but eventually both shook their heads. "Might I inquire your business with him, sir?"

"He and his crew of buccaneers attacked our slave ship last year, stole it and our cargo then set us adrift on his damaged and sinking ship." A wry smile smeared across his face. "But I have had partial satisfaction. I regained my ship. I sent its crew to the bottom of the deepest Gulf waters and sold the remaining slaves."

Anne's face reddened. An image of Nani flashed in her mind then the remnants of her crew.

She instinctively reached for her cutlass. All she felt was the frilly lace that trimmed the waist of her long dress. Angered she began to fidget staring straight away from him. Although her body jerked with quiet rage, she dare not release it. Not yet.

The proprietor placed her order on the countertop in front of her and noticed the scar on her forehead turning crimson. He babbled an apology, "I'm so sorry Miss Hebert for taking so long."

"And well you should be!" she barked into his face, releasing her anger and a fine spray of spittle upon him. She snatched up the merchandise and stormed from the small store.

Climbing into the buggy, she popped the horse with a whip. It whinnied and bolted. She whipped it into a run, moving with all haste to the waterfront. There she saw Windsong's Freedom and a group of strange men milling about her deck.

Removing the bonnet that hid her long hair and the pin holding the coiffure in place, she slung the tresses out, allowing it to tumble over her ears. She threw the headdress at her feet and whipped the horse to a full gallop back to Windsong.

As she related the story to Little Feather and Bear, it dawned on her how difficult just the telling of it was. Angered beyond good sense, she spouted incomplete facts buried within slobbery sprays. She stomped her feet and refused to see any situation that would end with the Frenchman alive. "Hell may be my destination, but I damn well will be seein' to it that he's there to meet me!"

"But Anne, beggin' your pardon ma'am," Bear said gently, "You've squared with that man before and could not match his speed or power with blades."

"Then I'll shoot the bastard!"

"Please," Little Feather said, stepping in and holding Anne's clenched fists, "The Frenchman did not know your identity. We maintain an advantage. Think about that. Maybe there is a better way to dispose of him without endangering our new way of life."

Anne yanked her hands from Little Feather and pounded a fist into an open palm. After a time pacing fast and choppy, her speed slowed. "You may be right. I need to be thinkin' on this for a time. I certainly don't want to endanger what we have dreamt of and built together."

She stopped the manic pacing altogether and whirled about. "But as God is my witness, before the sun reaches its noonday zenith tomorrow, I shall have had my revenge...somehow." Taking long breaths her anger seethed.

Hour after hour, Anne walked about the large house with no destination in mind just a reflexive by-product of planning, oblivious to everything and everyone around her.

Near dawn, exhaustion stalked her and eventually demanded the upper hand. She needed to sit. In mid-thought she slumped forward, muttering, "Damn you, Frenchman, for coming to ruin my life."

Her hands fell limp to her sides. She slept.

~ * ~

Awakening to the sound of agitated voices coming from the direction of the front door, she glanced to see the sun fairly high in the eastern sky through the window. Anne leaped to her feet and rubbed the blur from her eyes. She threw open the door to the parlor where she'd fallen asleep and entered the hallway and saw one of the plantation employees, hat in hands on the front porch, talking to Little Feather through the open door. "Oh, lawd missy. It's an awful tragedy," she heard him moan. "I don't know what be on his mind. He—"

"What's an awful tragedy?" Anne blurted.

Before he could speak again, Little Feather thanked him for coming with the information and sent him away.

"Little Feather, what in bloody hell's going on?"

Slowly closing the door behind her, Little Feather started to talk but choked. She looked to the floor.

"Please, love, tell me."

She pulled her eyes up to meet Anne's. "Bear is dead." Stoicism bred into her broke; her lip quivered as tears filled her eyes then spilled down her cheeks.

"Dead!"

"He thought you'd have no chance against the Frenchman because of your rage and went in your stead this morning. Even his strength could not match the speed of the Frenchman's rapier. According to the story, he took the point through his big heart."

A look of iron emblazoned Anne's face. She shrieked, slamming a fist down on a small table, knocking it over.

Again she screeched.

She reached for the seam on the top of her dress with both hands and ripped it away. Buttons flew. It fell to the floor. Along with the dress went the Anne Hebert alias, the more or less genteel Irish widow of Windsong. Springing forth, the ruthless, bloodthirsty Anne Bonny returned bent on revenge.

Leaving articles of under clothing in a trail up to her bedroom, she pulled a low trunk from beneath the bed and removed a pair of canvas pantaloons, a loose fitting linen shirt, her cutlass, rapier and a pistol.

Little Feather appeared at her door. "Please, Anne, don't go. He'll kill you, too."

"I think not." She stepped into the pants then slipped on the top. As she buckled the scabbard belt, "Before this day ends, he'll know who I am and be introduced to the eternal fires of hell!"

Anne poured fresh powder into the pan of the pistol then down the barrel. She followed that with a wadding patch and a lead ball then more wadding ramming it home furiously. She shoved the pistol under her belt beneath her shirt and trotted past her young friend.

"But Anne—"

"The time for talk is over."

She slung open the front door. It slammed back then trotted to the edge of the porch and leaped to the ground from the three-step-high platform. Anne never broke stride.

Quickly disengaging the horse from the carriage, she slung herself onto its back after it had already bolted.

She held fast to a rein with one hand while reaching down the side of the fast moving animal to retrieve the other, having no intention of letting the beast slow down. The horse was given its head to run full out. She whipped it with the tails of the long reins, pushing for more speed.

Racing through the streets of New Orleans, she pulled the horse up at the general mercantile store where she last saw the Frenchman. She yanked the sweat slickened horse's head down so suddenly dirt went flying forward from beneath its hooves.

Noticing the proprietor of the general mercantile rolling an oak barrel out on the porch, she performed a flying dismount, landing on her feet before the trailing dust cloud caught up.

Startled, the proprietor leaped back. "Miss Hebert?"

"Yes," she barked, "But Christian DeMornét knows me as Andrew. Where is that French dung beetle?"

The proprietor stood, mouth open, lip fluttering but had no voice to go with it. He clearly questioned whom to fear most.

People along the street backed away to safer places.

Anne's anger grew deadly.

Some onlookers stepped through open doorways and off the sidewalk. Faces crowded windows to view the goings on.

Pulling her cutlass, she charged the proprietor and grabbed his collar. She pulled him close until their noses touched. She slapped his crotch with the flat of the blade.

He groaned.

She then turned it so the sharp edge touched his testicles. Then she twisted his collar until his breathing became labored and red-faced, "Tell me now and tell me truly," she hissed through clenched teeth, "Or I'll see to it your wife has nothing to play with tonight."

"Behind you...across the street," he babbled tickling the air with dancing fingers. "Please don't hurt me."

She looked in the direction he pointed and glimpsed her target.

She released the storekeeper. He spiraled down on fear-weakened knees into a sniveling heap.

"Christian DeMornét!" she shouted, "Face me, you disgusting nasal slime!"

Having been walking away up the street, the Frenchman suddenly stopped and spun around. He stared, examining the source of the voice that shouted the insult.

The quizzical look told volumes. He had no idea why she'd be so rude and angry. "Missus Hebert?"

"Please allow me to introduce myself," she said, marching in his direction. "My name is Anne Bonny, alias Amber Flanagan, alias Anne Hebert, daughter of William Cormac of Charleston in the Carolinas. But you, sir, know me better as Captain Andrew the Protector of the ship Providence. And right now I shall have your life in exchange for the life of my friend. Friend, hell! He was family, by God! You have killed one of my family!"

"Andrew the Protector is a woman?" A smile crept across his face.

Anne didn't slow her step, cutlass in hand, though angered to the point of forgetting to unsheathe the rapier at her side. She broke into a dead run, bent on killing DeMornét where he stood.

His smile disappeared. Drawing his rapier, he struck the pose and braced for the assault but shock slowed his reaction time.

Anne overwhelmed him and quickly had him back stepping defensively.

He blocked each swing and thrust as quickly as he could. A split second late on positioning his weapon for a block, he left himself exposed and with lightning reflexes she stroked a gash in his forearm.

In the flash of time it took for him to glance at the injury, she back slashed another shallow cut across his belly, enough to draw blood before he jumped clear.

Suddenly, realization shined bright in his eyes. He'd die if he couldn't control her. He brought his formidable talents under control, parrying, thrusting, and moving to counter. He began moving offensively.

As Bear had feared, Anne's anger blinded her. Prudence dictated she back away defensively. Caution also dictated she pull her rapier. She did neither.

Instead, she stood her ground slapping aside repeated lightning thrusts. His speed was formidable but she matched it stroke for stroke.

Recovering from one block, he returned the point in time to run it through the bicep of her left arm.

She pulled away in agony, the rapier withdrawing with a slurp from her flesh. She grimaced.

It gave DeMornét time to thrust again. He aimed for her heart.

She deflected the point downward, but momentum was unimpeded. It skewered her thigh. Staggering back, she stumbled and fell. When her elbow hit the ground, the cutlass flew from her sweat-streaked hand.

Glancing toward the weapon, she caught sight of Laddy racing from the shadows of a nearby building. He screamed and waved to distract DeMornét.

"Laddy! Stay away!"

The Frenchman paid no attention and prepared for a killing thrust as the young boy jumped on his back.

He rode the big Frenchman and held on. His light frame flagged in a circle as the Frenchman tried unsuccessfully to sling the boy off.

With all strength, he choked the much bigger man. But his hands were small and too weak to inflict damage.

DeMornét finally slung him to the ground as easily as flicking a mosquito from his shoulder. "I have no time for a pickaninny." He slashed the point across the boy's throat then stabbed him squarely in the heart. The boy pathetically tried to scream but no sound came. His eyes froze. His mouth stopped moving and remained wide open. He was dead.

"Laddy!"

She didn't attempt retrieving the cutlass, flung some distance away. She reached into her belt and pulled the pistol, cocked it, pointed it, and fired at Demornét's head.

Urgency overrode precision.

Her aim was off.

The ball hit him in the throat.

He dropped his blade. He grabbed his neck with both hands and fell writhing on the ground.

Blood pumped in spurts between his fingers. He attempted to stand. It had to have been irrational reasoning of a dying mind telling him he might live, but he had to be on his feet.

He only managed to come up on his knees. The struggle ended there as he fell forward onto his face. One final convulsive quiver and he lay motionless—dead mere seconds after Laddy.

People tentatively emerged from doorways and alleys up and down the street—quietly at first.

Anne realized that in her anger she had given not only Christian DeMornét her true identity, but everyone within earshot.

Holding her shoulder and fighting pain in her thigh, she stood, careening sideways toward Laddy. She checked him but dull staring eyes told the tale. There was nothing she could do.

Her step hitched as she abruptly stopped and turned. She tried running but stumbled catching herself with an outstretched hand. Summoning reserves of strength, she ran unsteadily and mostly sideways back to her horse.

As she slung her leg over the still huffing and sweating horse's back, she heard a voice say, "Did you hear that? She said she is Anne Bonny."

"It had to be. Did you see the skill that went hand in hand with ruthless ferocity?" a woman said.

Another voice chimed in, "I thought Anne Bonny had been hanged."

A fourth voice questioned, "Do you think there could be a reward if that really is the infamous lady pirate?"

Not waiting to hear what else they had to say, she screamed and kicked the horse into a startled run.

Driving the animal hard up the carriageway at Windsong, the horse went down tumbling from a full gallop exhausted, ridden to death. She rolled from its slickened back in a cloud of dust on the ground but sprang to her feet. Staggering at first, she then worked into a limping run to the house.

Meeting her on the veranda, Little Feather said, "What has happened? What's wrong?"

"The Frenchman is dead. So is Laddy. If we don't abandon Windsong and get far away, we'll be hanged for sure."

Realizing the weight of those words, Anne paused. "Once again, it's just you and me, love."

Little Feather needed no further explanation and pulled three fresh horses from the nearby corral. She saddled two and prepared one to carry provisions. Within the hour, they began another journey—destination unknown. The only goal was to get as far away from civilization as possible into the wilderness. They rode northwest, intending to cross the Mississippi River into Baton Rouge then north once again with no plan beyond that.

As they galloped away from Windsong, Anne looked back as she had done so many times before. As Windsong shrank away, she couldn't visualize anything—a destination, a future—nothing beyond the snout of her racing horse. This time she saw no door opening just a last one closing. But the view over the rump of her racing mount, which she looked to one last time, told a quick clear story of a life ending. Vision tunneled, narrowing to the road ahead. Her life had just become a blank page.

# Chapter Thirty-one

Lying nearly flat upon the horse's back, its mane flagging in her face, Little Feather glanced over at Anne as they rode abreast away from Windsong. She wondered what evil shaded Anne's thoughts. The glimpses Anne stole behind them as they galloped away disturbed Little Feather. The look Anne bore changed with each blink of the young Iroquois' eyes. It ranged from fear to anger to love to loss. But it was the appearance of insanity Anne flashed that troubled the girl most—wild-eyed and vacant. Little Feather feared it had little to do with that French captain, nor the hangman's noose. The troublesome alternative was that maybe Anne wished for an end—a cry for it all to stop by any means—a lifetime of hurts and disappointments brought to a halt.

Anne whipped her horse to run faster. That forced Little Feather to do the same just to keep up.

Try as she might, the girl couldn't think of a better plan than this one—to run fast and far. If they could cross the big river, the one called Mississippi, it might provide breathing space. But they couldn't slow down until then.

Iroquois legend said the source of that river was heaven because they couldn't say where it began. Maybe that was the reason for the perceived comfort it provided. She thought if they could get across it things would improve.

The plan was simple; follow the river north into tribal controlled territory—country she was familiar with, where they might live and not be bothered by white people. Whites feared that country, and rightfully so. As a group, whites were unwelcome. Most Indian tribes did what was necessary to keep them away—even kill them. She and Anne had been unwitting participants in such annihilation two seasons past. But the wilderness was a place where her particular survival skills were appropriate. Together the two of them could live well the rest of their lives.

Pushing their mounts to the limit, in a single day's time, they came upon a ferry near a place Anne called Baton Rouge. Listening to Anne play the role of inquisitive conversation maker with the grizzled old man operating the ferry, she attempted to determine how far the name Anne Bonny had traveled.

The ferry operator waved to his helper across the river. Two large draught horses tightened the heavy rope. The ferry began its slow, meandering journey to get to the other side. The current tugged at the flat barge pulling it downriver. The trip across moved in an arc with the current, but the massive rope held fast. The barge continued on carrying the girls and their horses to the other side.

Monotony of his job kept the old man talking. He clearly welcomed questions and conversation with anyone about anything. He laughed, slapped his knees and peppered his conversation with wild gestures. He was a lonely man. Little Feather was sympathetically drawn to him. His long kinky gray beard hung to his belly. No razor had touched it in years, if ever. It looked like the moss dangling from Windsong's pecan and oak trees. After a period of trite conversation, Anne finally asked, "Have you heard if they've captured that lady pirate yet?"

With a groan the old man dropped to sit on a crate. "Ya mean Anne Bonny?"

"I think that's her name," Anne said.

"I hear that woman is a devil that'd rather kill you than converse with you." The old man snickered at the absurdity. "I can't say for sure but if she's still about, I wouldn't mind puttin' a bullet in her brain for some reward money." He burst into a belly laugh. The only teeth he still had in front were two on top and three on bottom that Little Feather could see. They showed clearly as he laughed slapping his knee and guffawing.

Little Feather cut a glance to Anne and saw her lips go white at the cruel joke, pressing the blood from them trying to hold her tongue. She looked away to the landing area. It was a slow go. Anne gripped the heavy rope that served as a rail around the barge in such a way Little Feather believed she might be fighting to control her temper, but she wondered if the old man may have simply hurt her feelings. Either way, Anne seemed on the verge of erupting with some type of outburst.

The rest of the ferry ride was quiet, at least on Anne's part. The old man chattered on.

Once across, they mounted up and rode north.

After a time, the pace slowed to a trot. Little Feather caught up to her. "Do not concern yourself with stories that swell beyond reality. That old man only knew what he'd heard. The story has grown grander with time and each telling. Tales told are of a mythical creature that happens to have your name. That person does not exist."

"What I have often told you as a simple unfounded inclination is now a fact. It might as well be carved on a bloody headstone," Anne said. "Anyone bold enough to tell the world they are my friend or even stand at my side for a time is a sentence of death for them."

"That's not true." Little Feather let the comment stand as the only reply to an irrational turn of mind. But Anne's statement answered Little Feather's question; the obsession in Anne grew.

Little Feather tried to think of ways to dispel the dangerous pattern Anne saw as indisputable. *I must put her mind to something else. But how? What shall I say?*

"And you have done that," Anne went on to say. "Although it has long been my suspicion, I now know beyond doubt that staying so close puts your life in jeopardy, regardless where we go or what we do. As long as I have breath in my lungs, your life shall have no value at my side. The world will view your presence with no more regard than an abscess on the rump of a forest creature." Anne looked squarely at the girl. "Do you understand what that means, love?"

Although Little Feather knew better, she shook her head anyway and let her eyes fall.

"It means someone somewhere will shoot right through you to kill me. If the curse continues, I'll survive. You won't."

"Please, Anne, don't let that thinking destroy you. You are no curse. You are my blessing. Say no more about it."

Although slower, the northward trek continued without breaks. Little Feather watched her friend closely. Anne's sense of guilt bottomed. It sucked energy from her, vigor drained away. Worse, Anne didn't care.

Nothing she said could snap Anne from the deep seeded curse she believed had befallen her. The once strong willed Anne Bonny whined that she'd been divinely denied happiness. Although deeply depressed, two forces drove her to continue the journey; not losing the last living love of her life and not being left to die alone—the two now inexorably entwined.

Camped at the base of rolling hills near a cold rushing stream, Little Feather tended a fire to cook a rabbit. All the while, she watched Anne sitting atop a boulder staring—just staring.

Anne coughed. There was hoarseness to it.

Breaking twigs, the young girl tossed a handful into the new flame and built upon it until it blazed hot. She skewered the rabbit on a stick and roasted it. As she tended to it, she studied Anne's pallor. No expertise was required to see deterioration. Anne had given up.

The chilled wind of early winter reminded Little Feather the time to run had again ended. Provisions must be made for winter. Colder days were coming.

Anne's obsessive behavior robbed her of that familiar take-charge attitude and ability to reason practically. Little Feather took the lead in preparing a winter home. Anne blankly accepted role reversal, readily taking orders in the mundane aspects of acquiring food and shelter. She didn't care. She just did what Little Feather asked.

Little Feather could not talk away thoughts that haunted Anne or find the right words to shake Anne from doldrums.

Anne's cough worsened. She had a problem expelling phlegm. When she did, spots of blood were in it. Pink in her cheeks disappeared. A grayish-green tint replaced the healthier color and was in sharp contrast to her bright red hair. She lost weight and was becoming gaunt. Her movements stiffened. She did not complain trudging on with day-to-day chores.

Little Feather experimented with herbs, looking to find a cure. With each failure, she looked for another. Every day she tried teas and poultices to stem Anne's deterioration to no effect.

With great sadness, Little Feather listened as fever born fantasies became real to Anne. Accounts of them gave physical life and characteristics to her fears. She spoke of them as literal beings she would have to fight and vanquish with pistol or cutlass. Delusions became frequent and frightening.

*How can I help?* Little Feather wondered. *I don't know what to do.* She cried but kept tears hidden away.

A blustery north wind sent a series of frigid blasts signaling the first true turn of the season. A small flurry of snow that began in late afternoon transformed into a blizzard in a matter of hours.

Realizing Anne's mind was not as it once was, Little Feather had to restrain her from wandering about.

Blood oozed from the corner of Anne's mouth. A dried streak of it had become a fixture on her face. Wildly fluctuating fever complicated things further. Little Feather's optimism waned.

Within the confines of the shallow cave she'd prepared, the fire warmed and dried the air while winter's worst beat against the entrance. Anne lay upon buckskin covering a soft grass pad, her head in the young girl's lap. She spoke of events and people of the past as if she were there with them. Anne's mind had become a multi-layered stew of disjointed memories, no longer distinguishing present from past.

"I think I'll have the men ready our ship so we might sail to Jamaica. Yes. That's what we'll do." Anne grabbed Little Feather's forearm and raised her head to look at her friend through swimming eyes. "We can fetch Calico Jack and Mary back to the colonies." Her head quivered under its own weight. She let it fall back into the girl's lap. She drew an uneven breath. "I think Bear and Laddy might really like them. Don't you think?"

Stroking perspiration from Anne's soaked forehead, "How could they not?" Little Feather said.

Anne jerked lifting her head abruptly from Little Feather's lap. "Do you think Peter has forgiven me?" She held it only a second and settled back down. "No matter. It's Michael's children I shall have, not Peter's."

Anne's voice trailed. She moaned then coughed. Her eyes rolled back; breathing became labored. She slipped from consciousness.

Then suddenly, as if her brain were switching off and on, she began talking again picking up where she'd left off. "We can all live together like a family...a real family. How about that? Doesn't that sound wonderful?"

Sadness clawed at the pit of Little Feather's stomach but there was nothing—absolutely nothing she could do to change the course of Anne's demise. Now, only a miracle could change where this would end.

Anne's eyes looked intently at an area above them. She looked at something other than the ceiling of a cave, a vision born of delirium. "Oh, Momma, you beautiful beast, you still watch over me. God bless you, love," she said then reached in the direction she looked as if she not only saw but could touch the wolf. Her hand moved in a stroking motion as if petting the canine.

Somehow, lucidity sparked. Anne whimpered pulling her frail body into a tight ball, rolling onto her side. Her head fell from Little Feather's lap.

The young girl snuggled down beside her and kissed her neck. She placed her lips to Anne's ear. "Someday, I'll share the story of Anne Bonny with a son or a daughter. My children will know, as I know, how special you are. In turn they'll tell their children, and so on. The truth will not be lost. I won't stop until the legend of Anne Bonny is one of a courageous young woman who took on the world and won. Everyone will come to know you as I do, a friend who never compromised, a woman who'd never leave a friend behind." She snuggled closer still and pulled a warm cover over them both.

Anne drifted in and out of consciousness. Little Feather stayed with her through the night as frigid winds howled beyond the mouth of the cave. The young girl treated the ailment best she could, herbal poultices, potions, and rubs but nothing eased fever-induced dementia. Anne slipped deeper.

Little Feather sat and leaned against the cave wall with a doe skin covering her. She wilted over against Anne's fevered body and closed her eyes to ease exhaustion. While thinking on it, sleep overcame her.

Awakening with a sudden sense of panic, she noticed the lack of warmth against her. Frantically she looked about the tiny space.

Anne was no longer in the cave.

Throwing the cover off she bounded to her feet and flipped back the buckskin drape that covered the opening to the cave to see a world blanketed in white. Frigid wind blasted her face numbing her cheeks but discomfort was not important. Trudging through waist-deep snow, she searched a tight arc in front of the cave, thinking Anne couldn't have walked far in her condition.

Within a snow bank piled high against the boulder Anne so often sat upon, the young Indian girl caught sight of long curly red hair whipping from a snowdrift. A few strands were all that was visible. Her frenetic attitude vanished. She slowed. The truth of it no longer required haste.

She dropped to her knees next to the wind-whipped strands and brushed snow away. The hardened stare of her liberator, her mentor, and her friend appeared.

As tears froze on her cheeks, she dug snow away from the body then pulled it into her lap. "My promise was not an idle one, Anne Bonny." She cradled and coddled the frozen corpse, still nurturing. "I will share your goodness with the world." Looking toward heaven she repeated, "I will. I promise I will."

Frost formed at her hairline and on her eyebrows. She didn't care. "You are free. Loved ones wait. Go be with them," she whispered.

She hung her head and cried.

She pushed snow back over Anne and chanted an Iroquois prayer of safe journey.

Little Feather could not remember ever having felt so alone. She coughed. A drizzle of blood escaped the corner of her mouth. Then she coughed again—a deep, hoarse cough.

# About the Author

A lifelong Texan, Daniel (Danny) Lance Wright is a freelance fiction writer and novelist born in Lubbock, Texas now residing near Waco. He lives with Rickie, wife of 40 years and has two children and three grandchildren. Having spent the first nineteen years of his life on a cotton farm on the South Plains and the next thirty-two in the television industry, he has seen the world from two distinctly different angles. Daniel has received recognition for writing skills from The Oklahoma Writers Federation in 2005, 2006, 2010 and 2011; from Art Affair in 2008; from Frontiers in Writing in 2004 and 2010; from Writer's Digest in 2008, and the Abilene Writer's Guild in 2004; Canis Latran of Weatherford College in 2011.

## VISIT OUR WEBSITE
## FOR THE FULL INVENTORY
## OF QUALITY BOOKS:

*http://www.roguephoenixpress.com*

Representing Excellence in Publishing

*Quality trade paperbacks and downloads*

*in multiple formats,*

*in genres ranging from historical to contemporary romance, mystery and science fiction.*

*Visit the website then bookmark it.*

*We add new titles each month!*